THE TENTH COMMAND

A WWII NOVEL OF LEADERSHIP, REDEMPTION,
AND THE 10TH MOUNTAIN DIVISION

JOE LOOBY

ISBN: 979-8-9991301-5-0

Published by 10TH MOUNTAIN FILMS, LLC

Mount Pleasant, SC, USA

Printed in the United States of America

DEDICATION

To our children, Kate, Jack, and CJ,

And the descendants of the valiant 10th Mountain Division—who stand in the light because others climbed through the dark.

ALSO BY JOE LOOBY

THE TENTH SERIES

The Tenth Trail Mark — *the story of the men who climbed.* A WWII Novel of Courage, Sacrifice, and the 10th Mountain Division.

The Tenth Station — *the story of the man who taught them how to fight.* A WWI Novel of Love, Courage, and the Rock of the Marne.

The Tenth Command — *the story of the men who led them.* A WWII Novel of Leadership, Redemption, and the 10th Mountain Division.

AUTHOR'S NOTE

This novel is a tribute to the soldiers of the 10th Mountain Division and the U.S. Army Rangers—men who defined themselves not by the ease of their path, but by the heights they were willing to climb in the dark.

While *The Tenth Command* is a work of historical fiction, its heart beats within the true, parallel journeys of two American leaders: Major General George P. Hays and Colonel William O. Darby. Their lives form an intersection of doctrine and daring, of the long, steady staircase and the vertical shaft of ambition.

The story of General Hays is anchored in his Medal of Honor actions at the Marne and his command from the hedgerows of Normandy to the peaks of the Apennines. The story of Colonel Darby grows from his founding of the 1st Ranger Battalion and the costly, brilliant campaigns that forged the Ranger spirit.

Private conversations, interior motives, and the thematic thread of the "Broken Tablet" are imagined. The operational record—the units, terrain, timelines, and outcomes—is drawn from the historical accounts that survived them.

This is a story about the calculus of sacrifice: the willingness to trade one life to buy time for another. It is dedicated to those who hold the line—and to those who dare to break the enemy's line.

A NOTE ON THE EVE OF WAR

By early 1945, the war in Europe was collapsing. Adolf Hitler, in a final, desperate gambit, dreamed of pulling his remaining forces back into a heavily fortified zone in the mountains—the "Alpine National Redoubt"—hoping it might prolong the war.

This concept hinged on a single lifeline: the Brenner Pass, the principal all-weather motor and rail exit from Italy into the Reich. The Allied objective was clear: seize the Brenner Pass and trap the entirety of German Army Group C, along with the estimated one million Axis soldiers and personnel in Italy.

But the road to the Alps was blocked. Standing in the way was one man and two monsters: Field Marshal Albert Kesselring and his twin creations, the Gustav Line and the Gothic Line.

The first monster, the Gustav Line, had already proven the futility of conventional war. Anchored on the historic monastery of Monte Cassino, perched nearly 1,500 feet above the Allied positions in the valley below, it had held the Allies in a brutal, bloody stalemate through the winter of 1943–1944. An attempt to bypass it—the amphibious "end-run" at Anzio—had also failed, devolving into a besieged perimeter, a second, separate front of desperate fighting.

Kesselring's lines had held. The U.S. Fifth Army was being "bled white" in a brutal war of attrition.

While this story spans both monsters—and the men forged in their shadows—its heart beats in the second: the Gothic Line, a "fortress built by a God of war," a "web of death" designed to guard Hitler's final Alpine lifeline.

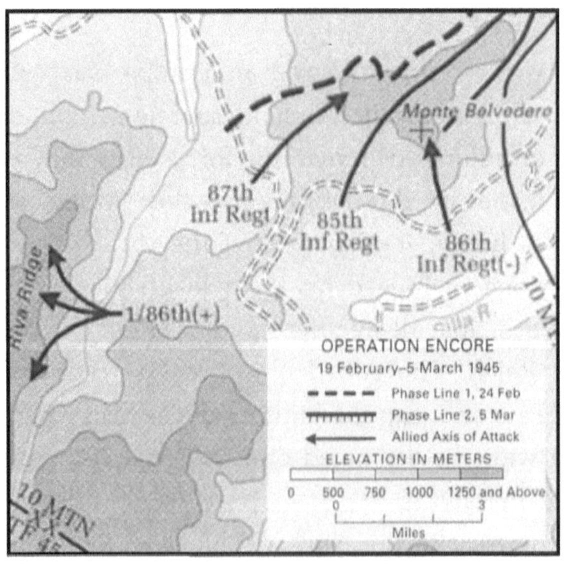

The terrain presented a tactical nightmare. At one of the line's most critical points, the jagged spine of Riva Ridge rose from the valley floor in a 1,600-foot sheer cliff to peaks topping out at 4,900 feet above sea level. Along with the adjacent summit of Mount Belvedere, it formed a natural citadel that barred the final road to the Alps. To the German

defenders, these heights were considered unscalable—an obstacle designed by nature itself.

Breaking the deadlock required a new approach. The mission would fall to two men whose paths, forged in the fires of earlier battles, were about to converge:

- **Major General George "Price" Hays** was a man forged in the mud of two world wars. A WWI Medal of Honor recipient and master of the guns, he had already endured the bitter stalemate of Cassino and the chaos of Anzio. After unleashing the artillery storm at Omaha Beach, the "Rock of the Marne" was returning to the mountain front. He wasn't just returning to command; he was returning to settle a debt with Field Marshal Kesselring for the tragedy at Monte Cassino.
- **Colonel William "Will" Darby** was a lightning bolt in a world of "paper men"—the founder of the U.S. Army Rangers, he had spent the war building a legend on the cliffs of North Africa and the beaches of Sicily. He was a leader who saw gravity as negotiable and commanded every room he entered. But beneath that "King of the Rangers" swagger lay a man who loved his Rangers too much to let them go—and who was now seeking a path through the fire toward redemption.

To understand the men who would face Kesselring's Gothic Line fortress, we must first return to the battles that forged them.

This is their story.

THE COMMANDERS

Major General George "Price" Hays (Left) **and Colonel William "Will" O. Darby** (Right). The Rock and the Ranger. Their converging paths—one of doctrine, one of daring—would help determine the fate of the Italian front.

PROLOGUE I - THE CLOCK TOWER

0130 HOURS, 1933

West Point, New York

The United States Military Academy was built of gray stone and black and white rules. A fortress of duty perched above the Hudson—it was designed to grind the individual into the whole, to replace personal ambition with the invincible, unified will of the Army. It was a machine designed to kill the ego.

For most, it was a crucible. For Cadet William "Will" Darby, it was a problem to be solved. Will had matured into a man who didn't just command a room; he owned it. He was a natural leader, his mind a brilliant, restless engine that saw the Academy not as a set of rules to be followed, but as a system to be mastered—or, if the opportunity arose, to be elegantly broken.

He was bored. The endless drills, the rote memorization, the suffocating emphasis on tradition—it all felt like a winding staircase of small steps. Will didn't want to just climb; he wanted to prove he could dismantle the stairs and rebuild them in his own image while the architects watched, helpless to stop him.

He needed a challenge.

He found it sitting by the flagpole on the east side of the Plain: the M1902 3-inch field gun.

It was the voice of the Academy, the iron throat that barked the Corps awake every morning at dawn and barked them to bed at dusk. It was the ultimate symbol of the Academy's rigid, unthinking control.

And Will wanted to move it.

He convened his "Black Hand," a small, secret club of like-minded cadets—engineers, athletes, and poets bound by a shared disdain for the "paper men" who simply endured. They met in a damp storage cellar beneath the barracks, the air thick with the smell of stone, mildew, and the acrid tang of disinfectant and lye soap.

"It's not enough to silence it," Will said, his voice a low, conspiratorial murmur in the lantern light. He unrolled a stolen blueprint of the old Academic Building across a crate of expired rations. "Any plebe can dump it in the Hudson. This... this is an engineering problem. It's a statement."

"A statement of what?" asked DeMarco, a nervous engineer whose glasses were perpetually foggy. "That we have a death wish?"

"That we have an appetite for the impossible, Mr. DeMarco," Will replied, his voice a low, intense rumble.

He leaned closer, the lantern light catching the sharp angle of his jaw.

"History doesn't ask if the plan was safe. It only asks if it worked."

Will tapped the blueprint, his finger landing on the clock tower.

"And tonight, we prove that gravity is negotiable."

The plan was audacious, a logistical nightmare that bordered on genius. They wouldn't just steal the cannon. They would disassemble the entire M1902 field gun—barrel, carriage, wheels—in the dead of night, haul the pieces unseen across the Plain, and reassemble it.

His finger landed on the final objective, the X on his map: the clock tower of the old Academic Building, the highest point on the Plain.

"It's a climb, gentlemen," Will said, a slow, wolfish grin spreading across his face. "A deconstructive climb. When the Academy wakes up, the cannon's voice won't be barking across the Plain. It will be booming down at them. From above. Like the voice of God, if God were a bored twenty-year-old from Arkansas."

This was Will's true nature. It was a prank, yes—a "spirit mission" in cadet parlance—but it was also a complex tactical operation executed for one purpose: glory.

The night they chose was starless, the air pregnant with the threat of rain. The post was asleep, the only sounds the distant cry of a loon on the river and the measured boot-falls of the cadet guards on their rounds.

Will was the conductor. He sent a two-man team ahead to "acquire" a tin of heavy axle grease from the cavalry stables, where a blind eye could be bought for a dollar. He posted lookouts. Then, he led the core team—twelve cadets, their faces blackened with burnt cork—across the Plain to Trophy Point.

They worked in a furious, disciplined silence. The M1902 was a 2,500-pound beast of steel, its metal freezing to the touch. The dominant smell was cold iron and gun oil. They muffled the metallic clank of the breechblock with oily rags.

Wrenches clicked, muffled by gloves. Pins were eased from their housings. Will, his hands sure and practiced, directed the disassembly, his mind working like a watchmaker's. The 800-pound barrel first. Then the 150-pound wheels, their axles already groaning despite the fresh grease. Then the 1,000-pound carriage itself. Each piece was a crushing weight.

The journey across the Plain was the gauntlet. They used the route Will had mapped—west along Cullum Road, a path shielded by a row of ancient oaks. They moved in shadows, their breath pluming in the damp air. At one point, a flashlight beam swept the grass ten yards to their left. They froze, thirteen shadows holding a literal ton of stolen government property, their hearts hammering against their ribs. The light passed. They breathed.

They reached the old Academic Building, a gray giant with battlements. The climb was the final act. Up the narrow, echoing concrete service stairs they went, their muscles screaming as they hauled hundreds of pounds of steel, flight after flight.

It was agony. The carriage slipped on the third landing, pinning DeMarco against the wall. He opened his mouth to scream, but Will was there instantly, his hand clamped over DeMarco's mouth, his eyes wide and hard. "Silent," Will hissed, straining to hold the weight of the steel back with his shoulder. "Pain is temporary. Getting expelled is forever. Lift."

In the turret of the clock tower, the wind whipped at their jackets, slick with mist from the river. The air up here was sharp, carrying the smell of the Hudson's waters and the distant coal smoke from the Academy's heating plants.

"Build it," Will commanded.

Under the faint glow of a hooded flashlight, they reassembled the gun. It was a resurrection in reverse. The steel, slick with grease and sweat, came together. The barrel was seated with a soft, satisfying *thunk*. The wheels were locked. By 0400 hours, it was done.

The M1902 reveille cannon, fully assembled, now pointed defiantly out over the Plain from its new perch, a mute, iron sentinel six stories above the ground.

At 0550 hours, the first notes of the bugle cut through the dawn. "Reveille."

The Corps of Cadets spilled from the barracks, forming up on the Plain, their movements groggy and automatic. The Commandant himself, a brigadier general with a gaze devoid of warmth, stood on the steps of Washington Hall, coffee in hand, watching the clock like a hawk.

The bugle call ended. A half-second of silence.

Usually, the boom came from the left. Today, the sky tore open.

BOOM.

The report was massive, a thunderclap that echoed off the granite walls and rolled down the Hudson Valley. But it was wrong. It was too loud. It was... above. The shockwave rattled the windows of the barracks.

A collective, unified gasp went up from the Corps. A thousand heads—cadets, officers, the Commandant— snapped upward. The Commandant spilled his coffee, a dark stain blooming on his pristine uniform.

There it was. The reveille cannon, a wreath of white smoke curling from its barrel, perched precariously in the clock tower turret, a king looking down on its stunned subjects. It looked absurdly majestic, a nonsensical piece of heavy artillery nesting like a gargoyle.

Cadet Darby stood in the front rank of his company, his face perfectly composed. He alone did not look up. He had already seen it. He had built his ladder to glory, climbed it, and fired a shot from the top.

It took the Academy engineers two days, a complex system of pulleys, and a team of horses to figure out how to get it down. They cursed the "ghosts" who put it there, unable to comprehend the physics of the prank.

Will had become a legend. But he saw the "paper men," the plodding, rule-following officers who graduated and moved on, and felt a sharp, hungry pang. He didn't just want to outsmart them; he coveted their rank, their unthinking authority.

He realized then that legends aren't issued with the uniform. You have to build them yourself, piece by heavy piece.

PROLOGUE II - THE ROCK

1918-1939

August 1918

Field Hospital No. 12, Near Paris, France

Survival felt less like a victory and more like a theft.

First Lieutenant George Price Hays lay in the narrow iron cot, the smell of carbolic acid and fresh cotton sheets doing little to mask the scent of gangrene drifting from the ward. His leg throbbed—a deep, jagged rhythm that matched the ache in his chest—but he was alive.

Seven horses had died under him. He remembered their screams. He remembered the Belgian draft horse, its honest eyes wide with terror before the shell tore the world apart.

But mostly, he remembered the boy.

A nurse moved silently between the cots, checking charts. Hays reached out, his hand trembling with fever.

"Sister?"

She stopped, her face worn with the fatigue of a thousand casualties. *"Reposez-vous, Lieutenant. La fièvre est tombée, mais vous avez besoin..."*

"Rest, Lieutenant. The fever is down, but you need..."

"The lists," Hays interrupted, his voice a dry rasp. "I need to check the casualty lists again. For the 28th Division. A Private."

The nurse sighed, a sound of gentle, exhausted patience. *"Lieutenant, nous avons vérifié. Les listes de la Marne sont un chaos de boue et de fautes d'orthographe."*

"Lieutenant, we have checked. The lists from the Marne are a chaos of mud and misspellings."

Hays sank back against the pillow. That was all he had. A name, a face smeared with mud, and a voice from the Adirondacks saying,

"Take him, sir."

The boy had given Hays his second horse—his ticket to deliver the coordinates so he could hold the line. Hays wanted to repay him, to learn if he made it to the aid station near Grèves Farm, or if the mustard gas got to him because he was now on foot.

"I have to find him," Hays whispered to the ceiling. "I owe him."

"Vous vous devez un peu de sommeil," the nurse said, dimming the lantern. *"Vous rentrez chez vous en héros, Lieutenant. Essayez de faire la paix avec ça."* "You owe yourself some sleep. You're going home a hero, Lieutenant. Try to make peace with it."

Hays closed his eyes. They were calling him a hero, but he knew what he did—he did not do it alone. He had help.

1924

Ithaca, New York

"And that, gentlemen, is the correct application of indirect fire solutions for the 75-millimeter gun."

Captain Hays, now assigned to Cornell University's ROTC detachment, tapped the blackboard. The chalk dust felt alien on his hands. In front of him, twenty young men in pressed uniforms looked back, their faces bright, earnest, and agonizingly naive.

"Sir," a young cadet in the front row asked. "My father says the war in Europe was a 'political failure' and that the 75 is obsolete." Price looked at the boy—a child of privilege who had never tasted the acrid burn of propellant—and felt a profound, weary sadness.

He thought of the men at the Marne, and of the private from the Adirondacks—gray and gone, a ghost that had followed him home from France, waiting for a debt to be paid.

"With respect to your father, cadet," Price said, his voice flat and cold, "battleships cannot hold a muddy railway embankment. And politics is what happens before the first shell lands. Your job is to be ready for what happens after."

1939

Army War College, Washington, D.C.

The teletype machine in the hall of the War College began to clatter, its sharp, insistent rhythm cutting through the academic quiet.

It was September 1st. Major George P. Hays stood with a group of other officers, all of them watching the paper spool out.

GERMANY INVADES POLAND. PANZER DIVISIONS CROSS BORDER.

A younger officer, an aviator, let out a low whistle. "Blitzkrieg. Lightning war. It's really happening."

Hays said nothing. He felt no shock. No surprise. He had been preparing for this day for twenty years. The "war to end all wars" had simply been a pause to reload.

He walked away from the teletype machine, his mind already calculating. The lessons of the Marne—the fluid, frantic, aggressive use of mobile artillery—were no longer history. They were the key to the future.

His preparation was over. The next Great War was about to begin.

1
———

THE PACK

1940

Fort Hoyle, Maryland

The braying of a mule was not the sound Lieutenant Colonel George P. Hays associated with the professional, ordered world of the U.S. Army. But here at Fort Hoyle, where he was organizing and commanding the new 99th Field Artillery Battalion (Pack), it was the constant, stubborn soundtrack of his new reality.

The air smelled of sweet hay, manure, and mule-hide. Hays, the "Rock of the Marne," was a master of the French 75 —a weapon of speed, precision, and firepower. This new command was a different beast entirely. This was a "Pack" unit, with artillery designed to be broken down and transported, piece by agonizing piece, on the backs of mules.

It was an infantryman's nightmare. He stood by a corral fence, packing a briar pipe and hiding a smile as he watched his new officers. They were a mix of eager reservists and frustrated career men who saw this assignment as a career dead end.

One of them, a young captain with a sharp West Point confidence, was currently in a losing battle with a packing harness. The mule, a dusty roan with a jagged scar on its flank, seemed entirely unimpressed by the captain's pedigree. Every time the officer reached for the cinch, the animal shifted its weight, pinning the man against the rails.

"You're trying to negotiate with it, Captain?" Hays called out, leaning casually against the fence. "You can't reason with a recruit who has four legs and tenure."

The captain spun around, snapping to attention, his uniform already stained with sweat and what looked suspiciously like slobber.

"Sir," Captain William Darby replied, his frustration barely concealed. "I am attempting to explain the chain of command to this animal."

Hays chuckled, a deep, warm sound that seemed to ease the tension in the humid air. "Oh, he understands the chain of command—and you're not in it. This is not a 155mm battery, Captain. And that isn't a cannon. It's a personality with hooves."

"I was expecting to command guns, sir," Will said, wiping his brow. "Not... donkeys."

"That 'donkey,' Captain, is the answer to a question the last war never asked," Hays said, his gaze fixed on the animal.

Hays looked at the roan mule, and for a fleeting second, the Maryland sun felt like the cold dawn of France. He saw the same honest, terrified trust in this beast's eyes that he'd seen in the Morgan that had carried him through the fire.

"On the Marne, we were two iron walls ground into the mud. The problem wasn't the guns, Will; the guns were loud and simple. The problem was the truth. We rode horses to be the wire—the living circuit—dragging coordinates through a storm of steel just so the batteries knew what to kill. This battalion isn't just about moving steel; it's about making sure the truth arrives in time to save the men."

He turned to face Will, his eyes locking on the younger man. "But the next war? It won't wait for us to dig a trench. It will be a war of movement, of violent speed. If the guns can't move as fast as the infantry, the infantry dies. And in the mountains or the jungle, trucks are just coffins with wheels. That mule is the only thing that gets the gun to the fight."

Will cast a skeptical look at the mule, which was currently chewing on a splintered fence rail. "It feels like a regression, sir. The rest of the world is building engines, and we're filling feedbags. We're betting our lives on a transport system that runs on oats and stubbornness," Will muttered. "It's a logistical nightmare with fuzzy ears and flies."

"The Army is a long, slow climb, Captain," Hays said. He tapped the bowl of his pipe against the top rail, knocking a clump of gray ash into the dust. "Fort Hoyle, Cornell, the Philippines. It's grueling work, and the air gets thin."

Will couldn't hide a small, dismissive smile. "With respect, sir, I've never been much for stairs. I don't have the knees for a slow climb. I'm looking for a ladder straight to the top."

The roan mule chose that exact moment to let out a wet, rhythmic bray that sounded suspiciously like a laugh. It nudged Will's shoulder hard enough to rattle his teeth.

"See? Even the livestock thinks you're overdoing it," Hays chuckled, his gaze sharpening. "You've got salt, Will," he said, his voice dropping to a low rumble. "But watch your footing. Ambition is its own kind of rip current. An old friend once taught me that if you don't learn to swim parallel to a rip current, the ocean will pull you under before you even know you're drowning."

Will straightened his cap, unfazed. "Parallel is for people who want to aim for the shore, sir. I'm aiming for something higher."

"Fair enough," Hays replied, leaning back. "But keep in mind that express elevators have a way of dropping... fast. Higher altitude means thinner air, Captain. And the higher you climb, the harder it is for the truth to reach you from the ground." He gestured with his pipe toward the line of mules. "I'll let you in on a secret—this isn't the dead end your classmates think it is. This is the missing link. While the rest of the Army is yoked to a paved road, this battalion can go places that are off the map. This unit isn't for parade-ground soldiers, Will. It's for the boys who grew up reading the woods instead of textbooks. Men who know that a trail mark is more than just paint—it's a promise of safe passage."

Will Darby stared at his new commander, then back at the mule, which was now chewing contentedly on his sleeve. The frustration in his eyes didn't vanish, but a dawning, restless drive joined it. "So, it's not about the size of the gun, then," Will mused. "It's about who can get it to the top."

"Exactly, Captain. Show me you can lead him, and I'll trust you with the rest of the battalion."

Will finally broke into a genuine grin, dusting off his uniform. "Challenge accepted, sir. On one condition."

Hays raised an eyebrow. "What's that?"

"Apples. Lots of apples."

2

THE HARBOR

1940

Fort Hoyle / Sullivan's Island

The Maryland heat was a physical weight, pressing down on the tin roof of the 99th's command hut. The air was a suffocating mix of brackish bay water and wet mule.

Lieutenant Colonel Hays sat alone at his government-issue desk, sweating through his khaki shirt. He had just dismissed Will. He saw the young captain's ambition, that familiar, restless fire to climb, and it made him think of the different path he himself had chosen.

On his desk, next to his reports, was a letter. The return address was not their row house in Charleston, but the summer cottage: Station 10, Sullivan's Island.

He opened it, and suddenly, the smell of the stagnant water of the nearby Chesapeake was replaced by the phantom scent of salt air and jasmine.

My dearest Price,

I am writing this from the porch. The tide is coming in, and the breeze is finally knocking back the heat. The house is finally still. Little Jack left a trail of sand and seashells all the way up the stairs before his mother finally wrangled him and his sister into bed. It is a joy to have the house full of life, but the noise makes the quiet moments without you feel even emptier.

I wish you were here to watch the sun go down over the jetties. I saw a young boy running into the surf today, fearless against the waves. It made me think of you. It made me think of the other path..."

Hays smiled, the memory of the ocean a cooling balm in the stifling heat of the hut. He picked up his pen, the nib scratching in the silence of the room. He loved writing every salutation to her, the distance between them erased by a twenty-five-year conversation.

My dearest Julia,

I saw a young captain today. Full of fire. He's climbing up the stairs just like the ones we used to talk about at The Citadel —all ambition and polished brass, desperate to get to the top.

It made me think of you. It made me think of the other path. The one you showed me in the library, all those years ago.

I can still see you, sitting in the archives, looking up from that old manuscript, telling me about St. Helena and her search for the truth. I was a boy then, feeling trapped by the world.

I've held onto that, Julia. It's been my anchor far more than the "Rock of the Marne" ever was. It reminds me that the real staircase, the only one that matters, is the one that leads you to your home.

Kiss the little ones for me. Tell them Granddad is coming

home eventually, but for now, September can't get here fast enough.

With all my love,

Price

He sealed the letter. A week later, her reply found him.

My dearest Price,

Your letter found me well. It is lonely here on the island without you. The family has gone back to the mainland for the school term, and the silence is deafening. The storms roll in off the Atlantic, rattling the screens, and I find myself listening for your step on the stairs.

It's amusing you remember the parable so clearly. My memory of it is far less poetic. I remember the literal one—the story you told me.

I remember you describing that day, standing on the beach as the storm rolled in. How you, a seventeen-year-old boy—an "ice boy" as the snobs called you—ran into a rip current that no one else would brave. How you had to improvise, fighting your way to the jetties to save those two women when everyone else, including the "storm warriors," thought it was a suicide run.

That boy... he wasn't a "Rock" yet. He was just a young man with a good heart, charting a new path when the old one didn't work.

By the way, I drove into town yesterday to gather a box for your regimental dayroom. I know you said the post library at Fort Hoyle is abysmal, so I am raiding the duplicates stack. I'm sending a crate of detective stories and Westerns. I suspect your mule-skinners will appreciate Zane Grey more than the manuals you're making them read.

It warms my heart, George, to think of a boy finding a

moment of peace in a story. It feels a world away from this quiet porch. Only two weeks left, my love. I am counting down the days until the season turns and brings me back to you...

Hays smiled, leaning back in his chair. Julia, with her books and her quiet strength, was holding the fort. She was keeping the harbor lights on.

3

THE PROTOTYPE

1941

Fort Hoyle, Maryland

It was a strange, anachronistic posting. Here, in an army motorizing as fast as it could, was a unit built entirely around the mule.

Will found himself fascinated. It wasn't just the animals; it was the engineering of disassembly, how an entire 75mm howitzer could be broken down into six precise loads. He studied the geometry of the pack saddles, the exact calculations of weight distribution, the intricate, impossible trails they practiced on.

Colonel Hays was a forward-thinker despite the backward-looking equipment. "Mark my words, Will," Hays told him during a grueling mountain exercise, "the future war won't be about who has the best roads. It'll be about high mobility in impossible terrain."

"It started with the Finns," Hays continued, his voice dropping to a conspiratorial register. "Winter of '39. They stopped the Red Army cold—literally—because they could move on snow when the Russians couldn't. That woke Washington up. Assistant Secretary Johnson sent a memo to Marshall last year, asking if *we* could fight in the cold. The answer was no. So now, Minnie Dole and the National Ski Patrol are out there recruiting a new breed for the 87th Infantry—volunteers, Ivy Leaguers, and ski bums. We aren't just building a unit; we're building a myth."

Will, ever the non-conformist, took to it immediately. He was learning how to move firepower where there were no roads, no bridges, only rock and mud.

A year later, the 99th was the sharpest, most mobile artillery unit on the post. Hays found himself having a drink in the Officer's Club with Major General Russell P. Hartle, commander of the 34th Infantry Division.

"George," Hartle said, swirling the ice in his glass. "I'm taking the 34th to Northern Ireland. It's the first deployment. I'll need an aide-de-Camp. But I don't want a secretary. I need a man who is not just smart, but fast. Someone who understands movement, not just maps. You got anyone like that in this mule circus of yours?"

Hays looked across the smoke-filled room. At a corner table, Captain Will Darby wasn't drinking. He was in a heated, lively debate with a group of mule-skinners and infantry officers, using a napkin to sketch out a map of a theoretical mountain pass. He didn't just command the table; he owned the room.

For a fleeting instant, Hays wasn't at Fort Hoyle; he was

on a moonlit beach, the salt spray on his face, watching a beautiful, unsurvivable wave he'd chosen not to ride. Will, he thought, was a man who would try to ride it all the way to shore.

"As a matter of fact, general," Hays said, the pride in his voice unmistakable. "I have just the man."

4

THE AIDE-DE-CAMP

1942

Northern Ireland

The air was a constant, cold, weeping mist. Captain Will Darby hated it. He stood at the window of the requisitioned manor house, staring out at the gray, Irish countryside. Through the mist, he could see a platoon of infantry slogging through the mud, practicing squad maneuvers. They were miserable, wet, and exhausted.

Will watched them with a naked, burning envy.

"Captain Darby?"

Will turned, arranging his face into a mask of practiced, easy charm before he even fully pivoted.

"Major," Will said, his voice smooth. "Don't tell me. The florist sent lilies again? I specifically told them Mrs. Hartle associates lilies with funerals."

The major, a man who treated a folded napkin with the gravity of a field dressing, didn't smile. He was holding a sheaf of papers like a weapon.

"The general's schedule for the reception with the Lord

Mayor," the major said, tapping the paper. "You've allotted fifteen minutes for the tea service. Lady Ashbrooke requires at least thirty. And the seating chart—you have the retired colonel sitting next to the Vicar's wife."

"Is that a problem?" Will asked, leaning back against the mahogany desk, feigning interest.

"They haven't spoken in ten years," the major hissed. "Since the incident with the pig at the county fair. If you put them together, there will be blood on the tablecloth before the scones are served. It's a minefield, Captain. Fix it."

Will took the papers. His hands, calloused from the reins of pack mules and the chilled steel of howitzers, felt absurd holding the linen stationery. He looked at the major—a man whose biggest risk today was a paper-cut. The thought burned on Will's tongue: *I was stripping field guns in the dark while you were still learning how to crease a trouser leg.*

He looked at the chart. He saw the problem instantly. It was a social puzzle, and despite himself, he was good at puzzles.

"A minefield, sir," Will repeated, flashing a disarming grin that had saved him from demerits back at the Academy. "Understood. I'll execute a flanking maneuver. We'll put the old colonel near the fireplace—he likes the heat—and the Vicar's wife near the window. I'll buffer them with the aunt who loves to talk about her cats. Neutralizes both threats."

The major blinked, disarmed by the efficiency. "Precision, Captain. That is what the general requires."

He walked away, leaving Will alone in the office with his competence and his boredom.

This was his war. While the world burned, while the Germans drove deeper into Russia and the Japanese fortified the Pacific, Captain Will Darby was fighting a war of doilies and protocol.

He sat at his desk. He was an aide-de-camp to Major General Russell P. Hartle. In title, it was a prestigious post for a young officer. He had gotten it because he was sharp, handsome, and could talk a hungry dog off a meat truck. He was a natural politician.

But in reality, it was a special kind of purgatory. He was a glorified secretary. A valet with a rank.

He looked at the "To-Do" list on his desk:

- Confirm menu for Officer's Mess (Lamb vs. Mutton – *The general hates gristle*)
- Review laundry requisition forms (*Starch levels unacceptable*)
- Draft thank-you note to the Women's Auxiliary

He picked up his pen. It felt light, useless. He thought of the Pack Artillery, the grit of the mules, the geometry of the mountains. He was a man built for vertical climbs, and he was currently drowning in two-dimensional paperwork. Will looked out the window at the shivering infantry platoon.

The world was starkly divided, Will realized. There were the people in this warm, dry room—the ones who took the safety, the rank, and the glory without paying the price. They got more than they gave.

And then there were the ones in the mud.

I am on the wrong side of the window, Will thought, the realization settling in his gut like a stone.

"Some people give more than they get," he whispered to the glass. "And some get more than they give."

He looked down at the seating chart for Lady Ashbrooke.

He felt the "paper" creeping in—the stifling, bureaucratic cotton wool that suffocated fire. He had too much fire for this cold, damp room. "You mistake patience for acceptance," he muttered to the empty office, staring at his reflection in the dark window. "I have the ambition. I just currently lack the war."

He aggressively crossed out the Vicar's wife and moved her to the other side of the table.

"Tactical redeployment," he muttered.

He needed a way out. He needed a war.

He needed a ladder.

5

THE DEPARTURE

1942

Charleston, South Carolina

The cottage on Sullivan's Island was shuttered for the winter. The wind off the Atlantic rattled the frames, a cold, restless sound that mirrored the mood of the nation.

General George P. Hays stood in the hallway of their small Charleston row house, his duffel bag packed by the door. The orders were in his pocket: Northern Ireland, commander of the 2nd Infantry Division Artillery, for a front that didn't even exist yet.

Julia came down the stairs. She wasn't crying. She was carrying a stack of books.

"I spoke to Mr. Abernathy at the Society," she said, her voice steady. "He says they're overwhelmed. With the men leaving, they need someone to manage the archives. And the donations. They're calling it the 'Victory Book Campaign.'"

Hays smiled, a sad, proud expression. "So, you're reen-listing."

"One of us has to hold the fort," she said, placing the books on the table. "I can't sit here, George. I can't just wait for the telegram."

He walked to her, taking her hands. They were older now. The fire of 1918 had settled into a deep, unshakeable warmth. "It's a different war, Julia. It's bigger. It's... industrial."

"But the men are the same," she said fiercely.

For a traitorous, fleeting heartbeat, she wished he had just walked away after the Marne. She wished he were a banker, or a clerk, someone who came home at five o'clock to a house that didn't feel like a waiting room for the next set of orders. She hated herself for the thought instantly.

He was a soldier; it wasn't what he did, it was who he was. "They're still boys, scared and far from home," she continued, pushing the selfish thought away. "They'll still need stories."

She had never been one for the nomadic life of the Army wife, packing trunks every few years to follow the flag. She needed the salt air of the island, the roots of the library, the stillness of the archives. She needed to be the anchor so he could be the ship.

She reached up and adjusted his collar, a familiar gesture that made his throat tighten.

"You're going to be a general," she whispered. "My 'Rock.' But don't forget the other part. The part that knows how to read the current."

"I won't," he promised. "I'll write."

"You better," she said.

He kissed her then, a kiss of shared silence and understanding. It wasn't the kiss of the library in 1919. It was the solid, enduring kiss of a husband saying goodbye to his harbor, to the love of his life.

He picked up his bag. He walked to the door, then turned back.

"Julia," he said. "If I... if I get lost over there..."

"You won't," she interrupted, her eyes bright and hard. "You have the compass. And you know the way back."

She watched him walk down the steps and into the waiting car. She didn't wave until he was almost out of sight.

Then, she turned back to the empty house. She didn't sit down. She didn't weep. She put on her coat, picked up her keys, and walked out the door.

She walked straight to the Charleston Library Society. She unlocked the tall oak doors, the smell of old paper and lemon oil greeting her like an old friend.

She walked to the main desk, picked up the phone, and dialed the director.

"This is Mrs. Hays," she said, her voice clear and commanding. "I'm ready to start. Send me the books."

6

THE RANGER

1942

Northern Ireland

Will stood in Hartle's office, a requisitioned room in a damp manor house that smelled of a hearth fire. "Sir, you sent for me."

Hartle grunted, not looking up from a dispatch. "Will. I was just on the horn with Truscott in London—he's sold Marshall on these British Commandos. Churchill's pets. The War Department wants an American version. A new, elite unit. Men who can move fast, hit hard, and raise hell. They're calling them... 'Rangers.'"

The general finally looked up, his gaze sharp and appraising. "I need a man to build it from scratch. A man who isn't afraid to get his hands dirty, who understands unconventional warfare."

Hartle leaned back in his chair. "I was talking about it with an old friend of mine. George Hays."

Will's posture straightened. Colonel Hays. His old commander. The "Rock."

"He's just up the road with the 2nd Division's guns, you know," Hartle continued. "We were discussing this very problem. Hays told me about you. He said you were the most brilliant, stubborn, and ambitious officer he'd ever trained. But that's not what sold me."

Hartle leaned forward, his eyes boring into Will. "He told me about the 99th. The mule-skinners. He said you took that 'dead-end' assignment and turned it into a laboratory. He said you mastered the one thing this new unit will need more than anything: high mobility in impossible terrain. Independence. Small-unit operations."

A strange mix of images flooded Will's mind: the jingle of mule bells on a dark switchback. The smell of pine and sweat. The precise, metallic click of a howitzer's breechblock being seated. He heard Colonel Hays's voice, clear as day: *"high mobility in impossible terrain."* He saw the cannon at West Point. Mules, cliffs, deconstructed guns—he'd been training for this the whole time and never knew it.

Hartle stood and walked to the window, looking out at the gray Irish rain. "This isn't a job for a conventional artilleryman. It's a job for a man who knows how to lead a pack of mules—or a pack of wolves—through hell and back. It's a doctrinal bridge, and you're the only man I know who's already crossed it. The job is yours, if you want it."

Will felt the familiar, intoxicating rush. The cannon on the clock tower. This was it. He heard the name again. "Rangers." He could see the headlines. "Darby's Rangers." He coveted the very sound of it, the deference it would command, the story history would be forced to tell.

This was the next, higher rung. This was the path he was born for. He didn't hesitate. "Sir," Will said, his voice electric with a confidence that was absolute. "When do I start?"

7

THE CASTLE

1942

Hut 6, Bletchley Park, England

Annie pulled her wool coat tighter. On the walk to the hut, she paused to rest her hand against the rough bark of the old chestnut tree, a brief, grounding ritual to remind herself that the world was made of more than just ciphers and rain.

She was an analyst, a 'crypt' in the jargon of the Park, and she hated the damp wooden huts that served as the brain of Britain's war effort. Inside, the atmosphere was a suffocating contradiction. While the English damp seeped through the floorboards, the air at desk-level was hot and dry, vibrating with the heat of coal stoves and overworked desk lamps.

It didn't smell of nature; it smelled of ozone, burning dust, and the nervous, sour sweat of people who sat still for twelve hours a day while their minds ran marathons. It also smelled of weak tea, stale cigarette smoke, and the biting, metallic tang of hot wiring and clattering typewriters.

Her SIS liaison, a man known only as 'Alistair,' set a

steaming mug on her desk. He was a thin, bird-like man seconded from MI6 to the Park, and he looked, as always, untroubled. "A new assignment for you, Annie. A field assessment."

"I'm an analyst, Alistair. I break codes. I don't 'do field assessments.'"

"This one requires your particular... insight," he said. He slid a slender file across the table.

"Major William Darby. American. He's bringing 600 volunteers to Achnacarry Castle for Commando selection. We're training them, arming them. We need to know who we're investing in and partnering with."

Annie opened it. A single photograph of a charismatic, smiling American officer was paper-clipped to the cover.

"He put a cannon on a clock tower at West Point. Brilliant, certainly. But is he a strategic asset, or is he a glory-hound who's going to get his men killed, and ours with them?"

"And I'm to find this out from a hut in Buckinghamshire?"

"No," Alistair said, a rare, thin smile touching his lips. "You're going home. Achnacarry is just outside Spean Bridge, is it not? Your village. You'll take a leave of absence to visit your family. It's the perfect cover. Go for the final week of their selection course."

"So I'm to psychoanalyze an American Major while on holiday."

"Precisely. The selection course is six weeks of hell. At the end, the survivors will get a 12-hour pass. They will be at the local pub. That is when you will... make a connection."

"This isn't Bletchley, Annie," Alistair said, his voice quiet. "This is a field assessment. Our New York station, the BSC, has had remarkable success doing this with the Vichy French government in southern France that is collaborating with the Nazis. This is the same principle. We need a vital connection to Major Darby. Use whatever... charming Scottish beauty... is required to make it. We need to know who he is. We need to know if he's a king, a cowboy, or just a fool. And, Annie," he added, his tone shifting, "we need him to trust one of us. If he's as good as they say, he'll be important. Your assessment will determine everything."

She would be building a profile of the man who would lead this new American force—and somewhere down the line, joint operations might stand or fall on whether she got him right.

Achnacarry, Scotland

Achnacarry Castle was not a training camp. It was a bleak, imposing stone fortress in the most desolate corner of the Scottish Highlands, designed for one purpose: natural selection.

The weather was a constant, miserable enemy of its own —a near-perpetual state of rain, mist, and bone-aching damp that seeped into everything. The 1st Ranger Battalion arrived, 600 volunteers hand-picked by Major Will Darby, all of them tough, arrogant, and utterly unprepared for what awaited them.

The castle itself was unheated. Men slept on the bare floorboards with a few thin blankets, their uniforms never truly drying. The air in the barracks was a thick, gagging mix of wet wool, mildew, and the acrid, choking smell of peat smoke from the few fireplaces.

They ate half-cooked, greasy mutton from cold tins and

drank chlorinated water that tasted of iron. Their instructors were battle-hardened British Commandos, men with quiet eyes who had already killed Germans at places like St. Nazaire.

Their commander, Lieutenant Colonel Charles Vaughan, greeted the Americans not with a speech but with a simple, cold statement of fact. "Gentlemen," Vaughan said, his voice clipping the damp air, "welcome to what our men affectionately call 'The Castle.' There is no welcome. This is not training; it is selection. We will be using live ammunition in nearly all exercises. You will be cold, you will be wet, and you will be exhausted. The man next to you will be the only thing that matters. Fail him, and you fail this course."

The training was six weeks of structured brutality—grueling, 25-mile speed marches in full combat gear, carrying 60-pound packs over the trackless, ankle-twisting heather and boggy terrain. Stragglers weren't just mocked; they were failed and sent back in disgrace.

Teamwork was beaten into them. They ran with 20-foot logs on their shoulders, six men to a log, learning to move as one. But it was the live fire that broke them and remade them. Instructors, demonstrating an assault on a bunker, would throw live, unpinned grenades with a 4-second fuse just behind the last man, the explosion physically kicking them forward, teaching them that hesitation was death.

Will, watching his men, felt a savage pride. This was not brutality; it was a crucible. He was not horrified by the live fire or the harsh conditions; he was exhilarated. This was how you forged a weapon. This was how you burned the weakness out of men and left only hard, sharp steel.

He saw their exhaustion, their fear, and their endurance,

and he knew, with an arrogant certainty, that the men who survived this would be invincible. They would be *his*.

The most notorious obstacle was the "Death Slide." It was an exercise in pure, calculated terror. A Ranger, in full kit, had to climb a 40-foot tree, hook a small wooden toggle and rope over a single cable stretched fifty feet across the raging, glacial currents of the River Arkaig, and slide down.

As the first Ranger launched himself into the void, his toggle smoking on the cable, Will heard a violent crack and the unmistakable zip of a bullet passing the man's head. He spun. A British instructor stood calmly on the riverbank with a rifle, firing live rounds into the water just to the side of the sliding American.

"Keeps their heads down, major!" the instructor shouted with a grin. Will's men stared in horror. This wasn't a prank. This was real.

One of his men, his hands slick with sweat and fear, fumbled his toggle. He fell, plunging into the rapids and breaking his leg on a rock. Another was wounded by shrapnel from a live-fire demolition drill. Of the 600 men Will brought to Achnacarry, only 500 would remain. This was the price.

Will looked at the live fire, at his wounded man, and at the grim, satisfied face of the Commando instructor. He accepted the cost.

This was how his elite unit would be baptized.

8

THE KING'S STONE

1942

Spean Bridge, Scotland

Six weeks later, Annie sat in the village pub. She nursed a dark stout and pretended to read a book of poetry. She had arrived home two days prior, her cover as a visiting daughter intact.

Her mission from Alistair was to "establish a vital connection." But if she was being honest with herself, the analyst was already compromised from the first time she saw Major Darby's photo.

The small pub was crammed with boisterous, drunk Commandos and Scots Guards celebrating their survival of the brutal training, the air thick with pipe smoke, damp tweed, and spilled ale. The six-week selection was over.

On their only 12-hour pass before graduation, Major Darby drove a borrowed jeep into the village. When he walked in, he didn't swagger; he just filled the space with a magnetic spark. He was wearing his dress uniform, clean and pressed, but he looked like he'd spent the day wrestling mountains.

He looked tired, happy—and dangerous. He scanned his men, who all straightened their posture when he entered, and his eyes were immediately drawn to Annie, sitting alone by the fire. She seemed utterly unimpressed by the throngs of uniformed men vying for her attention.

She looked up from her book. When her eyes met his, his face broke into a smile that was genuine, boyish, and utterly disarming. He walked over, dodging a rowdy group of Scots Guards. Will, used to women being charmed by his rugged looks and confident swagger, approached her.

"It's not often I see someone reading in a pub," he said with his easiest smile.

Annie looked up, closing her book but keeping her finger marking the page. She felt a flush of heat that had nothing to do with the peat fire.

"It's Burns," she said, her voice softening the edges, and in the most beautiful Scottish accent he had ever heard, replied, "And it's not often I see an American officer who thinks he's the first to notice."

Her eyes held his. "You're Major Darby. The one building the 'new Commandos.' That's all these boys in the pub, and the women in the Post Office, have been talking about. You look... ambitious."

He was thrown. She wasn't fawning; her assessment was immediate, intimate, and professional.

"Guilty as charged," he laughed, recovering. "And you are...?"

"Annie McKenna. And I am... skeptical."

"Skeptical of what? Americans?"

"Of men who look like they get drunk off themselves

racing up the ladder," she said, her voice soft, "but haven't checked to see what's at the top."

Will was hooked; he pulled out a chair, said "May I," and sat down. "And what do you suppose is at the top?"

"That depends on the ladder," she said, a small, challenging smile playing on her lips. "Are you a man who believes in destiny, Major Darby?"

"I believe a man makes his own," he countered.

"Spoken like a true American," she replied, her voice playful again. "We Scots believe destiny is a story that's already written. You're on a King's errand. You should know our stories of kingship. Come on, I'll show you something."

She didn't wait for an answer, grabbing her coat and walking out. Will, intrigued and entirely off-balance, followed.

Annie hopped up into his jeep parked outside the pub. The boisterous cheers of the Commandos faded into the cold Highland mist as she directed him through the seven-mile drive toward the Achnacarry estate.

Will pulled the jeep onto the soft verge at the entrance to the Mile Dorcha. Under the canopy of ancient moss-covered beeches and pines, the world turned silent and green, leaving the noise of the village far behind.

"It's called the Dark Mile," Annie whispered as they stepped onto the narrow road.

Will looked up at the ceiling of leaves, "I've spent the last six weeks training my boys to survive this wild place," he said, in the darkness. "I never thought it could be... beautiful."

"The trees here have long memories," she said, leading him past the Eas Chia-aig waterfalls. "Local legend says they grew together to hide a prince after he lost a battle to free Scotland."

The rainforest of thick moss and otherworldly ferns seemed to swallow their footsteps. As the dense woods finally gave way, the remote vista of Loch Arkaig stretched out before them, its waters mirror-still in the fading Highland light.

Annie led him to the quiet grove of ancient oaks overlooking the water. "This is a land of kings," she said, her voice taking on a hushed, reverent tone. She gestured to the large, flat rock sitting near the shore.

"It makes a man like you think of his destiny," she said, her sharp eyes fixing on his. "It makes him think of the Lia Fàil—the Stone of Destiny."

"The Stone of Scone?" Will said. "The one the English stole from Scotland for the coronations at Westminster?"

"The very one," Annie said. She fixed him with her sharp, knowing eyes. "You know the legend, then? The public one?"

"I know it's a coronation stone."

"It's more than that," she said, her voice dropping, pulling him closer. "Some say it's Jacob's Pillow from the Old Testament. The story says Jacob was alone in the desert, sleeping on the ground with nothing but this stone for a headrest. That night, he dreamed of a ladder reaching all the way to heaven—a path to the stars for a man who had nothing left."

She looked at him, a teasing smile playing on her lips. "The legend says it cries out—screams, really—when a true King sits on it. But it demands a heavy price for the heavy crown."

"A stone for a king," he repeated, liking the sound of it. "That's a legend I can get behind."

Annie laughed, a light, musical sound in the Highland mist. She saw the fire in his eyes, the ambition she had been sent to assess, and she found it undeniably attractive.

She was stoking the fire, and she knew it.

"Is that so?" she teased. "Well, let's see, shall we?"

She gestured to the large flat rock. "Go on. Sit."

Will, caught up in her game, grinned, "A ladder to the stars? And, all I have to do is sleep on a stone pillow? Sounds just like the infantry." He sat on the stone. "Well? Does it cry out?"

Annie stepped in front of him, her expression one of mock seriousness. She placed her hands on his shoulders, her touch sending a jolt through him.

"Be it known," she declared, her accent thickening in playful ceremony, "that this man, Will Darby, having climbed the high cliffs and braved the cold lochs, is hereby..."

She plucked a sprig of purple heather from a nearby bush and gently tapped his head with it, as if with a scepter.

"...crowned. King of the Rangers."

She smiled, her face close to his. "Does that suit you, Your Majesty?"

He reached up and caught her hand, the one holding the heather. "It suits me just fine, Annie."

He was silent for a long moment, about to make his move.

Annie, realizing her assessment had become something... else, gently pulled her hand back, but she left the sprig of heather in his grasp.

"For your glory, then, major," she said, her voice soft. "A trophy from Scotland. To remember your crown."

He looked at the small, tough purple flowers. A symbol of his destiny, given to him by the most intelligent, beautiful woman he had ever met.

"I'll keep it with me," he said, his voice firm, tucking it into his breast pocket. "To remind me of... the coronation."

She smiled, happy to have made a connection. "It is time for us to say goodnight, 'Your Majesty.' Even kings have to earn their keep in Scotland."

9

THE TWO LEGENDS

1942

Spean Bridge, Scotland

They retraced their steps, leaving the moonlit vista of the loch and entering the cathedral-like Dark Mile once more. The silence of the woods was absolute, broken only by the crunch of their boots on the road.

When they reached the verge where the jeep was parked, Will helped her up into the high passenger seat, a gesture that felt intimate after their walk through the shadows.

The engine roared to life, a mechanical intrusion into the Highland stillness. Annie directed him back along the winding seven-mile route, the jeep's headlamps cutting through the thick mist as they left the ancient estate and returned toward the village of Spean Bridge.

Will pulled the jeep to a stop near the pub, and they walked to her cottage in a comfortable silence, the mist clinging to their coats. Will didn't try to take her arm, but he walked close enough that their sleeves brushed every few steps, a rhythmic, electric contact.

"You're not just a local girl, Annie," Will said, looking at her. "You analyze people. You dismantle them."

"I'm an analyst for the government. I kind of listen and tell stories." She told him what she could, looking up at him with a smile. "And the American story is a bit loud, Will. You're shouting at the world. You all want to prove something."

"Maybe we just want to win," he said.

"Maybe," she agreed.

"But be careful. The Stone has two legends. One is the Coronation. The other..." She hesitated.

"The other?"

"The other is about what happens when the stone breaks," she said softly.

"Stones like that don't break, Annie," Will said, his confidence absolute.

"Everything breaks, Will," she replied.

They reached her small stone cottage, a single warm light glowing in the window. The pub was still roaring in the distance, but here, there was only the sound of the wind in the pines.

"Well," Will said, stopping at her small gate. "I should let you go. Thank you for the walk. And the history lesson." He gave her his most charming, disarming smile. "Even if I'm not sure I agree with the legend."

"Oh, you don't have to agree with it, major," Annie said, her hand on the gate latch. "You just have to be aware of it— the weight of the crown. The best legends show the dangers, not just the destinations."

"I'll stick with my legend, I think," he said, leaning

against the gatepost. "The one about a man making his own destiny. It's gotten me this far."

"It has," she agreed, her sharp, intelligent eyes appraising him in the dim light. "But it's a lonely path, chasing a throne. All that climbing. You must get awfully tired."

The playful jab hit its mark. He was tired. But he'd never admit it. "The view from the top is worth it."

"Is it?" she murmured. "Or is it just a way to keep from looking at what's all around you?"

He was captivated. This woman was a puzzle, and Will Darby loved a puzzle. "You're dangerous, Annie. You see right through a man."

"I just listen to the story he's telling," she said softly. "And you, Major Darby, are telling a loud one."

An impulse, something warm and genuine, seized him. "Achnacarry is six weeks of hell. I'm running one more class through. I'll be back in this village exactly once before we ship out. For a 12-hour pass. Will you have dinner with me? I'll... I'll try to tell a quieter story."

She looked at him, at this brilliant, charming man who was so clearly running toward the crown, and her heart softened. "Six weeks is a long time, major. Ask me then?"

"I will," he said. He hesitated, not wanting to leave. He leaned in, intending a charming, confident kiss. But Annie, seeing the move, turned her head at the last second. His kiss, meant for her lips, landed chastely and somewhat awkwardly on her cheek.

She smiled at his brief, surprised expression. "Goodnight, Major Darby."

She slipped inside, closing the door with a soft, final click, leaving him alone in the mist. He stood there for a moment, a bemused grin on his face. He looked at the heather. He thought of her Stone for a king. He smiled. Annie didn't know it, but she had just handed the "would-be King" his destiny.

"I'll see you in six weeks, Annie," he said to the closed door. He turned and strode back toward the pub, his confidence intact, his focus absolute.

Inside, Annie leaned against the door, her heart hammering. She had met the most compelling, brilliant, and dangerous man she had ever known. And he was, she thought with a sigh, absolutely chasing the wrong legend.

10

THE FAREWELL

SIX WEEKS LATER, 1942

London

Annie had spent the weeks since their walk at the loch at a Bletchley outstation in London, buried in ciphers and the relentless pressure of the "Paper War," but her mind kept drifting back to the American with the blue eyes. Her professional assessment of Major William Darby was complete and sat ready for dispatch in her satchel. He was, she had concluded, a "brilliant, ambitious, and a glorious king in his own mind, who will either win the war or die chasing it."

Her duty to the Crown was technically finished, but the distance between London and the Highlands felt like an unbridgeable chasm. She found she couldn't simply file her report and let the "King of the Rangers" leave without seeing him one last time. The analyst in her knew the risks of getting too close to an "asset," but the woman in her was already counting the hours.

She sought out Alistair in his smoke-filled London office.

He was looking over the latest intercept from the Mediterranean when she entered. "The report is finished, Alistair," she said, her voice steady despite the flutter in her chest. "Good," he replied without looking up. "I'll have a courier take it to the Admiralty."

"No," Annie countered, leaning against the edge of his desk. "The report is purely analytical. It lacks a final, live-environment verification. The Rangers graduate this weekend, and I believe a face-to-face confirmation of the Major's readiness is required before they ship out. It's a matter of... confirmation."

Alistair finally looked up, his one sharp eye fixed on her. He had been a handler too long not to recognize the personal note in her voice. He saw the way she clutched the strap of her bag, the subtle shift in her brogue that happened when she was being evasive. "A four-day field assignment to Spean Bridge," he mused, a thin, knowing smile touching his lips. "A bit excessive for a 'verification,' isn't it?"

"It is thoroughness, Alistair. Nothing more."

"Of course," he said, reaching for his stamp. "If the analyst insists on a final check of the asset, who am I to argue?" Annie didn't wait for him to change his mind. She caught the evening train north, the soot of the London yards still clinging to her coat as the locomotive began the grueling fourteen-hour climb into the Highlands.

Spean Bridge, Scotland

She arrived home on a Friday, the eve of the Rangers' graduation. It was the night of their only 12-hour pass, the one Will had promised her weeks ago. She told herself she was there as a liaison officer, but as she walked toward the village pub, her heart was no longer an analyst's; it was a woman's.

She pushed open the heavy oak door, the familiar warmth and noise of the pub washing over her—pipe smoke, ale, and the roar of Commandos and Scots Guards celebrating their survival. She scanned the room for her usual chair by the fire, the one that offered a view of the entire room.

And she froze.

He was there in her chair.

Major Will Darby wasn't holding court with his officers. He was leaning toward the firelight, his long legs stretched out, completely absorbed in a thin, worn book. She moved closer. It was her book. *The Poetry of Robert Burns.*

He looked up as if he sensed her. The easy, arrogant grin she expected wasn't there. Instead, his face lit up with a look of pure, delighted recognition.

"Annie," he said, standing up. He looked tired—the training had been brutal—but when he looked at her, the fatigue vanished. "I was hoping you'd come. I saved your seat."

"You stole my seat," she corrected, trying to keep her voice steady, but her heart was hammering. "And you're reading my poet."

"I am," he said, holding the chair for her. "I find I have a sudden interest in Scottish poets. Especially the ones about 'red, red roses' and women."

He sat down next to her, the small table creating an intimate island in the smoky room.

"I took the liberty," he said, signaling the barman. A moment later, a fresh pint of stout and a steaming plate of stew arrived for her. "Stout. And the lamb stew. You said it was the only thing worth eating here."

Annie looked at the food, then at him. He had remembered.

"You are dangerous, Will Darby," she said, sitting down.

"I'm just persistent," he smiled.

He had remembered her drink. He had ordered her dinner. Her entire mission—to assess, connect, and disengage—was in ruins.

"So, the King or the American?" he asked, his eyes, lit by the fire, never leaving hers. "Which one am I tonight?"

"Tonight, major," she said, recovering her wit, "you look like the tired man who's just finished a very hard school."

"I am," he said. "And I'm leaving tomorrow. For Africa."

The word landed with a thud. Africa. The war, which had been a game of maps and legends, was suddenly back.

"Then this is a farewell, Major Darby."

"This is dinner, Annie."

For the next three hours, the war didn't exist.

They ate. They drank. And Will Darby, the "King of the Rangers," proceeded to charm her completely.

He didn't brag about his tactics. He told her stories about the men. He made her laugh until her sides ached with a story about a mule that outsmarted a Brigadier General. He listened when she said what she could about her "boring" government job, asking questions that showed he was actually interested in her mind.

He was funny, self-deprecating, and warm. He was a gentleman who pulled out her chair and refilled her glass before she even noticed it was empty.

She watched him across the candlelight. She saw the way

his eyes crinkled when he laughed. She saw the way he treated the barman with respect.

And Annie, the careful analyst, realized with a jolt of panic and joy that she was falling in love with him.

"Last orders!" the barman shouted.

The bubble burst. The laughter died down.

"Well," Will said, his voice growing serious. "That's time."

"You leave tomorrow?" Annie said. The thought made her chest ache.

"0500 hours," he said.

He looked at her, his blue eyes searching hers.

Then, his gaze drifted to the side of her head. He reached out, his finger hovering just inches from her hair. "I didn't notice it in the dim light before," he murmured, his voice dropping to a low, private register. "The yellow bow. It's the only bit of sun I've seen in this whole gray country."

Annie felt a flush of warmth. "It's just a bit of silk, Will."

"No," he said, his eyes locking back onto hers with an intensity that made the noise of the pub vanish. "It's a marker. A reminder that there's a world outside this war."

"Will you walk me out?"

11

THE STORM

1942

Spean Bridge, Scotland

They stepped out of the warm, loud pub and into the cold Highland mist.

The silence was sudden and heavy. They walked toward her cottage, their footsteps echoing on the wet stones.

Will didn't try to take her arm, but he walked close enough that she could feel the heat radiating from him.

"You're different than I expected," Annie said softly. "The gossip said you were a wild man."

"I can be," Will admitted. "But tonight... tonight I just wanted to be the man who had dinner with Annie."

They reached her gate. The cottage was dark, save for the dying embers of the fire inside.

"This is it, then," Will said. He turned to face her.

The mist swirled around them. He looked at her—this beautiful woman with the bow in her hair—and he looked like he was memorizing her face.

"Annie," he said, his voice low. "I don't know when I'm coming back. I don't know *if* I'm coming back."

"Don't say that," she whispered.

"I have to," he said. "I can't make promises I can't keep. But I want you to know... tonight was the best night of this war."

He reached into his pocket and pulled out the sprig of heather she had given him six weeks ago. It was dried now, brittle, but he had kept it safe.

"I kept the crown," he said with a small, sad smile. "But I think I'd trade it for one more hour."

Annie looked at the heather, then at him. She saw the vulnerability behind the confidence. She saw a man who was going into the fire, and who didn't want to go alone.

She made her choice.

"You don't have to trade it, Will," she said softly.

She reached out and opened the gate latch. The click was loud in the quiet night.

"Come in," she whispered.

Will followed her up the garden path. He didn't rush. He waited while she unlocked the door, his presence behind her a solid, warm weight.

Inside, the cottage was cool. Annie moved to stir the fire, but Will stopped her.

"Leave it," he said softly. "Come here."

He reached out and took her hand. His touch wasn't demanding; it was asking.

Annie turned to him. In the dim light of the embers, his eyes were dark and intense.

"Will," she breathed.

He stepped closer and cupped her face in his hands. His

thumbs traced her cheekbones, his touch incredibly gentle for a man with such scarred hands.

"Annie," he whispered. "You are the most beautiful thing I have ever seen."

He lowered his head.

The kiss wasn't an ambush. It was a slow, deepening slide into warmth. His lips were soft, tasting of stout and the cold night air.

Annie melted against him. Her hands went to his waist, gripping the wool of his uniform. The analysis, the caution, the government secrets—it all fell away. There was only him.

Will groaned low in his throat, pulling her closer, his arms wrapping around her like steel bands, holding her as if she were the only anchor in a storm.

"Are you sure?" he murmured against her mouth, his breath hot on her skin.

"I'm sure," she whispered. "I don't want you to leave tomorrow. But if you have to go... don't go yet."

He picked her up as easily as if she were made of air, and carried her into the small bedroom.

He set her down on the edge of the bed. He didn't loom over her. He knelt before her, unlacing her shoes, his movements reverent.

When he joined her, it was with a tenderness that broke her heart. He wasn't the "King of the Rangers" taking a prize. He was a man sharing his warmth, his fear, and his hope.

They moved together in the firelight, slow and sweet, an urgent, wordless conversation. He made her feel safe. He made her feel seen.

Later, as the rain drummed against the roof, Will held her, his chin resting on the top of her head.

"I have to go," he whispered into the darkness, his voice heavy with regret.

"I know," Annie said, tightening her hold on him.

"But I'll come back," he promised. "I'll come back to this cottage. To this chair. To you."

"I'll be waiting," she said.

He kissed her one last time—a kiss that tasted of goodbye—and then he was gone, slipping out into the pre-dawn mist to lead his men to war.

Annie lay in the empty bed, clutching the pillow that still smelled of him. She touched her lips. She knew, with a certainty that terrified her, that she would wait forever if she had to.

12

THE CLIMB

1943

The Mediterranean (North Africa)

Will was on his path, and the Achnacarry training had given him the boot leather to climb it, two steps at a time. The Mediterranean was his stage. His first act was Operation Torch, the invasion of North Africa.

Will and his 1st Ranger Battalion were tasked with seizing the Vichy French batteries at the port of Arzew, Algeria. Though they flew the tricolor, these guns now served the Axis, commanding the harbor from atop steep bluffs. To the regular army, it was an obstacle. To Will, it was an invitation.

"We go up," he commanded. In the pre-dawn darkness, Will led his men from the landing craft, the salty spray cold on their faces. They slipped ashore not at the base of the cliffs, but a half-mile away near a place called Cap Carbon.

From there, they moved in a single, soundless column along the dark bluffs, just as they had practiced on the cold, wet stone of Achnacarry. They found the narrow ravine the scouts had identified and began to climb, their movements masked by the surf below.

The stone was cold, slick with sea spray and grit. Will felt for his next hold, his knuckles scraping against the rock face. Below, the surf crashed, a roaring chaos that masked the grunts and scrapes of his Rangers. He pulled himself up onto a narrow ledge, his lungs burning, the weight of his gear pulling him back toward the dark water.

For a fleeting second, he wasn't in Africa. He was back at the Point, the smooth, cold bronze of the cannon barrel leaving his fingertips, the familiar feel of the granite quad's stone under his palms, the breathless, stupid joy of pulling off the impossible.

He'd led that climb, too. The parallel was so sharp it almost made him laugh. But this time, nobody was laughing. This time, if he slipped, he wouldn't land in the Superintendent's bad graces—he'd land on corpses. He shook the memory away—one more heave. The fort and the war were just above them.

This was not a frontal assault; it was a stealthy infiltration. Will was one of the first men up, crouched at the top, his .45 holstered, his trench knife ready. This was not a drill. This was not a prank. This was his climb, made real, an assault from the rear for the highest stakes.

His men flooded the position behind him, a silent, disciplined wave of green. They seized the batteries before the French gunners could even get their morning coffee. He had taken his first castle. The guns were silent, Arzew's harbor was open, and the Rangers had done it with only a handful of men hit.

The flag of Free France now flew over Arzew, the red Cross of Lorraine standing defiant against the blue Mediterranean sky.

Will paced, cleaning his pistol, the exhaustion a heavy blanket. The staff officers back in England, the ones who had scoffed at his training methods, would have called the night assault up the bluff a suicidal, reckless gamble.

He smiled grimly. They didn't understand. West Point hadn't just been a prank; it was a prototype. Arzew was the field test. This victory wasn't a fluke; it was proof. Proof that his tactics—his belief in speed, surprise, and vertical envelopment—weren't just theory. It worked.

He felt the pull of it. The scream of the legend. He was building an army that could do what no one else thought possible, because he was willing to try what no one else dared. He clicked the pistol back together.

The first test was passed.

Wales

Thousands of miles from the North African coast, in a draughty hut in Wales, Brigadier General George P. Hays sat with a stack of reports. The after-action from Arzew lay on top, months old now but still bracing.

He was up to his neck in the slow work of building the 2nd Infantry Division for the cross-Channel D-Day assault —training tables, firing schedules, shipping diagrams—but he still had time to read about Rangers who climbed cliffs in the dark.

A slow, proud smile touched his lips. "He did it," Hays murmured, his mentor's pride unmistakable. "He learned the lesson from the 99th—high mobility in impossible terrain."

He read further down the report, and the smile faded, replaced by a hint of worry. His eyes scanned the details of the Sened Station raid: a march of thirty-plus miles, deep behind Italian lines, guided only by compass and starlight. The Rangers hit the post like ghosts and vanished before the enemy could even mount a counter-attack.

He was proud of his protégé, but he worried about the immense personal risks they were taking. "It was brilliant," he said to his aide, "but it was quite a gamble. He risked his whole unit on a single, glorious charge."

Hays turned to the map of France that covered his wall, a vast, complex problem he had to solve.

Will's legend was just beginning.

Then came the battle for Djebel el Ank pass. The Rangers, guided by Will's patrols, infiltrated the Italian positions on a tortuous 10-mile route through the dark hills. At dawn, they attacked from above while the 26th Infantry attacked from the front, seizing the critical pass.

Days later, at El Guettar, the Rangers found themselves dug in on bare rock, not prowling at night. When the German counterattacks came, they fought as ordinary infantry near Djebel Berda and paid for it – three killed and eighteen wounded in a handful of days, almost as many casualties as all their classic Ranger operations in North Africa combined.

But the German attack was shattered.

He reached into his breast pocket. His fingers brushed

the brittle, dried sprig of heather Annie had given him in Scotland. He thought of her warmth, her sharp wit, and the "secret legends" she tried to warn him about. But standing here, with the wind whipping his jacket and the ground secured, he didn't feel the warning. He felt the ascent.

The heather wasn't a caution. It was a trophy.

13

THE LEGEND

1943

Sicily / Salerno, Italy

Will's name was becoming a legend, a talisman whispered by Allied commanders and cursed by German ones. But legends are rarely written in ink; they are written in sweat and adrenaline.

The ink was barely dry on the maps of Gela, Sicily, when the reality of the invasion soured. The "soft underbelly" of Europe had teeth.

"Tanks!" a young corporal screamed, stumbling backward through the dusty olive grove, his face a mask of gray dust and terror. "Italian armor! They're breaking the line!"

Will grabbed the man by his webbing, halting his retreat with a jolt. "Hold fast, Corporal. Rangers don't run."

But the sound was unmistakable—the death knell of steel treads grinding against ancient stone. Will's Rangers were light infantry. They had rifles, grenades, and courage, but courage didn't dent steel.

A shell slammed into the earth fifty yards away, the

concussion knocking the wind out of the platoon. Through the smoke, Will saw the squad manning a borrowed 37mm antitank gun. The gunner crumpled, clutching his neck. The loader froze, staring at the lumbering metal beast bearing down on them.

Panic wasn't just knocking at the door; it was kicking it in.

Will didn't think. He sprinted. He shoved the wounded gunner aside and dropped behind the breech.

"Load!" Will roared at the frozen private.

The boy fumbled a shell into the chamber. *Clack.*

Will sighted. Fired. The small shell sparked off the Italian tank's armor plate like a stone off a pond. Harmless. The tank kept coming, its machine gun traversing toward them.

"Again!" Will screamed, shoving the loader's hand to speed him up.

He fired again. *Clang.*

"Again!"

He was firing point-blank now, a furious one-man stand against a machine designed to kill him. He poured round after round into the enemy until a lucky shot finally smashed the track mechanism. The tank shuddered, slewed violently to the right, and stopped, coughing black smoke.

The attack faltered. The beachhead held. But as Will leaned against the hot barrel of the gun, wiping grease from his face, he realized courage alone was a poor shield. He needed better tools.

He found them in the hills. When the 4.2-inch chemical mortars arrived, the manuals said they were for smoke screens. Will looked at the massive tubes and saw a hammer.

"Sir, these aren't precision weapons," a mortar sergeant argued as they set up on a rocky spur.

"They are if you aim them right," Will countered. "I want high explosives. Walk them up that ridge."

He treated the heavy mortars like a surgeon treating a scalpel. He raked the Italian strongpoints until the positions simply came apart. It was improvisation, pure and simple—Hays's old lesson in aggressive fire made real.

By the time they hit the mainland at Salerno, the Rangers weren't just a support element; they were the vanguard.

They landed at Maiori and surged inland, seizing the Chiunzi Pass by mid-morning. It was a stunning success, but holding it became a two-week nightmare.

"They're coming up the draw!" a radio operator shouted over the gale whipping the summit. "German infantry, battalion strength!"

Will grabbed the handset. He didn't ask for a forward observer; he stepped out onto the exposed rock and became one.

"Drop five zero," Will commanded, watching the gray shapes swarm up the slope. "Fire for effect."

He stood in the wind, walking the exploding twenty-five-pound shells up and down the German line like a conductor leading a symphony of destruction. He broke their assault, scattered their infantry, and forced them back down the mountain.

The German line broke. The pass held.

After the battle, Will leaned back against the rough bark of a chestnut tree to catch his breath. Below him, the Bay of Naples was a flat sheet of violet—a peaceful mirror to the black, oily pillars rising from the burning tanks in the plain. In the distance, Vesuvius smoked

The air smelled thick with the scent of crushed grapes where a mortar had pulverized a vineyard, mixing with the sharp tang of victory. Will took it in. This was not artillery work. This was mountain warfare. It was the 99th Pack Artillery's doctrine made real, and in that moment, he knew he was right.

Will lowered the binoculars. The wind whipped as he looked down at the armada filling the bay below. He reached into his breast pocket, his fingers brushing the dry, brittle sprig of Scottish heather.

He saw his reflection in the eyes of a nearby lieutenant—not just respect, but awe. He coveted that look. He had forged this brand in the fire of Gela and the rocks of Chiunzi.

He ran the tally in his head. At Arzew, he traded ten casualties to clear the way for twelve thousand soldiers coming in behind him. At Gela, his Rangers helped hold the beachhead against counterattacks so the entire Seventh Army wasn't pushed back into the sea. He was the master of the exchange rate—risking the few to save the many.

He was, in his own mind, untouchable. He wiped the grit from his forehead. The Italian sun felt like a crown.

It was the last time he would feel warm for a long time.

14

THE NEEDLE

MAY 1943

Hut 6, Bletchley Park, England

The war was a map on the wall, but for Annie, it was a needle in a haystack of static.

It was 0300 hours.

Annie rubbed her eyes, staring at the raw decrypt on her desk. It was a fragment of a *Kriegsmarine* transmission—the Shark key, used by U-boat wolfpacks in the Atlantic.

Usually, it was gibberish. But tonight, a single pattern had repeated. A grid coordinate.

"Jean," Annie whispered, not wanting to break the hum of concentration in the room. "Check the Atlantic shipping tables. Convoy UT-4. Where is it?"

Jean, a pale girl who looked like she hadn't slept in a week, flipped through the logbook. "Entering sector 44-North. Carrying the 1st Infantry Division reinforcements for Sicily."

Annie's blood ran cold. She looked back at the decrypt.

The U-boats weren't patrolling sector 44. They were *waiting* in it.

"They know," Annie breathed. "They aren't hunting; they're setting a table. Twelve U-boats. Twenty thousand men on those transports."

She grabbed her pencil. This was the "Paper War." There were no explosions here, no mud, no screaming sergeants. There was only the terrifying quiet of a pencil scratching on paper.

If she was wrong, she was just a tired girl in a cardigan hallucinating patterns in the noise. If she was right, twenty thousand mothers were about to get telegrams.

She thought of Price Hays's story—the one Will had told her. The Lieutenant who rode seven horses to death to deliver a message at the Marne. He had galloped through a storm of steel.

I am riding, too, she thought, her hand flying across the page as she decoded the intercept. *I am riding a beam of radio waves, and I have to get there before the torpedoes.*

She finished the transcription. It was a kill order.

She didn't walk to the Supervisor's desk—she ran.

"Priority FLASH," she said, slamming the paper onto the desk of the duty officer, Mr. Strickland. "Admiralty. Immediate. Re-route Convoy UT-4 to vector South-South-East. Now."

Strickland looked at the paper, then at her. "Are you sure, Miss McKenna? Rerouting a convoy of that size based on a partial..."

"I am not sure," Annie snapped, her Scottish brogue cutting through the polite English murmur of the hut. "I am certain. The wolves are at the door, Mr. Strickland. Turn the ships."

Two Days Later

The report came back in a grey, nondescript file folder.

CONVOY UT-4 ARRIVED SAFELY. NO CONTACT.

That was it. No medals. No headlines. No "Annie McKenna Saved the Division."

Just... silence.

The U-boats had waited in the dark, and the ships had simply sailed around them. The battle hadn't happened.

Annie sat at her desk, holding the piece of paper that confirmed "Nothing Happened." She felt a phantom vibration in her hand—the weight of twenty thousand lives that continued to breathe because she had sharpened her pencil.

She realized then the terrible power of her position. She could reach across the ocean and move mountains.

She placed the report in the "Complete" file.

She had saved thousands. And she could never tell a soul.

She thought of Will, somewhere in the Mediterranean. She prayed that if he ever walked into a trap, there would be someone like her, sitting in a cold room, watching the needle, ready to turn the ship.

15

THE WINTER LINE

AUTUMN 1943

Kesselring's HQ, Near Rome

Field Marshal Albert Kesselring, his face radiating an incongruous, smiling calm, stood before a massive map of the Italian peninsula. His staff was in a quiet panic. The Allies had successfully landed at Salerno. The "soft underbelly" of Europe had been cut open.

"They are celebrating, of course," Kesselring said, his voice the smooth, reasonable tone of a professor. He tapped the map at Salerno. "They have their beachhead. They believe the path to Rome is open. They believe we will run."

He smiled, a genuinely warm expression that chilled his officers more than any rage could have. "Smiling Albert," as the Allies called him, was never more dangerous than when he was polite. "But they are not fighting an army," he continued. "They are fighting a map. And this," his finger swept across the jagged spine of the Apennines, "is a fortress built by a God of war. They believe we will defend the cities. They are wrong. We will defend the *geography*."

He was not a fanatic; he was a master of the defensive war. He knew the Allies' weakness lay not in their arms but in logistics and imagination. They were a road-bound army. He would take the roads away from them.

His finger traced a line across the peninsula, from the mouth of the Garigliano River, up the Rapido and Sangro, to the coast. It was a line of sheer mountains and deep, muddy valleys. "Here," he said, his finger stopping on a single, dominant peak. "Monte Cassino. It commands the Liri Valley. It is the only flat, logical path to Rome. It is the gate."

An officer, brave or foolish, spoke up. "Field Marshal, the Führer's directive suggests a defensive line much further north. To hold a line this far south..."

"The Führer looks at a paper map; I look at the terrain," Kesselring corrected, his smile tightening. "That directive will not stand. Once he sees the terrain, he will choose my line. We are not holding a line. We are building one. A 'Winter Line.' We will use the mountains as our walls and the rivers as our moats. We will turn every village into a pillbox and every mountain pass into a kill zone. We will drag them into a war of attrition they cannot win. By the time they reach this... 'Gustav Line'... their army will be broken, their morale shattered, and their 'soft underbelly' will have been 'bled white.'"

He looked at the map, seeing not a retreat, but a masterpiece of defensive geometry. "They have landed in Italy," he said softly. "But they will die here. Send the order. Begin the fortifications. This will be their Verdun."

16

THE KILL BOX

JANUARY 1944

Bletchley Park, England

The "castle" Annie worked in seven days a week had no stone, no turrets, and no glory. It was a long, cold, damp wooden hut in the middle of Buckinghamshire.

This was Hut 6, the nerve center for breaking the German Army and Air Force Enigma ciphers. Annie was a junior intelligence officer in Hut 6, serving as liaison to Hut 3, one of the thousands of women who made up a majority of the Park's staff.

And, she was a single, vital cog in a massive, secret machine.

"More tea, Annie?" Jean, the woman at the next desk, whispered, holding up a chipped teapot. "God, yes, Jean. And make it strong enough to stand a spoon in," Annie whispered back, never looking up.

Her mind was a thousand miles away, in Italy. She was

trying not to think of Will. She was trying to hunt the mind of his enemy: Field Marshal Albert Kesselring.

For weeks, her section had been trying to build a "picture" of Kesselring's mind. He was a ghost, his communications disciplined, his movements masked. But he was also meticulous. And meticulous men, Annie knew, had patterns.

The decrypt on her desk was a logistical report, seemingly mundane. It listed fuel and ammunition requisitions for a "reserve" Panzer unit stationed near... Cisterna. Annie frowned and looked at her fingers—ink-stained and raw from onionskin paper.

She pulled a larger map, marked with her grease pencil, under the light. *Cisterna.* It was a quiet sector, south of the main Gustav Line. The Americans were at Anzio, and G-2 chatter was all about a "breakout" against a "thin screen."

"But why," she murmured, "is Kesselring sending so much fuel to a 'quiet' place?"

She went to the files and pulled the last three days of logistical intercepts for the same sector. Her blood went cold. The requisitions weren't just for one unit; they were for elements of the Hermann Göring Division. And they weren't being sent to a reserve area.

"Jean," Annie said, her voice suddenly sharp. "Look at this." She laid her map next to the decrypts. "The G-2 reports say the line is thin. But look at the routing on these fuel orders. They're not going to a rear depot. They're going here, here, and here— to pre-stocked depots overlooking the Anzio-Cisterna road."

Jean's eyes widened. "My God. They're not in reserve. They're in the rafters."

"It's a trap," Annie breathed. "It's a 'Kesselring Kill Box.' He's baiting them."

She didn't wait. She gathered her map and the flimsy decrypts and marched out of the clattering hut, splashing through the mud to the office of her section chief, Mr. Strickland.

Strickland was a man who lived by the book. His small, cramped office smelled of pipe tobacco, musty serge, and a wet umbrella. He looked up, annoyed, as she entered.

"What is it, Miss... Annie?" he said, pointedly looking at the clock. "I'm due for the daily briefing."

"Sir, it's about Cisterna. The G-2 report is wrong. It's not a 'thin screen,' it's a trap. I've found the 'plumbing'—fuel and ammo orders for Panzers, already in position." She laid the map and intercepts on his desk.

Strickland glanced at them, his expression one of profound boredom. He pushed the papers back toward her.

"My dear girl," he said, his tone a dismissive, patronizing sigh. "This is a hunch. A 'feeling.' We are not in the business of 'feelings' here. We are in the business of decryption. Your job is to decode the intercepts and pass them up. Their job," he tapped a thick binder on his desk marked 'AFHQ - G-2', "is to do the analysis."

"But sir, this is the proof!" Annie insisted, her voice rising. "The official analysis is wrong. They're reading the generals; I'm reading the supply sergeants. And the supply sergeants are stocking up to build a graveyard."

"That is quite enough," Strickland said, his voice suddenly cold. "You are a cryptographer, not a general. You are suggesting that the entire G-2 staff at Allied Force Head-quarters, with their own Ultra sources, is wrong, and you, a girl in Hut 6, are right?"

He stood up. "I will not be forwarding a 'hunch' that contradicts the official intelligence picture. It makes us look like a hysterical girl. You will file your decrypts through the proper channels and let the 'men at the top' worry about the strategy. Is that clear?"

Annie stared at him, her face drained of color, her hands clenching the useless papers. She was a Cassandra. She held the coordinates of the future, and he was telling her to file it in triplicate.

"Yes, Mr. Strickland," she said, her voice a dead monotone. "Perfectly clear."

She walked out of his office, back into the rain, her mind already racing. She had failed. The "by-the-book" man had shut her down. She had to find another way. She had to get to Alistair.

17

CASSANDRA

JANUARY 1944

Bletchley Park, England

Alistair's office was in one of the quieter, more permanent brick buildings, a sterile, wood-paneled room that smelled of his cherry pipe tobacco and musty old files—an academic's office, a world away from the mud and blood she had just seen in the decrypts.

He was on the telephone when she entered without knocking, and he raised a single, disapproving eyebrow before murmuring a polite "I'll ring you back" and hanging up.

"This had better be worth interrupting my call to Y Service, Annie," he said, tamping tobacco into his pipe.

"It is," she said, her voice tight. She spread the decrypts and her map across his desk. "Cisterna. The Americans think it's a thin screen. It's not. It's a trap."

Alistair sighed, a small, weary sound. "Annie, darling, we've been over this. The official G-2 reports from AFHQ, which include their own Ultra intercepts, are quite clear. The line is thin. The Hermann Göring Division is in reserve, yes, but well back."

"The G-2 is reading the generals, Alistair," Annie shot back, her finger jabbing the map. "I'm reading the supply sergeants. Look. Here. Fuel and ammunition requisitions for a full Panzer division. And they're not routed to the reserve area. They're routed here, here, and here—overlooking the Anzio-Cisterna road."

She looked him in the eye, her gaze fierce. "They're not 'in reserve,' Alistair. They're in the rafters, waiting. They're baiting them into a kill box."

A sudden, terrifyingly personal image flashed in her mind: Will's smile in the Highland mist. Her hand, tapping his head with heather. *King.*

She had done this. She had stoked it. She knew, with an awful, sickening certainty, exactly the kind of man who would volunteer to lead a "breakout" against a "thin screen." A man who believed he wore a crown.

"Alistair," she pleaded, her voice suddenly dropping, all professionalism gone, replaced by a desperate, personal urgency. "Please. Just send it. As a query. A 'low-grade' warning. I... I know the man who will lead this charge. He is... arrogant. He's ambitious. I know him. He'll see this 'thin screen' as the path to glory. He will not be able to resist. He *will* charge straight into that trap."

Alistair calmly lit his pipe, the smoke rising between them like a screen. He looked at her, his bird-like eyes devoid of sympathy. "You 'know' him? This is your 'vital connection' from Scotland speaking, is it? Not the analyst?"

"It's the analyst who sees the numbers!" Annie retorted.

"It's the woman who knows the man who will misread them!"

Alistair stood up, the friendly, tea-drinking handler gone, replaced by the detached, quiet authority of MI6. "You are compromised, Annie. You've lost your objectivity." He pulled open a drawer and slid a thick file, stamped TOP SECRET, onto his desk.

"This," he said, tapping the file, "is the Americans' operational plan for the breakout. This," he tapped it again, "is their complete order of battle for Kesselring's forces. It is the product of hundreds of hours of analysis from their G-2, combined with our high-level intercepts."

He looked at her, his gaze cold. "And you want me to ring up the G-2 chief at AFHQ and tell him his entire plan is rubbish because one of my crypts has a 'hunch' about a fuel order? And a 'feeling' about a particular American officer?"

"It's not a hunch! It's the plumbing! It's the proof!"

"No," Alistair said, his voice final. "We will not cry wolf. We will not compromise our relationship with Washington because you have a feeling. Our American partners are running this operation. Our job, Annie, is to listen to the enemy, not to second-guess our allies."

He began gathering her papers and handing them back to her. "The file is closed. You are to stand down. Is that clear?"

Annie stared at him, her face pale. She took the papers from his hand, her certainty now a cold, leaden weight in her stomach. She saw the grid clearly, and she was forbidden to speak.

"Yes, Alistair," she said, her voice a dead monotone. "Clear."

She walked back to Hut 6 in a daze, the sound of the rain

on the wooden roof mixing with the deafening, relentless clatter of the typewriters. The sound was no longer a comfort. It was the ticking of a clock. The sound of a trap she was now powerless to stop.

She sat at her desk, staring at the map of Cisterna, now a map of a graveyard.

She was no longer just an analyst. She was a silent, helpless accomplice to the slaughter that she knew, with an awful, sickening certainty, was about to happen.

18

THE ELEVATOR

JANUARY 1944

Anzio Beachhead, Italy

On the edge of the map table, a copy of *The Stars and Stripes* lay flattened beneath a heavy brass compass. The headline screamed in bold, optimistic black type:

ALLIES LAND AT ANZIO; ROME 30 MILES AWAY

It looked so simple in newsprint—a short hop, a quick victory, an express elevator to the top. A dark, circular coffee stain marred the word "ROME," dissolving the ink into a muddy blur, but to the men in the room, the promise of the headline was still intact.

The command tent was thick with cigar smoke. This was the meeting that would, Will knew, make his career.

Will didn't wait for the briefing to start. He walked straight to the massive situation map dominating the center of the room, his eyes scanning the jagged grease-pencil lines of the stalemate. He ignored the clutter of the beachhead and the chaotic mess of units trapped along the Mussolini Canal. He was hunting for a ladder.

His finger traced the German perimeter, looking for the break. It stopped at a small town sitting on the edge of the Pontine Marshes.

"Cisterna," Will murmured, his eyes narrowing. He looked closer. The heavy red markings of the German divisions—the iron ring that had been strangling them—thinned out right there. Where there should have been a solid wall of Panzer divisions, there was only a dashed line.

"It's a gap," Will said, looking up at General Truscott.

Truscott nodded, his face an expression hewn from stone. "G-2 thinks it's a 'thin screen.' The 715th Division. Static defense. They haven't had time to consolidate."

"It's not just a screen, general," Will said, his voice rising with the thrill of the discovery. He looked back at the map, but he wasn't seeing ink and paper. He was seeing the express elevator he had been waiting for. "It's a door. And they left it unlocked."

A staff colonel next to Will muttered, "Patrols have been disappearing out there, sir. It's... quiet. Too quiet."

"It's quiet because it's empty, colonel," Will countered, cutting him off, his ambition seizing the narrative. "The Hermann Göring and 26th Panzer are in reserve, yes, but well back. They can't reinforce in time if we hit them hard and fast."

Truscott's eyes scanned the room. "We need a unit that can move fast, in the dark. A unit that can infiltrate that 'thin screen,' seize Cisterna by surprise, and hold it until the 3rd Division and our armor can link up."

The room went silent. It was an audacious, borderline

suicidal mission, predicated entirely on the empty space Will was staring at. Truscott's gaze landed on Will Darby. "Lieutenant Colonel Darby. Your Rangers are the best night fighters we have. You believe you can do this?"

This was the moment. Will felt the familiar, intoxicating rush. He saw the "paper men" at this table, the conventional officers, hesitant and bound by doctrine. He looked at the gap on the map again. He saw the opening he had coveted since West Point.

"General," Will said, his eyes locking with Truscott's. "My Rangers can 'do this.' Done. We'll kick that door down, seize Cisterna, and hold it until the 3rd Division arrives to relieve us. We'll be waiting for you."

Truscott studied him for a long moment, then nodded, a grim smile touching his lips. "I knew you'd say that, Will. The mission is yours. This is the win we've all been waiting for."

Will walked out of the tent, the congratulations of the other officers ringing in his ears. He was no longer just a commander; he was the tip of the spear, the man everyone was counting on.

He had consciously, publicly, and proudly accepted the risk. He saw the opening. It wasn't a stairwell; it was a chute, straight to the top. He stepped into the void and pressed the button.

19

THE CHARGE

JANUARY 1944

Cisterna, Italy

The war in Italy had bogged down into a grim, muddy stalemate. The Anzio beachhead, intended as a lightning strike to seize Rome, had become a prison, hemmed in by a brilliant German defense.

Will's path had led him to this: a damp, cold command post south of Cisterna, the air electric with the promise of his greatest victory. He, the hero of Gela and Salerno, saw one more "impossible" objective, one more glorious charge that would make his name immortal.

He stood in the pre-dawn chill, lightly tapping the brittle sprig of purple heather in his breast pocket. It was a conscious, deliberate motion. He coveted this victory.

His mind went back to that grove in Scotland, to Annie's teasing smile. *King of the Rangers.* He thought of the scream in the rock Annie had described. He felt it vibrating in the ground beneath him.

He felt it crying out for him now.

This was it. The intelligence was clear: a "thin screen." It was a gap, a path to glory left open just for him. This was his destiny.

The unease he had felt, the quiet that was "too quiet," was just fear. He pushed it down. This is what kings do, he thought, his resolve hardening. They don't hang back. They lead the charge.

"They're light," Will had briefed his officers, his confidence absolute. "A screen. We'll punch through it, cut the main road, and be in Cisterna by dawn. We'll have dinner in Rome."

He committed his 1st and 3rd Ranger Battalions—his veterans, his brothers—to a night infiltration, a silent march down a deep irrigation ditch. The 4th Ranger Battalion would stand back in reserve.

Now, in the pre-dawn chill, he stood over the radio set, a cup of cold coffee in his hand, waiting for the victory report. The radio hissed.

20

THE TRAP

0130 HOURS, JANUARY 30, 1944

South of Cisterna, Italy

Private First Class Jimmy Tolliver, 1st Ranger Battalion, had never been this cold, or this quiet. He was 18, and his primary concern was that the sloshing of the water in the Pantano ditch would give them away.

But the ditch wasn't the flooded bog they'd feared; it was a half-dry irrigation channel, a sunken highway of damp earth that seemed to swallow the sound of their boots. It felt like a gift—a secret passage cut straight into the German rear, dry enough for speed but deep enough to hide an army.

He was one of roughly seven hundred and seventy Rangers—1st and 3rd Battalions, the elite—and they were moving like ghosts in a narrow, snake-like column.

"Keep it tight," Sergeant McCarthy whispered from up ahead, his voice a barely audible rasp. "And mind your feet."

To their left and right, in the moonless, cloudy night, the silence felt heavy, but deceptive. It wasn't empty. The wind shifted, and suddenly, Jimmy froze. He didn't just hear the enemy; he smelled them. The distinct, acrid scent of cheap German tobacco drifted down into the ditch.

Somewhere just above the embankment, a sentry laughed at a joke, the sound crisp and terrifyingly intimate.

Jimmy's stomach turned. They weren't sneaking past the line; they were walking down the hallway of the enemy's house. Yet the Germans didn't fire. The "thin screen" seemed real. He felt a surge of Ranger pride. They were doing the impossible.

For hours, they crept forward. The only sounds were light footsteps and the pounding of his heart. His pockets were heavy, stuffed with grenades; his shoulders ached from the bandoleers of ammo. This was it.

0500 Hours

The first, faint, gray light began to bleed into the eastern sky. They were still in the ditch, but the drainage ditch had given way to a large, open field on the southern edge of Cisterna. They were four miles deep behind the enemy's line.

"Out of the ditch! Out of the ditch!" Rollins hissed. "We gotta make the town before the sun's all the way up. Go! Go! Go!" Jimmy scrambled up the muddy bank, his legs burning, and began to run, his breath pluming in the damp air. The men fanned out, a running, stealthy wave of green, dashing for the first stone farmhouses on the edge of the village.

They were too late.

It started not with a rifle shot, but with a sound like a freight train. A single flare popped, high and bright, hanging in the gray dawn, casting everything in a sick, white light.

Then the world ended.

"TANKS!" someone screamed. "IN THE HAYSTACKS!"

The pastoral landscape betrayed them. A massive haystack to Jimmy's right began to move. The dried grass fell away to reveal the muzzle of a Panzer IV. The barn doors ahead swung open, not for cattle, but for the tracks of self-propelled guns emerging from their hiding spots.

The "gap" was a lie. They had walked into a staging area.

The shout came a half-second before the first 88mm shell hit. A stone house 50 yards to Jimmy's left simply... vanished. It didn't explode; it vaporized. The concussion threw Jimmy flat on his face, his helmet ringing like a bell.

He looked up, dazed. From camouflaged dugouts in the hills, from behind stone walls, from the town itself, the world erupted in fire. It was a trap.

German machine guns—MG42s, "Hitler's Buzzsaws"—opened up from three sides, their sound a terrifying, high-velocity rip that cut men in half. But then came a sound even worse—a mechanical, rhythmic *thump-thump-thump* that shook the ground.

Flak Wagons.

The Germans were lowering their Quad-20mm anti-aircraft guns to waist-height, using weapons designed to shred airplanes to butcher men caught in the irrigation ditches.

Self-propelled guns and tanks, which the "faulty Allied intelligence" said were miles away, were here. They were dug in. They were waiting.

"GET TO COVER!" Sergeant Rollins roared, shoving Jimmy toward a low stone wall. "GET—AGHH!" Jimmy watched, his mind unable to process it, as the sergeant's chest erupted in a red spray.

Rollins just stood for a second, a look of profound

surprise on his face, before collapsing. This was not a battle. This was a Ranger battalion's last stand.

"BAZOOKA! GET THE BAZOOKA UP!" a lieutenant screamed, his voice cracking. A Ranger team scrambled, loading their weapon. They were brave, but the physics were against them.

The Panzers were standing off at 300 yards—well outside the effective range of the light rockets. Before they could even aim, a shell from a Panzer IV hit the wall they were behind. The back-blast and shrapnel killed them all.

"They're everywhere! We're surrounded!" a man screamed, racing back toward the cover of the ditch. He made it three steps before a burst of machine-gun fire stitched its way up his back.

Jimmy huddled behind the wall, his whole body shaking. The air was a solid, screaming wall of noise. He was firing his M1, loading, firing, loading, not even aiming, just pointing it at the muzzle flashes.

The hardened German veterans—Hermann Göring Division, elite paratroopers—were closing the vise. He saw his friends, the men he'd trained with in Scotland, being systematically annihilated in the open field.

"Get to the White House!" a corporal yelled, pointing toward a large, whitewashed farmhouse complex near the rail line where the 1st Battalion survivors were trying to rally. "Fortify the White House! It's our only chance!"

But as Jimmy watched, a tank rolled right up to the window of the farmhouse and fired point-blank. The 'White House' collapsed inward, burying the last resistance in rubble.

The radio operator next to him was frantically calling. "Walcott to any station! Walcott to any station! We are surrounded! Cut to pieces! Panzers and self-propelled guns on all sides! Requesting immediate..."

A sniper's bullet hit the radio set, and it exploded in a shower of sparks. The operator stared at his useless equipment, and then, in a daze, he just sat down and started to cry.

Jimmy Tolliver looked over the wall. The sun was up now. The field was a sea of dead and dying Rangers. The Germans were advancing, moving from body to body. It was over.

He wasn't a Ranger. He wasn't a soldier. He was just an 18-year-old kid in a muddy field, a thousand miles from home, waiting to die. The floor had fallen out from under them.

There was nothing beneath his feet but the dark.

21

STATIC

0500 HOURS, JANUARY 30, 1944

Cisterna, Italy

The radio was quiet for hours as his men moved successfully in the dark. Then the voice crackled through. "Contact. Light resistance, as expected. Moving on the objective." Will smiled. He glanced at Annie's sprig of heather. The legend was holding.

Then, a new voice, frantic. "Contact heavy! My God, they're everywhere! We're in the open fields... they were waiting for us!"

Will's blood turned to ice.

"Walcott, what is your situation? What is your position?"

"Sir, this is Walcott. We are..!"

The sound of machine-gun fire, then static.

Will gripped the microphone, his knuckles white against the black Bakelite. The sounds coming from the speaker transported him instantly into the freezing mud of the Pantano ditch.

"Red Leader, this is Blue Three... we are... wait..."

The voice wasn't the calm, clipped tone of a drill. It was high, breathless.

"Contact!" the voice screamed, the word distorting in the speaker. "Heavy contact! My God, they're opening up! It's not a screen!"

Will pressed the transmit button, his voice steady, fighting to maintain order over the airwaves.

"Blue Three, clarify. What is your situation?"

"Panzers!" The scream tore through the speaker, followed by a sound Will knew too well—the high-velocity rip of an MG42. Then came a heavier, rhythmic thumping that made the speaker rattle. "Flak Wagons! They've got 20s! They're shredding the ditch!"

"Where are you?" Will shouted into the mic.

"We're making a run for the Isola Bella complex! The big white farmhouse near the rail line!" the voice screamed, distorted by static. "They're in the tree-line! Point-blank! They were waiting for us!"

Will stared at the map. He saw the cluster of buildings near the tracks. He grabbed his grease pencil, but his hand froze.

"Alspaugh!" Will barked. "Get McCarthy on the line. Tell him to flank right. Guide him to Isola Bella! Tell him 1st Battalion is making a stand at the white house!"

The radio hissed, then a new voice broke through—a young radioman, choking on smoke. "Sir... McCarthy is gone."

"What do you mean gone?"

"He took 1st Platoon for the farmhouse," the boy sobbed. "A Mark IV tank... it just rolled out of the haystacks. Point blank. An 88 shell, Sir. Direct hit. The Isola Bella... the 'Beautiful Island'... it just vaporized. McCarthy... the whole squad... they're just mist."

Will felt the blood drain from his face. He closed his eyes and saw Sergeant McCarthy, the steady, rock-solid NCO who had been with him since the beaches of Arzew. He saw McCarthy's slow grin, the way he cleaned his nails with a bayonet. *Vaporized.*

"Pull back," Will ordered, desperation creeping into his tone. "Get to the ditch!"

"We can't move!" It was a different voice now, the kid from Tennessee he'd shared a cigarette with just hours ago. The kid who had shown him a picture of his sweetheart in Nashville. "They're walking the mortars in on us! They're cutting us to pieces!"

"Jimmy, listen to me," Will pleaded, leaning over the radio set as if he could physically pull the boy out of the fire. "Keep your head down. Pop smoke. We're sending the 3rd Division. Just hold on!"

"Sir, there's no smoke left!" The kid's voice was barely a whisper now, drowned out by the mechanical squeal of tank treads crushing stone. "They're overrunning the perimeter. They're right on top of us. Tell my mom I—"

CRUMP

The line went dead.

"Jimmy?" Will whispered.

He clicked the transmit key. "Jimmy, report!"

Static.

"Alspaugh! Any station! Report!"

Static.

"Anyone!" Will roared, his voice cracking, slamming his hand against the table. "This is Darby! Sound off!"

The radio hummed—an indifferent, electric silence. The

screams were gone. The gunfire was gone. There was only the empty hiss of the frequency.

Will stood frozen, the microphone still clutched in his hand like an artery that had been cut. He looked at the map, at the red grease-pencil circle around Cisterna. It wasn't a gap. It was a mouth. And it had just swallowed 767 of his sons.

Red Leader..." he whispered into the dead air, his voice trembling. "Please. Anyone."

But the only answer was the static.

22

THE VISE

0545 HOURS, JANUARY 30, 1944

Anzio, Italy

Miles away, in a concrete command bunker on the Anzio beachhead, General George P. Hays stood as a high-level observer. He was on detached service from England, here to advise and observe on the breakout attempt.

He had known the plan. He knew Will was leading his Rangers on the breakout. He had felt a mentor's pride, mixed with his old worry. *He's a showman.* Now, the command post was in chaos.

"Sir, the whole right flank is collapsing!" a radio operator shouted. "We've lost all contact with the Ranger force. They've just... vanished."

Hays stared at the strategic map, where a blue grease-pencil line showed Will's intended path into Cisterna. That line was now being surrounded by a swarm of new red arrows labeled Panzer. He didn't need a radio to know what was happening.

He walked to the dugout's narrow observation slit and looked north toward Cisterna. The pre-dawn sky was lit by a hellish, silent strobing. German "Christmas tree" flares, white and red and green, hung in the air, illuminating the kill zone for their machine-gunners.

This was Kesselring's trap, sprung with brutal, German precision. The sound of his guns was a continuous, rolling thunder that shook the dust from the concrete ceiling.

The breakout had failed. The beachhead was still a prison. He thought of Will and all those brave souls under his command. Hays stood, his face stone, his hands clasped behind his back. But inside, his soul was cracking.

The vise had closed.

By evening, the annihilation was complete. Of the 767 men of the 1st and 3rd Ranger Battalions who had walked into the trap, only six men made it back. The remaining 761 were killed or captured.

Later, a young staff officer, trying to be helpful, placed a fresh copy of *The Stars and Stripes* on General Hays's desk. Hays looked down. The headline screamed back at him in bold type:

ANZIO BEACHHEAD FIRM

Firm. The word felt like a punch. It reduced the screaming death of countless brave men into a bureaucratic adjective. And, the sacrifice of the Rangers was not even mentioned.

23

THE FORGOTTEN FRONT

FEBRUARY 1944

London, England

Brigadier General George P. Hays stood in a cavernous, smoke-filled map room in London, the nerve center for Operation OVERLORD. The air hummed with the energy of the greatest industrial undertaking in human history.

The wall was dominated by a map of Normandy, a sprawling beast of grids, tidal charts, and logistics tables. The smell was of pipe tobacco, mimeograph ink, and the heat of a hundred vacuum tubes. This was the "real" war. This was the war everyone would remember.

Hays, as commander of the 2nd Infantry Division's artillery, was a master of its brutal mathematics. Twenty-six years ago, he had judged range by the feel of a horse's stride and the height of a hedgerow against the sky.

Now his job was a mountain of calculations: how many tons of shells per hour to saturate Omaha Beach; learning the firing tables for battleships he'd never seen; the coordination of a thousand guns that would, on a single day, fire in unison to open a path to Germany.

Tonight his "horse" was an army of steel—thousands of guns, rockets, and bombers yoked to a timetable measured in seconds. The work was the same—geometry and courage—but the scale was no longer flesh and leather. The Allies were building a symphony of destruction, and D-Day would be its debut.

An aide, a young major with the perpetually stressed look of a staff officer, hurried to his side. "General Hays? General Bradley's compliments, sir. He needs you at SHAEF headquarters. Immediately."

Hays frowned. A summons from Bradley, this close to the wire, meant a problem. He grabbed his trench coat, his mind racing. *Had the 2nd Division failed an inspection? Was there a flaw in his fire plan?*

He was driven through a London bristling with activity. The streets were choked with American jeeps, British lorries, and columns of GIs marching to yet another drill. The city was a coiled spring, wound so tight it felt it must snap.

He was ushered not into the main planning theater, but into a small, private office. General Omar Bradley didn't get up. He looked exhausted, his face gray with the burden of a continent.

"George," Bradley said, skipping the pleasantries. "Thanks for coming. I'm pulling you."

Hays felt his blood run cold. "Sir?"

"Not from OVERLORD," Bradley said, waving a hand. "From England. I'm sending you to Italy on temporary duty."

Italy. The word landed in the room with a dull thud. To Hays, Italy was a sideshow. A miserable, muddy, strategically questionable campaign fought in the mountains. It was the "forgotten front," a place where careers went to die in the rain.

"Sir," Hays said, his voice carefully neutral. "My Division is in its final phase of readiness. To leave now…"

"Your division will be fine," Bradley said flatly. "The 34th Division in Italy will not be. You've read the reports from Cassino?"

Hays had. A bloody, grinding stalemate. A WWI-style battle of attrition against a mountain crowned with a 1,400-year-old monastery. It was a meat grinder.

"They're stalled at the Rapido River, George," Bradley continued. "The 34th has been trying to take that monastery for weeks. They've been bled white, and their artillery is a mess. Their commander was wounded. They're failing. General Clark has personally requested 'an artillery expert' to break the stalemate. General Marshall's office submitted one name."

Bradley looked up, his eyes locking on Hays. "Your name. You're the best gunner we have, George. You're the Rock. Go to Italy. Fix the artillery support at Cassino. Then come back and help us fix France."

Hays stood at attention. It was not a request. "Yes, sir."

He walked out of the headquarters, back into the bustling London streets. He was being pulled from the center of the universe—the war that mattered—to go on a temporary-duty assignment to the one that perhaps did not.

24

MAKE THEM STOP

FEBRUARY 1944

Cassino, Italy

The C-47 transport plane bucked through the turbulent air, descending through a soup of low, gray clouds. When Hays stepped off the plane at the captured airfield near Caserta, the contrast to England was a physical shock. England had been a place of order, of massive, organized strength, of green parks and bustling, determined cities.

The approach to Cassino was a landscape of mud and misery, the air thick with the sweet-rot of mule carcasses blasted off the mountain tracks. In the cold, joyless drizzle, every road was a river of mire choked with exhausted, hollow-eyed GIs. This wasn't a modern war; it was 1918 all over again. For Hays, it was the Marne—a nightmare he had spent twenty-six years trying to escape.

A jeep drove him on a muddy road, forcing his driver to slow down. A truckload of dogfaces rattled past, half-drunk on exhaustion, growling out a sarcastic version of *"You are my sunshine."* Hays frowned, the tune jarring against the backdrop of the constant, dull thunder of the guns.

The 34th Division's command post was a sandbagged farmhouse cellar that shook with a low, continuous thunder. It wasn't the sound of a preparatory barrage; it was the random, spiteful crack of German 88s firing in ones and twos, a form of torture designed to break the mind.

He was met by a colonel whose face was covered in a three-day-old stubble, his eyes red-rimmed from lack of sleep. "General Hays. Thank God you're here. The 34th is... well, you'll see."

The colonel saw Hays looking at the passing truck. "The 'Soft Underbelly,' sir," the colonel said, his voice flat.

"That's the joke. Churchill promised us the soft underbelly of Europe. But the men... they know the world is looking toward France. They feel like a footnote. They wear it like a wound. Look around," he gestured to the landscape, "this 'sideshow' is killing them just the same."

Hays looked from the men to the endless rows of simple, white crosses by the side of the muddy road. He understood. This was not a sideshow. It was a place of sacrifice, and the world had already forgotten them.

The colonel took him on his initial 48-hour assessment. Not just to observation posts, but to the arteries. On the second day, Hays insisted on visiting a frontline aid station for the 34th.

"Sir, it's... not a place for a general," the colonel advised, his voice strained.

"It's the only place for one," Hays said, his voice flat. "I need to see the cost."

The "station" was a collection of canvas tents erected in a sea of ankle-deep, adhesive mire, barely shielded from the rain by a copse of shattered olive trees. The air was thick with the smell of canvas, phenol, and the coppery tang of blood. The wounded weren't carried in; they were dragged on litters, their stretchers caked with the same yellow-gray muck that covered everything.

A single, bare bulb, powered by a sputtering generator, cast a weak, yellow light inside the main tent. It was chaos. Medics, their arms stained to the elbows, moved with a frantic, exhausted urgency. The floor was a bed of straw that had long since turned to filth. Men lay in rows, side-by-side, their groans a low, terrible chorus beneath the constant, drumming rain and the *thump-thump-thump* of the distant guns.

Hays was a rock, an observer, his face granite. He walked slowly, careful not to step on the men.

"Water..." a voice rasped. "Please..."

Hays stopped. He knelt next to a medic, a kid who couldn't have been twenty, but whose eyes were ancient. He was old... in a young body, his face a mask of grime, his hands busily working as he tried to wrap a bandage around a wound Hays could barely bring himself to look at.

The medic, focused on the wound, didn't look up. "In a minute, soldier. Just... just hold on."

Hays's gaze moved to the man the medic was working on. No, not a man. A boy. A private from the 135th Infantry, his face ashen and waxy in the gloom. His eyes were wide, unfocused, staring at the canvas roof. The vacant, thousand-yard stare.

The boy's eyes suddenly locked onto Hays. He didn't see the general's star. He just saw a solid figure, an authority.

"Sir?" the boy whispered, his hand caked in mud, reaching out, grabbing the sleeve of Hays's pristine trench coat. "Sir... are you the doctor?"

Hays froze. The muddy fingers tightened on his arm. "I... no, soldier. I'm not."

"You gotta make 'em stop," the boy pleaded, his voice a dry, urgent rasp. The thousand-yard stare was gone, replaced by a terrible, raw clarity. "The guns, sir. Just... just make the guns stop. Please... just make 'em stop."

Hays couldn't breathe. He looked at the boy's pleading face, at the old-young medic beside him, at the rows of broken men in the mud. This was his "artillery problem." This was the cost.

He gently, wordlessly, took his canteen from his belt and, cupping the boy's head, gave him a sip of water. The boy drank, his eyes closing, his grip on Hays's coat finally relaxing as he slipped back into shock.

Hays stood up. The colonel was watching him, his face grim. Hays said nothing. He turned and walked out of the tent, back into the rain.

"Give me a minute, colonel," Hays rasped, waving the officer off. He walked past the waiting jeep, past the line of stretcher-bearers, and stepped behind the jagged remains of a stone garden wall.

The moment he was out of sight, the "Rock" crumbled.

He braced his hands against the cold, wet stone, his knuckles turning white. The smell of the tent—that cloying, sweet-rot stench of gangrene and mildewed canvas—was suddenly choking him. It wasn't just the boy; it was the Marne, it was the horses, it was twenty-six years of holding his breath.

He doubled over and dry-heaved, his body convulsing in violent, silent spasms against the wall. Nothing came up but bile and the bitter taste of helplessness. He stood there for a long minute, gasping, the rain mixing with the sweat on his face, shaking so hard his teeth chattered.

"Make them stop," he whispered to the wet stones, his voice cracking. He looked at his hands. They were trembling.

He closed his eyes, took a single, shuddering breath, and forced the tremor down. He wiped his mouth with the back of his hand, straightened his trench coat, and locked the granite mask back into place.

He stepped back out into the road.

The boy's words echoed with every *thump* of the German guns. *Make 'em stop.*

He realized, with a stark, sickening clarity, that the leaders were failing these men.

Next, the colonel took him to an observation post. Hays raised his binoculars. He saw it.

Monte Cassino.

It wasn't just a mountain. It was a fortress. A sheer, 1,500-foot wall of rock, snow, and ice, crowned by the ancient Benedictine monastery, its walls stark white against the gray sky. It dominated everything. It was a god's-eye view, and the Germans were the gods. Every road, every ditch, every ruin in the valley below was pre-registered by their guns.

"That's Kesselring's Gustav Line," the colonel said, his voice flat. "The 34th tried a frontal assault. They're still up there, some of them. Or what's left. They're pinned down in the rocks, just below the summit. We can't get to them. We can't supply them. The Germans just... pick them off. Day and night. For two weeks."

Hays scanned the terrain. He saw his artillery positions.

They were a mess. Batteries were poorly sited and exposed to counter-fire. Their firing was sporadic, uncoordinated. This was why he'd been sent.

"They're not shooting at the Germans," Hays growled, his frustration boiling over. "They're just making noise." He could hear the pattern in the sound: a random, scattered volume fire—a blind carpet. He mentally traced the cones of fire and saw only wasted effort, vast "dead ground" in the killing zones that guaranteed the German guns were untouched.

He saw the faces of the men in the trenches. They weren't the fresh, eager faces of the GIs in London. These were old men in young bodies. Their uniforms were filthy, their faces gaunt, their eyes dead. He saw the same vacant, thousand-yard stare he remembered from the faces of the gassed men in the aid stations near Château-Thierry. They were men who knew they were dying for nothing, in a place the world had already forgotten.

This was the "soft underbelly" of Europe. It was the hardest, most brutal, and most thankless fight of the war.

25

COUNTER-BATTERY

FEBRUARY 1944

Cassino, Italy

Hays spent his first forty-eight hours not firing a single shell. He walked to the front. He moved from battery to battery, his presence an unspoken rebuke. He tasted the fear, the mud, the exhaustion.

On the third day, he called his new officers to the command post.

"Gentlemen," he began, his voice a low, cold rumble that cut through the cellar. "You have been fighting this mountain. You cannot fight a mountain. You will, starting today, fight the *guns* on the mountain."

He unrolled a new map, his grease-pencil marks a stark, clean geometry. "This is not a siege. This is an artillery problem. Your batteries are exposed, your fire is scattered, and your observers are blind. You will move, tonight, to these new positions. You will coordinate all fire through this post. We will not fire another round until we have a plan for every shell."

For a week, Hays became the Marne liaison officer all over again. He was relentless. He re-sited every gun. He coordinated with British and New Zealand batteries. He established new, forward observation posts under the cover of darkness. He taught his men the brutal, forgotten math of counter-battery fire.

It was a deadly hunt, using complex trigonometry to locate the enemy's hidden guns, not just to return fire, but to *kill* them—silencing the storm and giving his infantry a chance to live.

He was a conventional officer, and this was the most unconventional problem he had ever faced. This wasn't about D-Day's overwhelming numbers. This was about skill. It was about finding a single, hidden German mortar and killing it with a single, perfectly-placed round.

Then came the day of the next push. The infantry, what was left of them, looked up, expecting the same, useless barrage.

Instead, Hays unleashed a storm.

This would not be another blind Cassino carpet-bombing, pulverizing the mountain and burying his men. This one would carve corridors. Scalpel, not sledgehammer. It was not a random carpet of shells. It was a surgical, terrifying, and methodical erasure.

He heard the barrage as a symphony in his head, the time-on-target synchronized to a terrible, flawless rhythm. He fired in rolling, concentrated waves.

He blinded the German observation posts with smoke. He hammered their known mortar pits with white phosphorus. He walked a curtain of high-explosive shells up the mountainside, a steel broom sweeping just 100 yards in front of his own advancing infantry.

It was the lesson of the 75mm gun, applied with the force of a hundred.

26

THE ARDEATINE CAVES

MARCH 24, 1944

Rome, Italy

SS Lieutenant Colonel Herbert Kappler, the head of German security in Rome, did not see himself as a monster. He saw himself as a policeman. And right now, he was a policeman with a logistical nightmare.

He sat at his pristine desk in the SS headquarters, a telephone receiver pressed to one ear, a pen in his hand. The day before, Communist partisans had detonated a bomb on the Via Rasella, killing 33 German soldiers from a column marching through the city.

The Führer's order, screamed from his Wolf's Lair in Prussia and funneled down with ruthless clarity from Field Marshal Albert Kesselring's command, was simple: Ten Italians for every one German. Kappler, a man of clinical detachment, was now trying to fill a quota.

He needed 330 human bodies.

"No," he said into the phone, his voice clipped with the annoyance of a man handling a supply requisition rather than a mass execution. "The official order allows for prisoners 'already condemned to death.' But I have checked the rolls at Regina Coeli. I don't have enough of them."

He listened for a moment, his eyes scanning the deficit on his ledger.

"I am short," he spat. "So improvise! Empty the political wing—the Communists, the syndicalists, the resistance suspects. Add the seventy-five Jews awaiting deportation. And if that isn't enough, take the civilians serving time for petty crimes."

He paused, his voice dropping to a terrifyingly practical register.

"I don't care if they are guilty of nothing but being in the wrong cell. Just fill the quota. Get me the names."

He slammed the phone down and looked at the list on his desk. He began to check off the names—political prisoners, Jews already in his custody, Catholic priests taken from their parishes, and teenagers pulled from their homes. This was not a passionate act of rage; it was a bureaucratic problem to be solved.

To him, it was paperwork.

That afternoon, the trucks arrived at the Ardeatine Caves. A miscount had brought the number to 335. When it was discovered, Kappler, a stickler for process, ordered them killed anyway. They had seen the site; they could not be allowed to leave.

Kappler stood at the mouth of the dark tunnels, clipboard in hand. He did the division in his head: 335 men marched in groups of five. That meant sixty-seven groups.

He watched the first five disappear into the damp, volcanic rock. He heard the muffled rhythm: *pop... pop... pop... pop... pop.* It took about three minutes. He looked at his watch, then back at the line of hundreds of bound men.

Three minutes per group. Sixty-seven repetitions.

Dread—cold and administrative—came over him. This wouldn't be a single volley of execution; it would be a workday. Hours of it. He felt a dry, bureaucratic annoyance; he had a dinner appointment in the city. He handed the clipboard to his adjutant, SS-Captain Priebke.

"Keep the count exact," Kappler said, as if he were auditing inventory. "No mistakes."

As the line kept moving, the sound inside the caves began to change.

In the early groups, there had been only the administrative silence, broken by a muttered creed or the name of a wife. But as the afternoon wore on and the tunnels filled, the survivors were forced deeper into the dark, made to kneel on the bodies of those who had gone before them to conserve space.

A sound began to rise from the darkness of the waiting line. It wasn't a scream or a plea. It was a single voice, thin and clear, starting the first notes of the *Inno di Mameli*.

"*...l'Italia s'è desta...*"
　　...Italy has awakened...

By the time the next group of five was marched forward, it wasn't just one voice; it was a contagion. One voice became fifty, then one hundred and fifty, until the entire tunnel was a single human instrument.

They were singing the Italian national anthem—a defiant claim of the living against a machine of the dead.

The Germans responded with boots and rifle butts,

trying to kick the music out of them, but as the loudest singers fell, the melody simply moved down the line.

It was a torch being passed from those who were finished to those who were next—a psalm of the dying that reached for the sky, even as they were made to kneel in the dirt.

Cassino, Italy

Miles to the south, in the mud-choked ruins of the Cassino front, General George P. Hays stood in his command tent, staring at his own list. It was a casualty report. Men from the 34th Division were dying in the frontal assault against the monastery.

Every name was a failure of his command, a price paid in blood for ground. This was the burden of his duty.

An aide entered, his face pale, and handed Hays a radio intercept. "Sir, from Rome. We... we've confirmed it."

Hays read the message. A partisan attack. A 10-to-1 reprisal. 335 civilians executed in the Ardeatine Caves, an order authorized by Kesselring.

The paper shook in his hand—not from a tremor, but from the force of his grip tightening until the blood left his knuckles. A sudden, violent wave of nausea rolled over him, tasting of bile.

"Three hundred..." he choked out, the number sticking in his throat like a bone.

He didn't just put the report down. He crushed it in his fist and slammed it onto his field desk with a force that made the lantern jump. The ink pot rattled; a pencil rolled off the edge. It was a spasm of pure, physical revulsion.

He turned away from the aide, his chest heaving, fighting the urge to throw something. He walked to the tent's opening and looked out at the rain, at the endless, grinding misery of the front.

He, too, was a general. He, too, sent men to their deaths. He lived by the terrible mathematics of command. But this... this was different. This wasn't war. This was murder. He had studied Kesselring and respected him as a brilliant defensive tactician. But now he saw the true, terrible end of a path of command devoid of honor.

Kesselring's "duty" was not to sacrifice, but to inflict atrocity. He had perverted the sacred duty of a soldier—to protect—into the cold arithmetic of a butcher.

Hays looked at his own casualty list, at the names of men who died fighting. He was horrified, not just as a man, but as a general. He had just seen the dark, perverted branch off the trail he himself walked.

Anzio, Italy

Lieutenant Colonel Will Darby sat in a wet, cold tent on the Anzio beachhead. He was no longer the hero of Salerno. After the Cisterna disaster, he had been relieved of his Rangers and given temporary command of the 179th Infantry. He was a broken man, signing requisitions for trench foot powder, a ghost haunted by the 761 men he had fed into the trap.

It wasn't just the silence of the dead that haunted him; it was the fate of the living. The intelligence reports had confirmed the final twist of the knife.

The survivors of his battalions had been marched through the streets of Rome by their German captors.

It was a propaganda coup for the Nazi regime. Will closed his eyes and saw the image that kept him awake: his

Rangers—walking past the Colosseum with their hands raised, paraded like trophies before the enemy cameras. He had promised them they would be in Rome by dinner. And they were.

A runner splashed through the mud and handed him a dispatch. Will read it. 335 civilians. An order from Kesselring. He didn't think of Kesselring. He didn't think of duty. His mind was a one-track loop. All he thought of night and day was Cisterna.

He dropped the dispatch into a half-filled burn bin. The number, 335, just seemed to blend with the 761 from his own failure. The paraded captives. The murdered civilians. It wasn't a parallel; it was just... more. More death. More proof that the entire war, from his own tactical failure to the enemy's cold-blooded atrocity, was nothing but a monstrous machine for devouring men.

The news of the Ardeatine Caves horrified him, but mostly it just numbed him even further, a final confirmation that the world he was in was built entirely of death, and his failure at Cisterna was his personal part in it.

27

THE ANCHOR

NIGHT, MARCH 1944

Cassino, Italy

The night felt contaminated. General Hays returned to his field quarters—a small, damp room requisitioned in a half-shattered Italian farmhouse—and the news of the Ardeatine Caves clung to him like the smell of charnel.

He was a general. He sent men to die. That was the terrible, lonely mathematics of his command. He accepted that burden.

But Kesselring's order... 335 civilians. A 10-to-1 ratio. That wasn't command. It was a perversion of the very duty Hays had built his life on. It was a map that led to madness, and for a terrifying moment, Hays felt the ground shift beneath his feet.

He thought of the grudging respect some of his staff officers had for the man. "Smiling Albert," they called him, a master of the defensive war. Hays himself had respected the professional, cold genius of the Gustav Line. But this... this was the other face. The same mind that built the Gustav fortress signed the order to create a cave of innocent corpses.

If being 'good at war' required this, Hays thought with a cold, sickening finality, *I'd rather be a failure.* He was shaken, not by the battle, but by the line that Kesselring had crossed.

He needed an anchor.

He walked to his footlocker, unlocked it, and pulled out a small, oilskin-wrapped bundle. Inside was a stack of letters, tied with a simple ribbon. He untied it and pulled one from the middle, the paper soft as cloth, the folds worn thin from countless readings.

He sat on his cot, the single lantern casting a small, warm circle of light, and read the familiar, elegant script.

"...my 'Victory Book Campaign' here at the library is becoming a positive siege. You would laugh, George. We received a crate of sermons from a well-meaning parish, but the soldiers are writing back asking for Mr. Dashiell Hammett and Mr. Zane Grey. It seems even in war, the heart craves a puzzle or a prairie more than a lecture.

It feels a world away from our quiet library, from the storms on Sullivan's Island. Our 'Tenth Station' seems a lifetime ago, doesn't it? But the work feels the same—trying to offer a small light in a gathering dark...

I trace the map of your journey every night. From Cassino, the path looks so hard. I think of the boy who ran into the surf all those years ago. That boy is still the man I love. Hold fast to your 'Staircase of Duty,' my love. But know that all staircases are meant to lead somewhere.

Yours leads home. It leads to me. I am waiting for you always."

Hays read the words, and the chill of Kesselring's order receded. Julia. Her keen wit, her unwavering faith in him.

Kesselring's duty was to a Führer, to an ideology, to a cold list of numbers. Hays's duty was to the men on his casualty list, and to the woman in Charleston who was waiting for him. His path was one of sacrifice, not atrocity. He had Julia's quiet story of endurance—the one she had given him from that old book of hours, the one she had lived by in her library—and he would always choose to follow it.

He was reaffirmed.

He took a deep, steadying breath, the first clean one all day. He reached for his pen and a fresh sheet of V-Mail. The first words were the only ones that mattered, the only compass he needed in the wilderness.

My dearest Julia...

28

THE TRUE CROSS

SPRING 1944

Cassino, Italy

The fight for Cassino was over, leaving only the smell of sulfur and pulverized stone. General Hays sat at the heavy oak table in the farmhouse, a stack of after-action reports in front of him. His failure at the Rapido River sat like a stone in his gut.

He'd gone over it a thousand times, looking for the flaw. His mind held the entire sector as a perfect, three-dimensional grid, every known German position locked into a precise fire mission, every elevation calculated to the foot.

He had executed the textbook solution, a model of mathematical warfare. The artillery plan had been flawless. The infantry was brave, as brave as any men who ever lived. And the attack still failed. It was a catastrophic, textbook failure. It was a failure of command, a failure of imagination, a failure of doctrine.

Kesselring's mountain fortress, in the end, was too

strong. The 34th Division was too broken. They were pulled from the line, shattered.

He realized, with a cold clarity, that being a "Rock" was not enough if it meant being immovable. Doctrine was paper, but the battlefield was a storm. If he were to win, he couldn't just be a rock; he had to become the water. He had to learn to adapt, to listen to the men on the ground, to find a new path when the old one was paved with bodies.

It was in this dark frame of mind that he read the full, classified report on the Cisterna disaster. He'd requested it. He needed to know. He knew Will—knew his brilliance, his drive. He'd seen it back at Hoyle. The report was cold, but the tactical diagrams were a nightmare. They showed a perfect ambush. The intelligence analysts at AFHQ, he noted with a grimace, had dubbed the trap a 'Kesselring Kill Box.'

He put the report down, the contrast chilling him. The Cassino and Cisterna. Two faces of the same coin of catastrophe.

Hays re-read the after-action report from Cisterna. He thought of his protégé, now a ghost somewhere in a tent at Anzio. He couldn't go to him. But he could send a message. He pulled a sheet of V-Mail toward him.

Will,

I've just read the report from Cisterna. And I've spent the last month watching my own men from the 34th break themselves against this mountain. I'm in no position to lecture a man on failure. But I am, perhaps, in a position to offer a guide for what comes after.

I came to tell you a story. Two of them.

Years ago, I had a friend in the old Life-Saving Service. Silas

McGuire. A mentor. He had a young protégé named Coste. The strongest man he ever saw. Arrogant. Thought he could fight the ocean itself. A woman and her child got caught in a rip current. Silas warned him, "Don't fight the rip head-on. Find the angle. Use your head, not your strength."

Coste didn't listen. He charged straight in. He fought the rip until he had nothing left. The ocean took him, the woman, and the child. He died for his pride, Will.

When I read your report, all I could see was Coste. You're him. You've been fighting the tide your whole life. The cannon at West Point. Arzew. Gela. You let your own legend and desire to win pull you under. And it cost you 700 men.

But you are lucky, Will. You're not dead, which brings me to the second story. The one that saved my life.

My wife, Julia, gave me a story once. A story about St. Helena. She went to Jerusalem, a faithful old woman, looking for the True Cross. But when they dug where the story said, they found three. How could they know which was real? They were all just... wood.

So they brought a dying woman. They touched her with the first cross. Nothing. The second, nothing. But the third... the True Cross... it healed her. It gave her life.

You've been chasing one of the other crosses, Will. Glory. It looked like the real thing, didn't it? But it broke. It didn't heal anyone. That and the faulty intel got your men killed. It's not the True Cross.

The real guide, the one that saves you, is the other one. Julia once showed me that in the traditional Way of the Cross, the Tenth Station is about being stripped of everything and still finding the strength to endure.

For us, it is the moment where the soldier is stripped of his rank, his pride, and his illusions, and finds that service is all that remains. That's the map that will get you home. Your failure at Cisterna... that's your Tenth Station. It stripped you bare.

The question is, what will you do now that you're free?

Don't be Coste, don't race back in. And, don't drown in the failure. Own it, learn from it, and get back up—you are stronger and braver than you know. Find your True Cross, Will.

Your friend,

Hays

He folded the V-Mail. Outside, the guns of Cassino began their nightly barrage, a grinding, hateful thunder. He had sent his message into the storm, praying it would find a safe harbor.

He now recognized that his failure was one of rigid adherence. He had been sent to salvage something already doomed, to throw men at a problem that must be solved, even if the cost was total.

He'd somehow let doctrine bind him.

But Will... Will's was different. He hadn't been bound; he had been unleashed. Will had *chased* something. He had coveted the victory, seen the "gap" that was really a kill box, and let his legend, his ambition, perhaps blind him.

Hays leaned back, rubbing his eyes. *One man let ambition blind him. Another let doctrine bind him. Either way, men died.*

He picked up a pencil, staring at the map of Italy. The lesson was brutal. This war wasn't going to be won by the rulebook. But it couldn't be won by personal glory, either.

It required something new—a balance he hadn't yet found, a way to temper doctrine with the right kind of intuition, the right kind of human trust. He was beginning to see that the old rules and the new ones were both failing.

He would have to find a third way.

His job done, he was recalled to England. He stood at the airfield, waiting for his C-47. He looked back at the monastery, now a bombed-out ruin after the Allies, in desperation, had dropped tons of bombs on it. But the stalemate at the Gustav line was still unbroken.

He climbed into the plane, his heart heavy. As the C-47 prepared for takeoff, Hays pulled out his V-Mail. He found the letter from Julia and read the words, written months earlier in Charleston, that stripped away the tactical failures and the mud. She told him that *the steep staircase he saw others rushing up was not his. ...Hold fast to your path, my love. It is long, but the footing is solid. Your path leads home. It leads to me. I am waiting for you always.*"

The words hit him every time with the force of a perfectly aimed artillery round, reorienting his spirit. If his path led home, he could not afford to waste the lives of the men he was about to command on blind doctrine.

He was returning to what he no longer thought of as "the real" war—in England, preparing for the landing in France —he now intimately knew that this was a miserable war on many fronts, including especially, Italy.

And he knew that he was leaving behind a front of mud-caked, forgotten men who were fighting perhaps a different but no less hard war—a war of pure, desperate courage against an impossible objective, with no promise of victory at all. He had been sent to fix a problem, but he had, in truth, just borne witness to tragedy.

29

THE LIAISON

SPRING 1944

London, England

Alistair met her not at Bletchley, but in a sterile, wood-paneled office in London. He sat behind the heavy mahogany desk, taking a slow, deliberate draw on his pipe before sliding a thin file across the blotter.

It was her report from Achnacarry.

"He's been recalled, you know," Alistair said, the pipe stem clicking against his teeth as he exhaled a thin stream of smoke. "Your Major Darby. After the Cisterna disaster."

Annie said nothing. She had seen the intercepts. She knew.

"Your assessment was... prescient," Alistair continued, tapping the file. "You wrote that he was a 'glory-hound who may either win the war or get all his men killed.' It seems you were right."

Alistair's words hit like a physical slap. "It was an intelligence failure," Annie said, her voice tight. "The intel was wrong."

"He was arrogant," Alistair countered, his voice void of sympathy. "Now he's in Washington. A ghost. A broken asset, sitting in that new Pentagon they built."

"So he's of no more use to us," Annie stated, her tone flat, masking the ache she felt.

"On the contrary," Alistair said, a thin smile touching his lips. "He's more useful than ever. A broken man is a blank slate. And we need to know what the Americans intend to write on it. Or better yet, why don't you be the first to write on that slate?"

He leaned forward. "Since the BRUSA Agreement was finalized, we're sharing everything, which means we're sending a full liaison team to Washington. You'll be our chief crypt-liaison for European intercepts, posted to the Pentagon."

Annie processed this. The biggest intelligence hub in the world. It was a massive promotion. "My official cover," she realized.

"Precisely," Alistair said. "Your... 'vital connection'... to Lieutenant Colonel Darby is a unique, unofficial asset. Your official duties are your own, and they are vital. But unofficially... find out if the man is salvageable. He's too important to be left a ghost."

30

D-DAY

1800 HOURS, JUNE 7, 1944

Little America

Hays's journey to the "Hell of the Hedgerows" had begun months earlier, in the damp, tense green of England. His orders had led him not to a front-line command, but to a critical, frustrating role in the planning for Operation Overlord. His job was to manage the artillery—the most massive, complex concentration of firepower in human history.

He'd spent his days in a blur of command tents and staff meetings, but his nights were often spent with the men, visiting the sprawling airbases in East Anglia, a "Little America" built on English soil.

He'd see the Women's Army Corps (WACs) in the control towers, young plotters like Sergeant Gerry Hill, their eyes tracking the bombers returning from raids, their voices a calm, steady presence in the chaos of the air war.

He'd share a cup of coffee and a doughnut with the women of the American Red Cross, the "Clubmobile" crews like Liz Richardson's, who served as the last bit of home for aircrews heading into the flak-filled skies over Germany.

This "Little America" of logistics, plotting, and morale, run by men and women alike, was the crucial, unglamorous work of the war. It was, he often thought, Julia's library campaign, magnified a thousand times.

Now, the planning was over. The 'Longest Day' had passed.

Omaha Beach, Normandy

The landing craft bucked in the heavy surf, its steel ramp grinding against the sand with a sound like a dying animal. The air was a toxic cocktail of diesel fumes, salt, burnt copper, and the sweet, sick-metallic smell of death.

General George P. Hays stood on the ramp, his face set in lines of stone. "Omaha Beach" was no longer a beach. It was a graveyard choked with the wreckage of the battle that had raged 24 hours earlier. Burned-out Sherman tanks sat like hollowed-out iron tombs in the surf. Smashed landing craft and bulldozers littered the shingle. The tide, stained pink, lapped gently around the bodies of men who had died before they even had a chance to fight.

Hays stepped off the ramp, his boots sinking into the wet, bloody sand. He began the long, hard climb up the captured heights, a route marked by discarded helmets, shell craters, and the unseeing eyes of the fallen.

At the top, he entered the "Hell of the Hedgerows."

This was the Bocage—a thousand-year-old maze of sunken lanes and massive, ancient earthen walls, each one topped with impenetrable thickets of thorn and oak. It was a landscape that made a mockery of modern warfare, a fortress built by medieval farmers that was now bleeding the U.S. Army dry. Each field was a self-contained kill zone.

A German 88mm shell cracked overhead, and Hays didn't even flinch. He was "The Rock." His presence was a calming anchor in the chaos.

He saw the problem immediately. The infantry was pinned, and the tanks were useless. This was not a war of maneuver. This was a war of artillery. This was his war.

"Get me a line to the 12th Field Artillery," he commanded, his voice a low, steady rumble that cut through the noise. "I want a rolling barrage on these coordinates, timed increments. We're not going to fight these hedgerows. We're going to erase them."

His climb would be a bloody one, a brutal, yard-by-yard ascent. It would lead him through the savage, close-quarters butchery of the Bocage, through the grinding breakout at Saint-Lô, and, months later, to the attack on the fortress of Brest, where he would command the massed guns that finally pulverized the German defenses.

He stood in the rain, his command a physical weight on his shoulders, and did his job. His gaze was fixed on the path that would, one day, lead him home to Julia.

31

THE D-DAY DODGER

JUNE 7, 1944

The Pentagon, Washington, D.C.

Across the Atlantic, in a quiet room in the Pentagon, the air was cool and still.

Will, the hero of Gela and Salerno, sat at an empty steel desk. After the Cisterna disaster, he had been recalled, his command stripped, his purpose extinguished. He was a ghost in a uniform, haunting the halls of a building dedicated to the war he was no longer allowed to fight.

The Pentagon didn't even smell like war. It smelled of floor polish and the yellow haze of cigarette smoke trapped in windowless rooms. It was the sterile, recycled scent of air-conditioned bureaucracy, hermetically sealed, and far removed from the sweat and fear of the line.

A young, starched captain from the public affairs office entered, holding a stack of papers and radiating an eager, boyish admiration. "Colonel Darby, sir! It's a genuine honor. Gela, Salerno, sir—the Rangers! The whole staff is talking about your legend."

"Thank you, Captain," Will said, his voice flat, unable to meet the boy's eyes. He accepted the papers with a grim nod. He thought: If this kid knew how many Rangers were still lying outside Cisterna, he wouldn't be smiling.

It was meant as a sarcastic rebuke to a world that had forgotten them. Now, it was his literal, humiliating reality. He, Will Darby, founder of the Rangers, was a D-Day Dodger, stuck in a mausoleum while real Rangers...

...His phone rang. It was the public affairs office.

"Colonel Darby, sir. Just a reminder that your car picks you up at 1400. You're the guest of honor at the War Bond rally in Philadelphia. They're expecting 5,000 people. The press will be there."

"Thank you, Captain," Will said, his voice a dead monotone. He hung up.

He looked at the speech on his desk, written by the PAO. It was full of words like "valor," "glory," and "the Ranger spirit."

It was a lie. And he had the proof sitting right next to it.

He opened the classified folder that had arrived that morning—the official Fifth Army After Action Report on the battle of Cisterna. He didn't need to read the casualty counts; he knew them by heart.

He turned to the command summary, the final verdict signed by Lieutenant General Mark Clark.

The words seemed to burn off the page, cutting through the praise of the PAO officer like a scalpel.

"This was a definite error in judgment," Clark had written.

Will stared at the sentence. He knew Clark was criticizing the Division command—blaming Truscott or Lucas for sending light infantry to do a tank's job. A kinder man would have read it and felt vindicated: *See? Even the Army Commander says we were misused.*

But Will didn't feel vindicated. He felt sick.

He read on, the report dissecting the battle with cold, forensic logic: "...for the Rangers do not have the support weapons to overcome the resistance indicated."

It was a professional autopsy of his own arrogance. He had seen the maps. He had known the odds. But he had been so in love with his legend, so convinced that "Ranger spirit" could bend physics, that he hadn't pushed back. He hadn't demanded tanks. He had just saluted and led them into the grinder.

He had brought a knife to a heavy artillery duel. He stared at the casualty count: 761—killed or captured. The exchange rate had finally turned on him. He hadn't traded a few men for a victory. He had risked everything... to buy... nothing.

Clark called it an error in judgment. Will knew it was something worse.

It was a breach of the trust his men had placed in him

He was a fraud. He was the "King of the Rangers," being paraded on a speech circuit as a hero, while the official record marked his battalion's sacrifice as a tactical mistake.

He closed the file, hiding the truth, but the words stayed burned in his retina.

Error in judgment.

He closed his eyes, and he wasn't in his office. He was back at the radio set, listening to the screams of his men as they were annihilated in the "iron vise." *Heavy contact! My God, they're opening up!*

A clerk silently placed a fresh copy of *The Stars and Stripes* on the stack of old newspapers on his desk. It landed heavily, burying the previous day's edition, which peeked out from the bottom of the stack—a June 5th headline that read:

WE'RE IN ROME

That victory had enjoyed exactly two days of sunlight before the shadow fell. The new paper covering it screamed in massive, world-altering block letters:

INVASION! ALLIES LAND IN FRANCE

The Italian campaign had literally been papered over. Will reached out to push the invasion news aside, trying to find the war he belonged to, but his hand froze on a sub-headline in the fresh edition. The headline, in massive black letters, screamed:

RANGERS STORM CLIFFS AT POINTE DU HOC

Will's hands trembled as he read the report. Men scaling 100-foot sheer cliffs under a storm of German machine-gun fire. A heroic, "impossible" climb that had saved the landings on Omaha Beach.

It was the "greatest moment" of the war. It was Arzew and Chiunzi Pass combined, magnified into legend.

And he had missed it.

The knife-twist was this: they weren't his Rangers. They were the 2nd and 5th Battalions. His 1st and 3rd—the men he had personally forged at Achnacarry, the men who had followed him to glory—were gone, their names on a list he knew by heart.

The war's greatest moment was happening without him. He thought of Annie and her warning about the weight of the crown. He had scoffed at it, at the story of a relic of failure. Now, sitting in his office under fluorescent lights while other men fought for freedom, he finally understood.

He was the man who had coveted glory and been left with nothing.

32

THE VICTORY BOOK

MID-JUNE 1944

Charleston, South Carolina

The Charleston Library Society was no longer a quiet harbor; it was a command post. The air, once still and smelling of old paper, was now a chaotic bustle of activity, smelling of newsprint and the heady, chemical sweetness of mimeograph ink.

Julia Hays, her hair pinned up, stood at the center of it all. This was her war.

Where George commanded artillery at Cassino, Julia commanded an army of volunteers. As head of the Victory Book Campaign for the Lowcountry, she was engaged in her own complex, frustrating war of logistics.

"No, Senator," she said into the telephone, her voice a model of strained patience. "I cannot, in good conscience, send another crate of 19th-century sermons to the boys at the Anzio beachhead. They are writing to us, sir. They are asking for Dick Tracy and Flash Gordon."

She reached across the desk and snatched up a ragged, coffee-stained clipping George had sent her—a 'Mail Call' letter from *The Stars and Stripes*. It referenced the bitter rumor circulating at the front that some bigwig had called them 'D-Day Dodgers,' implying they were shirking the real war in France.

She read the soldier's angry, printed plea:

'We're dodging nothing but death in this mud, and we'd appreciate it if the folks back home knew the difference. They call us "D-Day Dodgers" because we aren't in France,' a corporal wrote. *'But tell the folks back home that the crosses here in Italy stand just as straight as the ones in Normandy. And there are just as many of them.'*

She crumpled the clipping in her free hand, the paper biting into her palm. These men were being erased by the headlines while they were still fighting, and she refused to let them be buried by boredom on top of it.

She listened for a moment, her knuckles turning white on the receiver. "With respect, sir, I believe our Chaplains do a fine job tending their souls at weekly service. But for the rest of the week, when they aren't dodging 88s, they are hungering for home. They need a story that reminds them of the world they're fighting to save—and what a happy ending feels like."

She hung up the phone with a quiet, forceful click.

Just as Julia was sealing a box of Zane Grey novels in the APO shipping box, a society matron, Mrs. Pinckney, stopped by with a donation of forgotten poetry. "It's such a lovely thing you're doing, Julia," Mrs. Pinckney simpered, adjusting her pearl necklace. "At least our boys aren't facing anything like what's coming in France. Italy must be a real holiday compared to that."

Julia forced a polite smile, but her hand clenched the twine. Italy was killing them, too. The letters told her. Cassino, Anzio, mountains with names the papers barely bothered to print. She turned back to the stack.

The bell above the library's heavy oak door tinkled. Julia looked up, expecting another volunteer with a sack of donations.

Instead, it was Eleanor Ravenel. One of the oldest, proudest names in Charleston. She was dressed in a perfectly tailored black suit, her gloves and hat perfectly pinned. She was the very picture of Charleston society, except for the small, gold star pinned above her heart. Her son, John, had been killed at Salerno.

The cheerful bustle of the library seemed to freeze. Mrs. Alston and the other volunteers fell silent.

"Eleanor," Julia said, walking over, her voice soft. "How good to see you."

"Julia," Mrs. Ravenel said. Her voice was not sad. It was brittle, like thin ice. She was not crying; her stoicism was a fortress. She was holding a small, neat stack of books, tied with a bit of kitchen twine.

"I was... cleaning," Mrs. Ravenel said, her gaze fixed on the books, not on Julia. "John's room. I... I found these. They were his favorites."

She held out the stack. Julia saw the worn, cracked covers. A set of Zane Grey novels. *Riders of the Purple Sage. The Thundering Herd.*

"He read them until the covers fell off," Eleanor whispered, her iron control cracking for just a second. "He always wanted to be a cowboy."

She pushed them into Julia's hands. The books were heavy, a physical, tangible weight. This was not a donation. It was a sacrament. This was Julia's casualty list, walking through her door.

"He'd want the other boys to have them," Mrs. Ravenel said, her voice firming again. "The ones... the ones who are still there. He'd want them to have a good story."

"We will find them a good home, Eleanor," Julia said, her voice thick. "I promise."

Mrs. Ravenel gave a single, sharp nod, as if completing a transaction. She turned, her back perfectly straight, and walked out of the library, her footsteps echoing in the silence. The bell tinkled again, and she was gone.

Julia stood there, holding the dead boy's books. She looked at the 'APO shipping' box for the cowboys. Her "Burden of Command" was no longer a mountain of paper. It was the weight of these books in her hands. She was not just shipping stories; she was managing the last wishes of the dead, offering a small, fragile comfort in the face of an unbearable cost.

"He died at Salerno," she thought, the reality a cold, hard knot in her chest. "His books are going back to Italy."

That evening, long after the volunteers had gone home, she sat at her desk, the library silent again. The news from the radio was grim. She thought of George, somewhere in that hell.

She worried about his relentless drive. She worried that his duty would consume him, that "The Rock of the Marne" would be ground down to dust by this new, more terrible war.

She pulled a single sheet of V-Mail paper toward her. She had to write him. She had to send him an anchor.

She thought of the life they had built, the quiet, intellectual partnership that was her entire world. She thought of his integrity, the unshakeable core of the man.

She remembered a conversation they'd had, a lifetime ago, about the grand staircases of Charleston society. He had hated them. He had always felt more at home in her library.

She picked up her pen. *My dearest George, The library is in chaos...*

She wrote, her hand moving quickly. She told him about the books, the senators, the funny, human requests from the front. She told him that she saw his name and Will's in the papers. She told him that the stairs he saw others climbing were not his.

It was a path of duty, a path she understood. And she reminded him where that path ultimately led. *...Hold fast ... my love. But know that all paths are meant to lead somewhere. Yours leads home. It leads to me. I am waiting for you always. Love, Julia*

She folded the V-Mail, sealing her love and her faith into the small, fragile packet. It was her own form of artillery—a single, precisely aimed round of hope, fired into the darkness, praying it would find its target.

33

THE GHOST

JUNE 28, 1944

The Pentagon, Washington, D.C.

Will held the receiver of the black telephone against his ear, his voice calm, clipped, and utterly hollow. "No, major, with respect, you cannot route the hospital ships through that sector. Not yet."

He was performing the role he had played two years ago in Northern Ireland—the efficient staff officer, the master of logistics—but the man who had once charmed Lady Ashbrooke with a smile was gone.

"I don't care what the morning briefing says about the sea lanes being clear," Will continued, staring at the steel of his desk. "If you send unescorted medical transports into a zone that hasn't been swept for submarines in forty-eight hours, you aren't sending aid. You're sending targets. Reroute them. Darby out."

He hung up the phone. The silence that rushed back into the room was immediate and oppressive.

He swiveled his chair to the window. Below, in the

perfectly manicured courtyard of the Pentagon, a squad of MPs was changing the guard. Their uniforms were pressed, their gait synchronized, their boots gleaming in the summer sun.

They looked like toy soldiers. They looked like his Rangers had looked at Achnacarry before the mud, before the blood, before the ditch.

Will watched them with a detached, cold grief. He had come full circle. He was back in a well-lit, warm room looking out the window, imprisoned by the safety he had once fought so hard to escape.

He looked down at his collar. The silver eagle of a full colonel glinted in the fluorescent light. It was shiny, heavy, and new.

It was also the punchline to a joke only he understood.

The memory hit him, sharp as the Sicilian sun. He was back in Gela, standing in the dust beside a command jeep. General George S. Patton was leaning out, slapping a riding crop against his palm, his high-pitched voice cutting through the noise of the shelling.

"I'm offering you a way out, Will," Patton had barked, squinting against the glare. "I'm giving you the 180th Infantry. I'll make you a full bird colonel today. Right now. You take the Regiment, you get on the fast track to a star."

It was the golden ticket. The regular army. The "Royal Road" to becoming a general.

Will remembered his own smile—arrogant, assured, invincible. He had looked at "Old Blood and Guts" and shaken his head.

"With respect, general," Will had said, thumbing the Ranger scroll on his shoulder. "I'd rather be a Lieutenant Colonel of Rangers than a General of the

Infantry. I built this battalion. I'm staying with my boys."

Patton had looked at him with a strange expression—part admiration, part pity. He leaned in close, the smell of leather and sweat heavy in the air.

"You're a fool, Darby," Patton had growled. "You love them too much. And special units... they burn bright, but they burn fast. You stay, and you'll burn with them."

Will closed his eyes in the cool Pentagon air.

Patton had been right. Will had refused the crown of a colonel to stay a King of the Rangers. And because he stayed, he led them into the ditch.

Now, the Army had made him a colonel anyway. They had given him the rank as a consolation prize for the massacre of his kingdom.

He touched the silver eagle again. It didn't feel like a promotion. It felt like thirty pieces of silver.

He turned back to his desk. A single document lay on the blotter, awaiting his authorization. It wasn't a shipment of supplies. It was a deployment order for the 4th Replacement Battalion to the Pacific.

Will picked up his fountain pen. The nib was black steel, sharp as a bayonet. He read the attached G-2 summary one more time. The intelligence assessment for the landing zone read: *"Area secured. Light resistance expected. Expedited insertion recommended."*

Light resistance.

The words seemed to vibrate on the page.

His hand froze.

The paralysis wasn't a tremble; it was a terrifying clarity. He looked at the map coordinates on the document, and his mind didn't see a tropical beach.

He saw Cisterna.

He saw the "gap" in the line that General Truscott had pointed to. He saw the "thin screen" that was actually an iron vise as seventeen Panzer IVs waited in the dark.

His intuition, the "gift" that had built his legend, had turned on him. It whispered now that the intelligence on this paper was a lie.

If I sign this, the voice whispered, *and the intel is wrong again, who dies? If I sign this, am I sending a thousand more boys into a kill box just to keep the schedule moving?*

His hand remained rock steady, suspended over the paper, but he could not force the pen to move. He was locked in the memory of the radio static, listening to his men scream for help he couldn't give.

He pressed the nib down on the signature line, not writing, just pressing. The ink began to bleed into the high-grade linen paper. It spread slowly, turning the blank space into a dark, widening blot.

To his tired eyes, it didn't look like ink. It looked like a shell crater.

"Damn it," he whispered, the sound harsh in the quiet room.

He didn't throw the pen. He simply set it down, the metal clicking against the desk like a bolt sliding home.

A soft, rhythmic tapping came from the door. Not a military knock—a playful, familiar rhythm. *Shave-and-a-haircut.*

Will didn't answer. He stared at the wall.

The door opened, and the gray world of the Pentagon suddenly flooded with color.

Annie stepped in.

"Annie," he breathed, stunned. She was in the crisp,

tailored uniform of a British intelligence liaison. "Hello, Will," she said, her voice soft but her gaze as sharp as ever.

"May I come in?" She walked into the stifling room.

"How..." he finally managed, closing the door. "How are you here?"

"Since the BRUSA agreement, they've started sending us over as liaison," she said simply. "And my angling for a transfer was to see you."

She brought the weather of the living world into the sterile room—the scent of sunshine, ozone, and the faint, sweet smell of vanilla.

She took in the room in a glance—the pristine uniform, the overflowing wastebasket, the paralyzed man. But she didn't look at him with a cold analyst's eye. She looked at him with those deep, luminous brown eyes—the biggest, warmest eyes he had ever seen—and her face broke into a small, breathless laugh. It wasn't that anything was funny; it was the sheer, overwhelming relief of seeing him standing there, real and solid, after months of imagining him as a ghost.

"Well," she said, her voice rich with a Scottish lilt that wrapped around him like a blanket. "I've breached the perimeter. The guard downstairs was quite insistent, but I told him I had vital supplies for the colonel."

"She held up a brown paper bag. "Fresh donuts. And this terrible drink you all consume—coffee."

"Look at you," she said softly, walking around the steel desk.

Will looked at her, and the rigor mortis in his jaw loosened just a fraction. "You shouldn't be here, Annie."

"And you shouldn't be sitting in the dark," she countered. She didn't wait for an invitation. She reached out and pulled him into a fierce, sudden embrace, her arms wrapping around his neck to pull his head against her shoulder. Will remained rigid for a heartbeat, his body a statue of granite, before he finally broke. He leaned into her, his breath hitching as he buried his face in the crook of her neck, his hands clutching her waist as if she were the only solid thing in a world made of smoke.

She held him in the silence of the office, letting the warmth of the embrace settle before she stepped back just enough to look him in the eye, her hands remaining firmly on his shoulders.

"You're stiff as a board," she said, her voice rich with a Scottish lilt. "You look like you're waiting for a firing squad, Will."

"I am checking tables," Will rasped, his voice unused and rusty. "I am... trying to work."

"You're trying to hide," she corrected, but she said it with such warmth that it didn't sting. She leaned against the desk, invading his sterile space with her vibrant presence. "You've lost your nerve to be wrong, haven't you?"

Will looked away from her, his gaze falling back to the dark ink blot on his desk that looked so much like a shell crater. "I've lost the right to be right," he whispered. "General Marshall wants my 'Ranger instincts.' But that man is dead, Annie. I killed him at Cisterna. The man sitting here... all he sees is the casualty list."

He reached out to touch the deployment order on his desk, his hand beginning to tremble slightly as he stared at the words "Light resistance expected."

"I failed seven hundred and sixty-one men, their parents, their families, and my country." He looked up at her, his eyes raw with a terrifying clarity. "You don't navigate by a compass that spins, Annie. You throw it overboard."

Annie didn't offer a platitude. Her eyes filled with a fierce, protective light. She reached across the desk and firmly covered his trembling hand with hers, her skin warm and steady against his. The physical contact was an anchor, pulling him back from the static of the radio room at Cisterna.

"You are not a compass, Will," she said softly. "You're a man. And you're hurt. But you are not throwing yourself overboard. Not while I'm here."

She squeezed his hand one last time before releasing it to reach for the brown paper bag she had placed over his ruined papers. A twinkle of the old Highland Annie returned to her eyes. "Coffee," she commanded gently. "Then we tackle the past."

34

THE SILENCE

EVENING, JUNE 28, 1944

The Pentagon, Washington, D.C.

The rain against the office window wasn't soothing; it was relentless, a drumming reminder of the mud thousands of miles away.

Annie sat on the edge of the desk, the box of donuts unopened between them. She had tried to get him to eat, to smile, but the weight on his shoulders seemed to be pressing Will to the floor.

"Just breathe, Will, let it out," she said softly. "You're safe."

"Safe," he repeated, the word tasting wrong. He stood and walked to the window, his back to her. "That's the problem, isn't it?"

He turned, his composure cracking. The polished colonel was gone; in his place was a man vibrating with a grief he had been suppressing for months.

"A Lieutenant stopped me in the hallway this morning," Will said, his voice quiet, almost hollow. "Bright-eyed.

Fresh out of OCS. He wanted to shake the hand of the 'Hero of Gela.' He asked me what it felt like to be a legend."

Will ran a hand through his hair. "I couldn't even look him in the eye, Annie. He was standing right there, smiling at me, expecting wisdom... and I found myself staring and talking to the wall behind his left shoulder."

He leaned back against the window frame, looking defeated.

"I mumbled something about 'teamwork' and walked away. I couldn't look at him because if I did, I was terrified he'd see it. I was terrified he'd see what I am."

"He didn't see that," Annie said gently. "He saw a Colonel."

"He saw a lie," Will said, his voice sharp with pain. "Nobody knows! They haven't even told the families the whole truth yet."

"Do you know what the telegrams say? The ones going to Ohio and Tennessee and New York? They list them as 'Missing in Action.' Not killed. Not captured. Just... missing."

He looked at her, "We retook the battlefield at Cisterna last month, Annie. The Graves Registration units are out there right now. The Army knows who is dead. But the families don't."

He paced the small room. "For months, mothers have been walking to their mailboxes, reading the papers about the victories in France, looking for a sign from Italy. They think their boys are hiding in a barn somewhere, waiting for rescue. They think there's hope."

"But the Germans know," he hissed. "Kesselring knows. The crowds in Rome who lined the streets... they know."

He closed his eyes, the image haunting him. "They

paraded them, Annie. My Rangers. The ones who survived the ditch."

"I know," Annie whispered.

The words stopped Will in his tracks. He opened his eyes, staring at her. "What?"

"I know, Will," she said, her voice trembling but her gaze steady. She slid off the desk and stood before him, refusing to look away from his pain. "We have a source who smuggles propaganda films out of Rome. It came through the diplomatic bag to London. I saw the reels."

Will looked at her, his breath hitching. "You saw them?"

"I saw the march," she said, stepping into his space, her hand reaching out to touch his rigid arm. "I saw them walking past the Colosseum. Like trophies. Dirty, bloody... walking past the ruins of the Caesars while the cameras rolled. I watched it in a dark room in London, Will. I witnessed it."

Will crumbled. The isolation that had been choking him—the belief that he was the only one holding the visual horror—shattered.

"They must have looked so small," he whispered, his voice breaking. "Next to that stone."

"They looked brave," she corrected fiercely, gripping his forearm.

"And there was one... a boy in the rank. Dirty, exhausted, a German guard right on his heels. But he raised his hand to the crowd, Will. He held up two fingers. A 'V'—for Victory."

She looked Will in the eye, her voice trembling with the intensity of the image.

"They were marching into captivity, surrounded by guards, and he was still fighting. They haven't given up, Will. Why have you?"

The image pierced him. Will closed his eyes, and the static in his head finally cleared. He didn't see a victim. He saw a brother holding the line.

"He's daring them," Will whispered, a tremor in his voice. "He's telling us he's still there."

"He is," Annie said softly. "And I know where 'there' is."

"We've tracked the rail movements. Stalag II-B. Stalag III-B. They are freezing right now, but they are alive."

He looked at her, tears finally spilling over. "But their families have no idea. They are living in a silence that I helped create. And every time one more bright-eyed junior officer gushes over me, thinking I'm some kind of hero because they don't know the truth... I feel trapped. I feel like a fraud."

He slumped against the wall, sliding down until he was sitting on the floor, his head in his hands.

"I wish I were in the camp with them," he confessed, the admission barely audible. "I would trade places with any of them. I'd take the lice, the cold, the starvation... to not be the 'hero' sitting in a warm office while the mothers wait for a letter that isn't coming."

Annie didn't offer platitudes about duty or rank. She knew the intelligence estimates; she knew the survival rate.

She sat on the floor beside him, her shoulder pressing firmly against his. She didn't try to fix it. She just sat with him in the silence, acknowledging the terrible, heavy truth on his shoulders.

She knew then that before she could help him stand, she had to let him mourn the lie he was being forced to live.

35

______

THE BROKEN TABLET

JULY 4, 1944

Washington, D.C.

The apartment was a sauna, and Will was its willing prisoner this night. Outside, the humidity of a D.C. summer pressed against the city.

Through the open window, the sounds of honking horns and a distant celebration drifted in—the pop and crackle of fireworks, the faint cheers of a populace celebrating a war they thought was already won.

Will stood by the window, his shirt unbuttoned, sweat slicking his skin. He wasn't watching the fireworks. He was staring at his dark reflection in the glass.

It had been six days since he crumbled on the floor of his office. Six days since Annie had told him she *knew*.

"You can't stand there all night, Will," Annie said.

"It's Independence Day," Will muttered, "Everyone is celebrating. They think because we took Rome and hit the beaches in France, it's over."

"They're allowed to hope," Annie said gently.

"They're celebrating a halftime score," Will countered, turning from the window. "They don't know the game we are playing."

"You turned down the transfer?" Annie said. She sat on the single armchair, her legs tucked under her.

Will didn't turn around. "The Pacific needs officers, Annie. It doesn't need ghosts."

"They need *you*," she countered gently.

"No," Will muttered, the word scraping his throat. He turned from the window, his face a map of exhaustion. "I can't lead men, Annie. I can't look a nineteen-year-old boy in the eye and make the promise anymore. The 'follow me' promise. I broke it."

He walked to the nightstand. There, sitting next to a bottle of whiskey he hadn't touched in two days, lay the small, dried skeleton of the heather sprig.

He picked it up. It was brittle, gray, and dead—just like the legend he had tried to build.

"I coveted the glory, just like you warned me," he whispered, rolling the dry stem between his fingers. "I wanted the crown. And I marched 767 men into a ditch to get it. I shattered the pact, Annie. I didn't just lose a battle. I lost the right to stand in front of a formation."

"You're still there, aren't you?" she whispered.

Will looked up. Annie's eyes were filled with a profound, knowing sadness.

"You're still in that ditch with them," she said.

"I never left," Will admitted, his voice cracking. "Every time I close my eyes, the static clears. I hear them screaming for the support I couldn't give. I hear the Panzers, the Buzzsaws, the 20s, and the 88s—Hitler's whole damn symphony."

Annie stood up. She didn't rush. She crossed the room

slowly, stepping into his personal space, invading the cell he had built for himself. She wrapped her arms around his waist, resting her head against his chest.

Will stood rigid for a moment, afraid that if he softened, he would shatter. But the warmth of her pressed against him was undeniable. Slowly, his arms came up to hold her.

"Listen to me, Will," she whispered into his shirt. "It's not all on your shoulders. The intel failed you."

"I was the commander," he rasped. "The intel is just paper. The decision was mine."

She pulled back, forcing him to look at her. Her eyes were swimming with tears, but she was smiling—that heartbreakingly beautiful smile that had disarmed him in a Scottish pub a lifetime ago.

"You want to know who else failed you? The Army," she said fiercely. "You went from captain to a full colonel in roughly three years. They pushed you too fast." She took a breath, her voice trembling. "And you know who else failed you… I did."

Will stared at her, confusion cutting through his grief. "You? Annie, you're the only thing that *hasn't* failed me."

"No," she said, shaking her head, the guilt pouring out of her. "I was sent to assess you, remember? And I... I was charmed. I thought you were a king. I liked you. I stoked that fire. In Scotland, I... I only told you the first part of the story."

Will frowned, stepping back slightly. "What story?"

"The Stone of Scone," she whispered softly. "I only told you the public legend. The one about 'Jacob's Pillow' and the 'King's Stone.' The ladder to the stars and the stone that screamed for royalty. That was the story that fed your ambition, Will. And I fed it to you. I crowned you with that…" She pointed to the dead heather. "I helped send you into that trap."

"Annie, that's superstition," Will said, trying to comfort *her* now. "That's not why they died."

"It's not just superstition!" she insisted, her desperation rising. She took a step back, wrapping her arms around herself as if she were suddenly cold. "I saw it, Will. At Bletchley. I saw the intercepts."

The room went deadly silent.

"What did you see?" Will asked, his voice dropping to a whisper.

"They wouldn't let us share the intel with you," she sobbed, the secret finally breaking loose. "But I saw the trap! I saw the supplies for the Panzers moving into place at Cisterna. I knew it was a kill box, not a gap. And I was ordered to sit on it, knowing that you... that *you* and your men were probably charging straight into it."

Will felt the blood drain from his face. He leaned back against the dresser, his legs suddenly weak. "You knew?"

"I tried to send a warning," she pleaded, reaching for him, but stopping short. "They wouldn't let me. They called me just a 'girl.' But don't you see? It wasn't just your arrogance. It was the machine that chewed us both up."

Will looked at her—really looked at her—and saw the same haunting in her eyes that lived in his mirror—his beloved Annie was a fellow casualty. The anger flared and died in the same second, extinguished by the shared weight of the tragedy.

"Oh God, we are both so broken," he whispered and began to weep.

"Yes," she said, tears streaming down her face. "But we don't have to stay that way. There's another legend, Will. A

'Secret Legend' of the Stone I didn't tell you. I should have. God, I wished I had."

"Annie, I don't want any more legends," Will said wearily, turning away. "I just want to forget."

"No, you need this one," she pressed, moving around him, forcing him to engage. "The secret legend says the stone is not Jacob's Pillow at all. It's a relic from the Temple of Solomon. It's the foundation stone for the Ark of the Covenant—the box that held the Ten Commandments."

Will paused. "The Ark?"

"The legend says that when Moses came down the mountain, he saw the Golden Calf—the coveting of his people, their desire for glory and easy gods—and in his rage, he shattered the tablets."

She took his hands, her grip fierce.

"That, Will... that was your Cisterna. The 'Broken Tablet.' The moment of failure. The moment the glory shatters."

Will looked down at his hands. He didn't see the stone tablets. He saw the map of Italy. He saw the casualty lists he had memorized.

"Then I'm done," he said softly. "Moses broke the law. He failed his God."

"You think because Moses broke the tablets, God fired him?" Annie whispered, bringing her face close to his. "You think He sent him to a desk job in Egypt?"

Will blinked, the absurdity of the image piercing his gloom.

"No," Annie said, her hands framing his face, holding him together. "God called him back. He ordered Moses to go back up the mountain and cut two new tablets. He gave him a Second Chance."

The words hung in the air between them. *A Second Chance.*

"That, Will, that is the true legend of the Ark," she continued, her voice gaining strength. "It's not about the glory of the king. It's about the redemption of the man. It's not a story about failure; it's a story about what you do *after* you fail."

A single, tiny, flickering flame lit in the vast, hollow emptiness of Will's guilt. He looked at Annie, and for the first time in months, he didn't see the end. He saw a path.

"He went back up?" Will whispered, his voice raw with a terrifying hope.

"He went back up," Annie confirmed, smoothing the hair back from his forehead. "He had to face the same mountain. The same burden. But this time, he didn't do it for the glory. He did it for the service. He did it to carry the Law."

Will stared at her. The paralyzing fog that had choked him for months began to thin. He looked at the map on the wall, then at the darkness outside the window. He thought of the film Annie had described—the march past the Colosseum, the trains heading north.

"They're still there," Will realized, the thought crystallizing into a hard, sharp point. "My men. They aren't just missing, Annie. They're waiting."

He stood up, the lethargy of the heat vanishing.

"They're in those camps because of me," he whispered, the realization fueling him not with guilt, but with purpose. "If I stay here... and the clock runs out on them..."

He took a breath, and it went deeper than it had since the day the radio went silent at Cisterna.

"And because he went back up," Annie whispered, "his people made it home."

Will reached out and pulled her to him. He kissed her—not a desperate collision of grief, but a slow, deepening affirmation of life. She tasted of vanilla and rain and forgiveness.

He pulled back, resting his forehead against hers.

"You're not a King, Will," she murmured against his lips. "You're a soldier. And by God, right now, the world needs soldiers like you more than anything."

Will nodded, the movement slow but sure.

"A soldier," he repeated, testing the weight of the word. It felt heavy. It felt real. It felt right.

"I'm going back up the mountain," he said, looking at the map one last time. "I'm going to get my men."

36

THE PENANCE

MORNING, JULY 5, 1944

Washington, D.C.

The morning after, the heat had broken. A cool breeze drifted off the Potomac, washing the city clean. Will sat at his desk in the gray dawn light. The room was clean. His mind was sharp.

He pulled a single sheet of V-Mail paper from his drawer. He began to write, not to the War Department, but to his general.

General Hays,

Your letter about Coste and the 'True Cross' found me weeks ago. I wasn't ready to read it then. I am now. You were right. About all of it. I was Coste, chasing my own glory, my 'King's Stone.'

I let that ambition pull me under, and it cost me my men. My legend died in that ditch. An analyst here... a friend. More than a friend; her name's Annie McKenna. We've been seeing each other since Scotland. She told me the other half of the story.

She saw the trap, general. She called it a kill box when we all saw a gap.

She told me the story you knew all along. The one about the 'Broken Tablet.' About a second chance, a path that isn't about glory, but about what comes after you fail. I'm not the man you knew at Fort Hoyle. That man is gone.

I'm not asking for a command, general. I'm not asking for anything but a chance to serve, in any capacity. I'm just trying to get back on the right path. I am working my way back, sir.

Very Respectfully,

Will

He sealed the envelope, a man with a new, quiet purpose. He would pull every string, call in every favor, not for a promotion, but for a posting. He didn't care where. He just had to get back to the war, back to the men, back to the path of service.

37

THE CAGE

JANUARY 1945

Stalag II-B, Hammerstein, Poland

The wind coming off the Baltic Sea didn't just freeze the skin; it seemed to crack the bones. Inside the wire, the ground was a sheet of gray ice.

Private First Class Jimmy Tolliver—or what was left of him—shivered violently in his thin coat. He was only nineteen, yet he felt ancient.

He had learned to count life in inches and ounces. He had survived a year on hot water for breakfast and exactly seven small potatoes for dinner.

He had even survived Hauptmann Springer. Jimmy closed his eyes and could still see the Kommando Officer—the "Nazi fanatic" in charge of the work details—red with rage the day the Americans had refused to volunteer for labor.

The Rangers had stood tall, quoting the Geneva Convention rights they had memorized in training. Springer hadn't cared about rights. He had just screamed, "I make the rules!" and ordered his guards to charge them with fixed bayonets.

Jimmy remembered the glint of steel, the shock of unarmed men being herded like cattle by blade-point, realizing in that terrifying second that honor was a word their captors did not understand.

He had seen Private Harry Galler, the speaker they had elected from their own ranks—the only voice they had—stripped of his authority the moment the Germans discovered he was Jewish. He had watched soldiers throw their dog tags into the latrines, desperate to hide the 'H' for Hebrew stamped into the steel—a single letter that could strip them of their rights and mark them for torture.

They had taken everything. They had even confiscated their Red Cross cigarettes, ripping them from the men's starving hands because the packs bore the slogan: "For Victory."

He had survived it all. But now, standing in a formation of ghosts, hundreds of men huddled together against the gale, he wondered if his luck had finally run out.

To the east, the horizon flickered with a dull, rhythmic orange glow—the Red Army. Salvation was ten miles away.

But the gate didn't open to the east. It opened to the west.

"Raus! Schnell!" the German guards screamed, their voices edged with a panic Jimmy hadn't heard before. They wielded rifle butts, driving the prisoners toward the road.

"Where are we going, Sarge?" Jimmy whispered, his teeth chattering uncontrollably.

The sergeant next to him, a man who had once climbed cliffs at Arzew but now walked with a limp, didn't look back.

"Away from the Russians, kid. Into the storm."

Jimmy looked at the road ahead. It was a ribbon of white

snow disappearing into the blizzard. He wrapped his arms around himself, feeling the sharp ridge of his ribs.

He didn't know they were about to walk nine hundred miles. He only knew that the war wasn't over.

It was just getting colder.

38

THE NEW COMMAND

JANUARY 1945

Fifth Army Forward HQ, Italy

Major General George P. Hays arrived in the frozen, vertical hell of the Northern Apennines as the second commander of the 10th Mountain Division. He was inheriting an elite, untested unit of skiers and mountaineers, and a tactical nightmare.

The U.S. Fifth Army was exhausted, bled white by a series of costly assaults against Field Marshal Kesselring's masterpiece: the Gothic Line. As the Fifth Army stepped back, the 10th Mountain Division stepped in.

In early January, Major General Hays traveled to the Fifth Army forward headquarters at Traversa to meet with Lieutenant General Lucian Truscott.

The command post did not smell of victory; it smelled of damp earth, burnt coffee, and the constant chill of the Apennines seeping through the stone walls. The three-star general looked more like a man managing a bankruptcy

"We're starving, George," Truscott said, pacing the

small room. "We are at the end of a 5,000-mile supply line, and the well is dry. Washington has us on an 'active defense'—which is a polite way of saying we don't have the shells, the weather, or the men to move an inch. We are paused."

Truscott walked to the situation map, a massive sheet covered in grease-pencil markings that dominated the room. He tapped the jagged contour lines of the Northern Apennines.

"This isn't just a line on a map," Truscott muttered. "It's a fifty-mile-wide wall of rock separating us from the Po Valley. There are only a few ways through it that can handle armor and logistics: Highway 12, Highway 64, and Highway 65."

Hays stepped closer, his eyes tracing the black line of Highway 64. It wound through the Reno River valley like a snake. He knew the logistics; without that road, they couldn't push fuel or tanks north.

"Highway 64 is the key," Hays observed.

"It is," Truscott agreed. "But right now, it's a shooting gallery. Look here." He pointed to two dominant peaks looming over the highway. "Mount Belvedere and Mount Gorgolesco. As long as the Germans sit up there, they have total observation of the road and the valley floor. We can't move a single truck without them calling in an 88."

He slid his finger west to a jagged spine of rock. "And here. This ridge allows them to fire into the valley from the flank. They have us in a chokehold."

Truscott turned to Hays, his expression grim. "Operation Encore. I want you to lead it. It's a limited offensive. A surgical lunge to grab this chain of peaks. We aren't trying to win the war here, but we need that high ground to secure an anchor. If we don't hold this high ground when the snow melts, the spring offensive is dead on arrival. You have to reset the board."

"And the support?" Hays asked, sensing the isolation in Truscott's tone. "No one," Truscott said, the answer chillingly blunt. "No one is going to share the bullets with you, George. You take the mountain alone."

Hays looked at the map. He saw the peaks Truscott was pointing to—Belvedere, Gorgolesco, and the jagged spine of Riva Ridge. They weren't just terrain features; they were a fortress built by nature, a fifty-mile-thick wall designed to stop an army cold.

"I understand, general," Hays said, his voice a low rumble. "You want an anchor. You want the 10th Mountain Division to take the whole damn mountain range."

39

THE GOTHIC LINE

JANUARY 1945

Northern Apennines, Italy

General Hays stepped out of the farmhouse to inspect his new command.

It was a strange beast, and yet it felt familiar —like the 99th Field Artillery. In the muddy courtyard, a squad was struggling to lash the barrel of a 75mm pack howitzer onto a sullen mule.

"Easy, Socrates," a grizzled sergeant muttered, patting the animal's neck. "This isn't Kiska. The wind doesn't bite as hard here, even if the mud is deeper."

The sergeant's face was wind-burned leather—a veteran of the 10th's earlier Aleutian Island campaign.

The private wrestling with the cinch strap, a kid who looked more like he belonged in a library than a foxhole, adjusted his glasses.

"Actually, sergeant, the mud *reduces* friction. The animal is struggling against the viscosity. It creates a vacuum seal around the hoof, so we're fighting atmospheric pressure every time he lifts a—"

"Just tie the knot, Professor," the sergeant sighed.

The private cinched the strap, his eyes drifting to a tattered piece of newsprint tacked to the stable post. It was a Bill Mauldin "Up Front" cartoon clipped from *The Stars and Stripes*, featuring the haggard, unshaven infantrymen Willie and Joe standing in the omnipresent Italian slush.

Happy Anniversary, Joe. I was gonna get you flowers, but I decided to give you the side of the foxhole that don't drip.

The caption cut through the misery with a dark, weary humor that no manual could teach. The Professor chuckled, a dry, intellectual appreciation of the irony. The grizzly sergeant looked at the drawing, then down at the sucking mud around their boots, and gave a grim, approving nod.

It was the first time they had agreed on anything all day.

As the Professor turned back to the mule, hoisting a crate of ammo that would break a lesser man's back, he started to hum. It was a tune that had haunted them since Camp Hale —"Bell Bottom Trousers"—but the words were their own.

"*Ninety pounds of rucksack, a pound of grub or two...*" he sang softly, patting the mule's flank in rhythm.

The sergeant shook his head, suppressing a grin, but he joined in on the downbeat, his voice a gravelly bass that carried across the courtyard.

"*He'll mush, mush, mush, in the slush, slush, slush...*"

Hays watched them—the college boys quoting physics and the Aleutian vets who knew the cold better than they knew fear—bonding over the absurdity of their burden.

They weren't complaining; they were boasting. They owned the weight.

They moved on hooves, not wheels, dragging mountain guns where no truck could go. It was the only full division in the Army organized like this—a fourteen-thousand-man experiment in total specialization.

Hays lit his pipe, the melody of the "singing division" drifting through the damp air. He was betting the war that this odd, brainy collection of climbers was the key to picking the lock.

Kesselring had built a fortress in the mountains. The lynchpin was Mount Belvedere, a peak that gave German observers a god's-eye view of every Allied approach. For months, conventional assaults had been chewed to pieces by a "ring of fire"—a perfectly registered, unending storm of German artillery.

Hays stood in his drafty command post and stared at the maps. He saw the frontal assault on Belvedere for what it was: a kill box. His failure at Cassino, where he had followed doctrine perfectly and been butchered for it, was a fresh, hot wound. He would not make that mistake again. His duty demanded another path.

His eyes drifted to the west, to a long, sheer ridge that flanked Belvedere. Riva Ridge.

"What about this, gentlemen?" Hays said, his finger tapping the map.

"Find me the instructors from Seneca Rocks," Hays commanded, his voice a low, steady rumble.

"Find me the men who lived on those cliffs. I want a plan to put an entire battalion on Riva Ridge. At night. In silence."

40

THE SECOND CHANCE

JANUARY 1945

Washington D.C.

Will stood over his map table. The room was lit by lamps and the glow of Annie's presence in the corner. He wasn't looking at the map of Japan. He was looking at a personnel file. His own.

"I can't ask for a command," Will said, his voice steady for the first time in months. "I can't ask General Marshall for a regiment. I haven't earned the right to lead yet."

"So how do you go back?" Annie asked. She was curled up on the sofa.

"I have to find a way to serve that doesn't require them to trust me with their lives. Not yet."

He flipped through a stack of Pentagon circulars—the boring, administrative detritus of the war. Notices of inspections. VIP visits.

His hand stopped on a memo from the Army Air Forces.

Subject: General H.H. "Hap" Arnold Inspection Tour. European Theater of Operations. March 1945.

It was a junket. A glorified sightseeing trip for the top brass to inspect airfields, shake hands, and look busy. It was the kind of assignment a combat colonel would usually scoff at—a "dog and pony show."

But Will looked at it, and he saw a door.

"The Hap Arnold tour," he murmured. "They need a senior ground officer as an observer. To advise on air-to-ground coordination."

He looked up at Annie, and the fire in his eyes wasn't about ambition. It was about justice.

"It's not just about my penance, Annie," he said, his voice dropping to a low, intense pitch. "It's about what is happening over there. You saw the intercepts. The Ardeatine Caves."

Annie stiffened. She knew the report well. "335," she whispered. "Executed in the dark."

"Murdered," Will corrected, his knuckles white on the table edge. "Ten Italian civilians for every one German soldier," Will said, his voice trembling with a new kind of fury.

"Kesselring takes ten lives for every one. That is the pure, distilled evil coming out of Germany. A soldier is supposed to give his life so ten others don't have to. That is the difference, Annie. That is the math. That is dignity and human decency. I spent my early career trying to get the victory, the glory, the headline. Now... I just want to balance the ledger the other way. I would gladly give back tenfold what I lost."

He walked over to the window, looking out at the safe,

rain-slicked streets of D.C., but seeing only the darkness of those caves.

"I did covet glory," he said, turning back to her. "But Kesselring covets death. If I sit here in this office, safe and warm, while that man is turning Italy into a graveyard... then I haven't learned anything. I have to go back. I have to perform a service to end that evil."

He tapped the circular.

"It's not a command. It's a ride. I'd be carrying luggage and holding doors. I'd be a tourist in my own war. But if I carry the luggage, I'm still in the theater. I'm still helping."

"Is that beneath you?" Annie asked gently.

Will smiled—a genuine, humble smile that crinkled the corners of his eyes.

"Nothing is beneath me, Annie. Not anymore."

He picked up the pen. This time, his hand didn't shake. He signed the request form.

"I'm going to apply for the observation tour," he said. "It gets me to Europe."

Annie walked over and wrapped her arms around his waist from behind, resting her chin on his shoulder.

"A humble step," she whispered. "The stonecutter's path."

"It's the only way up the mountain," Will said. "I don't know where I'll land. Maybe France, maybe the Alps. But I'll find a shovel, or a rifle, or a map. I'll find a way to help stop him."

He turned in her arms, and the love in his eyes was fierce and clear.

"Thank you," he whispered. "For helping me get back up."

"Just come back to me," she said, burying her face in his neck. "When your work is done, you come home."

"I will," he promised.

41

THE SILENT CLIMB

1900 HOURS, FEBRUARY 18, 1945

Riva Ridge, Italy

The night of February 18th was one of impossible silence. The air up here was different—thinner, sharper. It didn't smell of the battlefield mud below; it smelled of ozone and crushed pine resin. There was a metallic taste to the rarified air that coated the back of their throats, cold and clean like the blade of a knife.

Following the intel from the February 15th recon patrol's free climb to the summit, the 86th Mountain Infantry began their "unscalable" ascent into the sudden, total blackness.

This was not a charge; it was a vertical infiltration.

At approximately 1900 hours, under a deep, moonless sky, Staff Sergeant Johnnie Grey and the original recon team led one of five companies of the 86th—140 mountain soldiers in all—as they hiked silently toward the base of Pizzo di Campiano, deep in the Dardagna River valley.

At the same time, the other four companies made the

same approach along parallel routes. In total, 700 men would make the climb.

As Johnnie ascended in the lead of the men, his hand trailed along the thin communication wire he and his recon patrol had laid three days before, every knot at 100-foot intervals telling him precisely where he was. It was also his only communication link to the world below, a black thread snaking up the cliff that promised a way back—or a path straight into the unknown.

Under his boots, the ground was a treacherous crust of ice and hard-packed snow. Every step was a battle against the crunch, a fight to keep his numb toes from slipping on the 1,600-foot cliff that rose sheer above the valley floor.

For hours, the parallel teams moved like shadows up the five parallel summits of the sheer face of the ridge. The cold rock sucked the heat from their fingertips. A boot scraped; the sound was a thunderclap in the thin air. Every man in the trail party had wrapped the head of his hammer in heavy cloth to stifle the ring of steel against steel to drive the pitons in the rock.

They paid out the new nylon climbing ropes—a critical technological edge over the heavy, water-absorbent hemp of the past. The lightweight lines allowed the lead climbers to carry the sheer volume of rope needed to rig the length of the face for the main assault force.

The Ridge, topping out at 4,900 feet above sea level for some of its ascent routes, was famously deemed "unclimbable" by the Germans.

However, these were the men who learned to climb at the Army's school at Seneca Rocks, West Virginia, and this was the cliff they were born to climb. By dawn, they were on the summit. The German defenders, who had relied on

God's creation and gravity as their sentries, awoke to a nightmare. The assault was silent, brutal, and a swift success.

The 10th had seized Riva Ridge, the western anchor of Kesselring's line. But the victory was precarious. The 86th was now isolated on a high, narrow, and exposed spine of rock, with no way to get supplies up or, more critically, to get their wounded down.

The pack mules, the backbone of mountain supply, had been defeated, broken by the ascent of even the most forgiving trail. Only one animal—a small Italian mule carrying the heavy tube of a 75mm pack howitzer—made it all the way to the summit of Mt. Cappel Buso.

It stood trembling while the gunners unloaded the steel, and then, its heart having burst from the strain, it simply lay down and died.

42

—————

THE STAND

DAWN, FEBRUARY 19, 1945

Riva Ridge, Italy

The euphoria of the ascent evaporated with the rising sun, replaced by a cold, terminal reality.

Staff Sergeant Johnnie Grey and his small band of men from the 86th were not just holding a position; they were clinging to a knife's edge.

They were isolated on Pizzo di Campiano, the easternmost spur of Riva Ridge. To their backs was the sheer, 1,600-foot drop they had just scaled. To their front was an angry, waking enemy.

The Germans, realizing they had lost the high ground, were throwing everything they had to take it back. A specialized mountain company, elite and furious, launched counter-thrust after counter-thrust against Johnnie's ragged platoon.

For hours, the Americans fought without food, without water, and with their ammunition dwindling to a terrifying few rounds.

The wind whipped over the exposed peak, a relentless, biting force that searched for any gap in their white camouflage gear.

Mineo huddled low behind a rock outcropping, his breath vanishing instantly in the gale. His face was gray, the stubble on his chin frosted white.

"I can't feel my feet," Mineo stammered through chattering teeth, his eyes scanning the mist below for the next gray wave of uniforms. "I think my toes are gone, Johnnie."

Luby, crouched beside him, chipped a layer of rime ice off the receiver of his rifle with a manic, exhausted grin.

"This is a beach compared to the D-Series," Luby rasped. "Remember Camp Hale? Thirty-five below? At least here the air doesn't kill you."

"Yeah," Johnnie muttered, checking his last remaining magazine. "And at least here, we get to shoot back."

But shooting back was becoming a luxury.

"Sarge!" A young voice yelled from the left flank. It was Private Rega. "Movement! They're coming up the draw!"

The Germans surged again. Machine gun fire stitched the rock around them, sending stone shards flying like shrapnel. The air filled with the sharp *crack-thump* of incoming mortars.

Johnnie didn't have to give the order. His squad opened up, their fire disciplined and short. They couldn't afford to spray and pray. Every bullet had to be a kill.

Rega stood up to throw a grenade, his arm arcing back. *CRACK.*

A sniper's bullet caught the kid in the shoulder, spinning him around. He crumpled to the hard-packed snow, a bright bloom of red instantly staining the white.

"Man down!" Luby roared, scrambling over the rocks, dragging Rega back into the defilade.

Johnnie fired two rounds, dropping the German who had taken the shot, then ducked back as the rock above his head shattered.

He crawled over to where Luby was pressing a bandage against Rega's shoulder. The wound was bad. Not immediately fatal, but up here, in this cold, shock would kill him long before infection did.

"He needs a doctor," Luby said, his hands slick with blood. "We gotta get him down."

Johnnie looked at the cliff edge behind them. It had taken them hours to climb up with ropes and specialized gear. Lowering a wounded man down that sheer face under fire was impossible. It was a death sentence for the wounded and the bearers.

"We can't go down," Johnnie said, his voice tight.

He looked at Mineo, who was shivering violently but still holding his sector. He looked at Rega, whose face was turning the color of ash.

They were trapped. They had taken the unscalable mountain, but now the mountain was threatening to become their tomb.

"We hold," Johnnie commanded, gripping his rifle until his knuckles turned white. "We hold until they build us a bridge."

He looked out toward the valley floor, miles below, praying the engineers were as good as they said they were.

"Dig in!" Johnnie yelled over the wind. "Nobody dies on this rock! You hear me? Nobody dies!"

They dug their fingernails and boots into the frozen

earth, waiting for the next wave, knowing that on this peak, there was no retreat.

There was only the rock, the brotherhood, and the desperate hope for a miracle from below.

43

THE LIFELINE

1200 HOURS, FEBRUARY 19, 1945

Vidiciatico, Italy

"They're cut off up top, general," Lt. Col. Hampton reported to Hays, his voice grim. "They're running low on ammunition, and they can't evacuate their wounded. We have to get them a lifeline." Hays's gaze was fixed on Riva Ridge. His men had done the impossible; now, he needed a miracle.

He turned to the commander of the 126th Mountain Engineer Battalion. "Get me your tramway," Hays commanded.

The engineers of the 126th began their work under sporadic but lethal German mortar and sniper fire. They drilled into the rock, their tools a jarring staccato against the raging battle. They hauled massive steel cables up the most forgiving ascent, their muscles straining, their faces masks of concentration, as they built an aerial tramway up the sheer face of Mount Cappel Buso. It was D Company of the 126th

—men who had trained for this exact moment—rigging a cable that stretched 1,700 feet across the void.

A young private, straddling a girder to drive a pin home, was suddenly blown from his perch by a nearby mortar blast. His squadmate, a boy from Ohio with tears mixing with the sweat on his face, didn't even have time to shout. He just wordlessly clipped his own safety line and took his place on the girder, his wrench tightening the bolt, his knuckles white and bleeding.

In eight hours of relentless, death-defying labor, they did it. The Light Tramway M-1 was operational. A single cable, stretching 1,700 feet and climbing over 600 feet in elevation, with a small, open car suspended beneath it. The first car that ascended was not filled with men, but with crates of ammunition and cans of water.

The sight of it, slowly, steadily making its way up the cliff face, brought a ragged cheer from the exhausted men on the ridge. It was more than just supplies; it was a promise.

A promise that they were not alone.

The first car to descend carried two stretchers. On one lay Rega—his face gray from blood loss—staring up at the cable like it was a lifeline thrown from heaven. Before the engineers drove those stakes, his wound was a death sentence—an eight-hour agony of being jostled down a cliff, bleeding out in the cold. Now, it was a five-minute glide. That cable wasn't just steel; it was the difference between a telegram home and a life.

This was the lifeline. It was a testament to the grit of the 126th Engineers, a steel artery that now pumped life into the assault.

From their new perch, the artillery observers on Riva Ridge began to call in devastating, accurate fire on the

German positions, "blinding" the mountain. In his command post, General Hays watched the tramcar move, a steady, unwavering presence against the indifferent mountain. Riva Ridge was secure. The lifeline was in. Kesselring's flank was broken.

Now, and only now, could he turn his full attention to the main objective. The heart of the fortress. Belvedere. He turned to Hampton, his face a mask of stone. "They're secure on the ridge. God bless the engineers. Now, prepare the men. We move on Belvedere tonight."

44

THE PHYSICS

1815 HOURS, FEBRUARY 19, 1945

Vidiciatico, Italy

The main classroom of the stone schoolhouse, commandeered as the 87th Regimental CP, was crowded. The air was thick with cigarette smoke and the heavy, suffocating weight of imminent violence.

General Hays stood at the head of the map table. He had come forward from the Division headquarters at Lizzano to look his commanders in the eye. Before him stood the regimental commanders of the 85th and 87th—the men who would have to lead the main assault into the teeth of the fortress in less than six hours. They looked tired. They looked cold. But mostly, they looked skeptical.

"Gentlemen," Colonel Walker of the 87th broke the silence, his voice tight. "With respect, the plan has us crossing the line of departure without a preparatory barrage. We are walking up a fortified mountain in the dark, naked— soldiers against artillery, machine gun nests, and gravity. It goes against every lesson we've been taught since Fort Benning."

Hays slowly lifted his eyes from the map. He did not pace. He did not shout. He reached for his steel helmet, sitting on the corner of the table, and placed it in the center of the map, right over the contour lines of Mount Belvedere.

"Doctrine," Hays said, his voice a low rumble that seemed to vibrate in the floorboards, "assumes we can hit what we aim at."

He placed a spent shell casing at the base of the helmet's brim. "Your men are here." He placed a second casing on the opposite side, hidden by the curve of the steel. "The Germans are here. In the defilade. On the reverse slope."

Hays picked up a pencil.

"It is a problem of physics, gentlemen. Think of a baseball. If I stand on the front lawn and throw a ball over the roof of a house, gravity pulls it down. But it comes down at an angle."

He traced an arc in the air over the helmet. "It lands in the backyard. But it cannot hit the back wall of the house. The angle is not sharp enough. The wall protects it."

He tapped the casing hidden behind the helmet.

"The Germans are living against that back wall. We can throw a thousand tons of standard shells over this mountain. They will explode in the valley behind them, or they will bury themselves in the mud. The German gunners will simply sit in their bunkers, drink their schnapps, and wait for the noise to stop. And when it stops, they will climb up to the ridge, set up their MG42s, and slaughter our men as they climb."

The room went deadly silent. The logic was brutal and irrefutable.

Hays nodded to his Division Artillery Officer, Brigadier General Ruffner, who stepped forward and placed a wooden crate on the table. He pried the lid open with a bayonet. Inside, packed in straw, sat an artillery shell. But the nose cone was different. It wasn't the standard tapered steel point. It was a bulbous, green plastic cap.

"The Army calls it the POZIT fuze," Hays said. "We call it VT. Variable Time."

He picked up the heavy shell, holding it like a chalice.

"Inside this nose is a radio transmitter. It sends out a signal. When that signal bounces off the ground—or a roof, or a German helmet—and returns to the fuze, it detonates."

"Washington is terrified of these, general," Ruffner said, his voice low. "If a dud lands and the Germans reverse-engineer the radio transmitter in the nose cone... we lose our edge in the Pacific. They were only released for the emergency in the Battle of the Bulge. We had to fight like hell to get them released for this theater."

Hays looked at Walker. "We don't have to hit the ground anymore, colonel. We don't have to hit the back wall. We just have to get close."

He moved the shell over the helmet, hovering it in the air above the hidden casing.

"We fire these over the ridge. They don't wait for impact. They sense the ground rising to meet them, and they detonate here." He held the shell above the helmet's 'reverse slope.' "Forty feet in the air. An airburst. It rains shrapnel straight down into their foxholes. It turns their reverse-slope sanctuary into an open grave."

He set the shell down with a heavy thud.

"But this only works if we catch them in the open," Hays

said, his voice dropping. "If we fire a prep barrage now, they will stay deep in their concrete bunkers where nothing can touch them. To kill them, we must lure them out. We must wait."

Hays leaned over the table, his face illuminated by the harsh light of the lantern, the shadows of his fatigue carving deep lines around his eyes.

"And that means there will be no preparatory artillery for the assault on Belvedere," he said, his voice hardening. "None. We will not tell them we are coming."

He looked directly at Walker.

"The order for the assault is brutal, but simple: From the moment you cross the line of departure until you breach the enemy perimeter at the summit, every rifle in this Division will be empty. Chambers unloaded. Magazines out."

The shock was palpable. An infantryman without a loaded weapon was naked.

"Sir," a colonel breathed, "you're asking them to climb past machine-gun nests with empty rifles?"

"I am," Hays said, his voice hard as flint. "Because I know soldiers. I know fear. It takes only one nervous boy, one accidental discharge, one shot, one muzzle flash, to wake up the entire mountain. If we lose surprise, we lose the division."

He looked at the officers, seeing the dread in their eyes.

"We climb in the dark. Bayonets only—grenades if you have to. A rifle flash is a flare that says 'I am here.' It paints a target on your chest. A grenade explodes in *their* foxhole, not yours. It kills the enemy without giving them your address."

"Until first light, we take that summit with cold steel."

"Then, and only then, will our guns speak," Hays continued. "When your men breach the perimeter... when the

Germans scramble from their bunkers to man the walls...
that is when we unleash the VT fuzes. We will catch them in
the open."

He straightened up, the "Rock of the Marne" settling
over him like a cloak.

"It is a gamble," Hays admitted softly. "We are betting
everything on the discipline of our soldiers to hold their fire
until they can see the whites of their eyes."

He paused.

"And there is one more thing."

This was the hardest part. The order that went against
every instinct of brotherhood these men possessed.

"The incline is steep. The enemy fire, once it starts, will
be intense. We cannot afford to stall. Momentum is our only
armor."

He looked at them, his eyes conveying the terrible
burden of his command.

"The order is: Always Forward. If a man is hit... you do
not stop. If your buddy falls... you step over him. You leave
him for the medics coming behind. You do not stop to
bandage him. You do not stop to comfort him. You keep
climbing."

The officers stared at him. To leave a fallen brother was a
sin in the infantry.

"I know what I am asking," Hays said softly. "But if you
stop to help one man, the squad stops. If the squad stops, the
platoon is pinned. And then everybody dies. We buy their
lives with our speed."

He looked at his watch.

"You step off in four hours. No rounds chambered.
Complete silence. The order is: Fix bayonets... and move
out."

Hays met Walker's eyes one last time.

"Make them understand, colonel. We are not throwing a baseball over the roof. We are bringing the roof down on top of them."

45

ALWAYS FORWARD

2200 HOURS, FEBRUARY 19, 1945

Assembly Area, Near Vidiciatico

The wind had died down, leaving a silence that was heavier than the gale. Hundreds of men were moving into position, a shifting sea of shadows in the snow.

Hays walked the line. He had left the warmth of the farmhouse. He couldn't remain sheltered by the map table's cold abstraction. He needed to see the faces.

He moved through the staging area. The men were ghosts in their camouflage, checking gear, tightening straps. They looked like boys. They looked like old men.

He stopped near a platoon huddled behind a stone wall. He stayed in the shadows, unobserved. A lieutenant had just finished whispering to his platoon sergeant. The officer looked sick. He patted the sergeant on the shoulder and moved on, leaving the NCO to do the hard work.

The sergeant turned to his men. He was a big man, his

face obscured by a wool cap and scarf, but his voice was a low, gravelly anchor in the dark.

"Alright, listen up," the sergeant whispered. "Change of plans. We're dropping the rounds. Clear your chambers. Drop your mags."

A confused murmur rippled through the huddle. One soldier, a kid who couldn't have been eighteen, looked up.

"Sarge?" Rubinski whispered, his tone hushed but analytical. "I understand the muzzle flash discipline. But the order permits grenades. Won't the detonation compromise our position?"

"Grenades for machine gun nests only," the sergeant corrected, a grim appreciation in his voice. "It's about the vector, kid. Your rifle flash puts a big red 'X' on your chest—it gives the German spotters your home address. A grenade flashes in the machine gun nest—right on *their* front doorstep."

"But... what if we run into a patrol?" Rubinski asked, his voice rising in panic. "What if they see us?"

"Then you stick 'em," the sergeant said, tapping the bayonet on his hip. "We go in quiet. We don't shoot until we're inside their living room. The general wants surprise. We're gonna give it to 'em."

He waited, letting it sink in. Then he leaned closer, his voice hardening.

"And listen to me. The slope is steep. The snow is ice. When the shooting starts, it's gonna be bad. If I get hit... you step over me."

The silence in the huddle was total.

"If Rubinski gets hit... you step over him. You don't stop to bandage. You don't stop to hold hands. You keep climbing.

You get to the top. That is the only way any of us get home. Do you understand?"

"Yes, Sergeant," the men in chorus affirmed.

"Good. Now clear those weapons. Fix bayonets."

Around them, the reality of the order took hold. It wasn't just Rubinski. All along the assembly area, the movement rippled down the squads like a contagion.

Clack. Clack. Clack.

It was a surreal, disjointed choreography. Hundreds of men pulled their bolts back, catching the ejected live rounds in their gloved palms.

Then came the sound that seemed to stop the heart—the collective, hollow slam of bolts sliding forward on empty chambers.

It wasn't the sharp, reassuring snap of a weapon ready to fight. It was a dead, flat noise.

Rubinski looked at the man to his left, then the man to his right. They locked eyes—a silent, grim nod passed between them. It was the look men give when they think they are seeing each other for the last time.

Rubinski gripped his rifle. Without a bullet in the chamber, the heavy steel and walnut didn't feel like a rifle anymore. It felt like a club.

The terror settled in, like the cold seeping through their coats. They were walking into a fortress of machine guns, armed only with a spear.

Hays watched from the darkness as the metallic *clack-clack-clack* of bolts being pulled back echoed softly in the night. He watched them eject live rounds. He watched them fix cold steel to the ends of rifles.

He felt a weight press against his chest. He had drawn the line on the map. He had explained the physics of the artillery. But it was this sergeant and the soldiers—the men in the dark—who had to carry the soul of the order.

The sergeant looked up, scanning the dark line of the woods, and for a second, his eyes seemed to meet Hays's in the gloom. There was no salute. No recognition. Just the shared, crushing knowledge of what was about to happen.

Hays turned away, walking back toward his jeep. His part was done. The physics were set. The geometry was calculated.

"It's up to the soldiers now," he whispered to the night.

He climbed into the jeep and looked up at the black silhouette of the mountain.

"May God help them."

46

THE CURRENT

2250 HOURS, FEBRUARY 19, 1945

Vidiciatico, Italy

The schoolhouse cellar was cold.

A single lantern cast a pool of yellow, wavering light over the maps, making the grease-pencil contours of the Gothic Line seem to shift like living things.

General Hays sat alone on the edge of an old desk, a cup of hot coffee in his hand, one boot resting on the floor.

It was quiet.

He checked his watch. He knew the 87th was staging just outside these walls, but he felt the urge to push even further forward, closer to the slopes of Belvedere where the 85th would soon be fighting.

Outside, the wind howled. The guns were silent. It was the silence he had ordered.

Sitting in the dark, waiting for the first report, was suffocating.

His mind drifted back to Cassino.

He was standing in the aid station again, the smell of blood and mud in his nostrils.

He saw the face of the dying boy from the 34th Division, his hand grabbing Hays's coat, his voice a rasp: *"Sir... just make the guns stop."*

They had failed that boy—followed doctrine—and his artillery had been a useless symphony against an immovable mountain.

They had sacrificed men to a map, and the guilt of it was a cold, hard knot in his gut.

Make them stop.

"I stopped the guns," Hays whispered to the empty cellar. "God help me, I stopped them tonight."

He had silenced the guns tonight in a last-ditch hope to save his men, but in doing so, he had sent them naked into the tiger's den.

He looked down at his hands, calloused and chapped. He wasn't just at Cassino.

He was at the Marne in 1918. He was a young lieutenant, the world exploding, the air thick with mustard gas.

He heard the screams of his seven horses, creatures of fire and spirit, running to death because he had ordered them to "hold the line."

The "Rock." The title had always felt wrong. It was a monument built on the bones of horses and the sacrifice of many men.

He had been a rock his whole life. Immovable. Unyielding. A man of duty, of doctrine.

But to win tonight, he had to be the water. He had to flow around the obstacle.

He had to trust the ghost path.

He had bet everything on the unconventional skill of his

men, on the one thing Kesselring—a man of doctrine himself—would never expect: a division that moved like shadows up a mountain in the night instead of conventional soldiers.

Hays reached into his breast pocket. His fingers brushed the oilskin packet containing Julia's letters.

Hold fast to your path, my love, she had written. *It is steep, but the footing is solid.*

He closed his eyes. He wasn't praying for victory. He was praying for the soldiers.

He was praying for the boys with the empty rifles who were, right at this second, cutting the German wire in the dark.

The silence in the room stretched, heavy and physical.

Riiiing.

The field telephone screamed.

Hays opened his eyes.

The moment of reflection was over. The gamble was cast.

He picked up the receiver, his hand steady.

"Hays."

47

THE DISCIPLINE

0200 HOURS, FEBRUARY 20, 1945

Slopes of Mount Belvedere

The 3rd Battalion of the 85th Mountain Infantry was a ghost army moving through hell.

They were halfway up the slope when the first boot found the tripwire.

It wasn't a click. It was a roar. A German "S-mine"—a Bouncing Betty—sprang waist-high and detonated.

The blast was a blinding flash of orange fire and jagged steel that tore through the lead squad. Three men went down instantly, their bodies shredded.

By every instinct of warfare, this was the moment the screaming should have started. This was the moment the survivors should have dropped to the dirt, racked their bolts, and opened fire into the darkness to kill the ambush.

But the bolts were forward on empty chambers.

And the screaming didn't happen.

A wounded private, his leg mangled by shrapnel, bit into

the wool of his sleeve, stifling the agony into a wet, guttural whimper.

His squad-mates didn't shoot. They didn't yell for a medic. They remembered the order: *If a man is hit, you step over him.*

They stepped around the living wreck of their friend, their boots crunching on the blood-soaked snow, and kept climbing into the dark.

A squad of engineers moved silently to the front, unspooling a roll of white canvas tape, staking it into the frozen mud. In the darkness, that thin strip glowed like a spectral vein—the only safe ground in the world.

"Stay on the tape," the sergeant whispered. "You step one inch off—Bouncing Betty gets you."

They formed a single, shivering line, following the white ribbon up the mountain.

Three hundred yards above them, in a hardened bunker on the crest, a German sentry from the 232nd Infantry Division lowered his binoculars.

"*Nichts,*" the sentry muttered to his partner. "*Minen. Wildschweine.*" *Mines. Wild boars.*

He had seen the flash. He had heard the boom. But there was no return fire. No muzzle flashes. No American voices.

If it was an attack, the Americans would be shooting. Everyone shoots.

The sentry shrugged, lit a cigarette, and turned his back to the slope.

Below him, hundreds of men with bayonets fixed continued their silent, terrifying ascent. The bluff had worked. The darkness held.

48

THE LIGHT

0635 HOURS, FEBRUARY 20, 1945

Below the Summit of Mount Belvedere

The sun didn't rise; it struck.

First light hit the peaks of the Apennines like a hammer, burning away the protective cloak of the dark.

For more than seven hours, the men of the 85th had climbed in a terrifying, unnatural silence. They had stepped over friends torn apart by mines. They had held their breath while German sentries smoked cigarettes yards away. They had carried their rifles as dead weight.

Now, they were near the objective. And the sun was up.

"Time!" the sergeant roared, his voice cracking the silence wide open.

He didn't whisper. He screamed it, a sound of pure, feral release.

"LOAD AND LOCK!"

The order rippled down the line, chasing the light.

SHHH-CLACK.

SHHH-CLACK.

It was a metallic symphony—the distinctive, aggressive sound of hundreds of eight-round en-bloc clips being shoved down into the receivers of M1 Garands.

Rubinski drove his clip home with the heel of his hand. The bolt snapped forward, stripping a live round from the clip and slamming it into the chamber with a solid, heavy warmth.

He felt the vibration of it in the wooden stock.

He looked at the man next to him. The terror of the night had evaporated, replaced by the hard, cold capability of daylight.

They weren't naked anymore. The club was dead. The rifle was alive.

"Rover Joe is on station!" a radioman shouted. "Batteries are hot!"

The sergeant turned back to where the German counter-attack was already forming in the mist.

"Let 'em have it!"

49

THE ANVIL

1200 HOURS, FEBRUARY 21, 1945

Vidiciatico / Querciola, Italy

The "silence" of the initial assault was a distant memory.

The sun was high over the Apennines, but the light brought no relief—only exposure.

The attack had stalled.

What was supposed to be a dawn victory had ground down into a bloody, terrifying stalemate. The 85th and 87th Regiments had breached the initial line in the dark, but as the sun rose, the German defense hardened into concrete.

For more than twenty-four hours—the air was a solid, vibrating wall of noise.

The German artillery on the reverse slopes of Belvedere and Gorgolesco had found their range, and they were hammering the exposed Americans with a ferocity that shook the dust from the command post ceiling.

"They're holding, general," Lt. Col. Hampton said, his voice rasping with exhaustion. "But they aren't moving. The

87th is pinned on the western face. The 85th has secured the ridgeline, but every time they try to crest the summit, the mortars chew them up."

Hays walked back to the map table. He didn't look at the tactical markers; he looked at the casualty returns.

Company A: 40% effective. Company K: Commander killed. XO wounded.

He was feeding men into a thresher.

They were surviving—but they were bleeding to death.

"Get them water," Hays muttered, staring at the map. "And get them ammo. If we stop firing, we die."

85th Regimental Command Post, Querciola

1400 Hours

The stalemate had calcified into a crisis. General Hays had left the relative safety of the 87th's headquarters in Vidiciatico hours ago. It wasn't close enough. To the horror of his staff, he had moved his personal command forward to Querciola—a hamlet sitting right at the foot of the mountain, dangerously within range of the German mortars. It was a calculated risk, a flag planted in the mud to show the men he was there.

Standing in the doorway of the ruined Querciola farmhouse, watching the stretcher jeeps rumble down the muddy track from the front, he could smell the cordite from the German guns.

The wounded and dead were coming in convoys now—a steady, grim procession of muddy canvas and blood-soaked boots sticking out the back.

The 85th Regiment was exhausted. They had spent the

last forty hours clawing their way up rock faces under direct fire.

They were running on adrenaline and terror, and they were beginning to falter.

"General," the G-3 officer said, placing a new report on the table. "Some units of the 85th are combat ineffective for offensive operations. They can hold, maybe. But they can't push. If we don't reinforce them, the Germans are going to push them off that mountain."

Hays looked at the map. He looked at the 86th Regiment, sitting in reserve in the valley below.

He had been saving them. They were his fresh legs, his exploitation force for the breakthrough.

But there would be no breakthrough if the line broke now.

He realized then that he couldn't wait for the perfect moment. The perfect moment was a myth.

There was only the necessary moment.

He needed a hammer.

He stood up, his joints popping, his face a mask of granite resolve. He walked to the field phone.

"Get me Hampton," Hays barked.

The line crackled.

"Henry? It's George. I've made the decision. I'm sending elements of the 86th held in reserve to reinforce the 85th on Belvedere. We have to widen the breach."

Hays paused, looking at the map where Riva Ridge loomed above them. From here in Querciola, the ridge seemed to hang right over their heads.

He remembered the impossible shot that had blinded the German observers.

He remembered the report—the staff sergeant who had

led the Recon, the one who knew the terrain better than the Germans did.

"And one more thing," Hays added, his voice dropping to a low, iron rumble.

"Get me that staff sergeant and his squad who led the Recon and assault on Riva. I'm at Querciola. It's a fast descent for them. I want them off Riva and here by 1700. I'll be in the briefing tent. Hays out."

50

THE RING OF FIRE

2345 HOURS, FEBRUARY 21, 1945

Querciola, Italy

Major General George P. Hays stood in the center, holding on to the map table—the ground itself did not stop shaking—a deep, guttural, continuous *thump-thump-thump*.

At the 85th's forward CP, the noise was deafening. They were practically underneath the artillery duel. The sun had set over the Apennines hours ago, plunging the mountains into darkness. But on Mount Belvedere, there was no night.

The Germans, spotting the 86th assembling to reinforce in the twilight, had unleashed a hellfire reprise—the "ring of fire"—the storm of perfectly registered German artillery that was systematically pulverizing his Division on the slopes.

His men were lying on the mountain, wounded, cold, dying in the dark.

"General," Lt. Col. Hampton said, his voice tight, his face ashen. He had just come from the radio set.

"The 85th is stalled. The 87th is pinned. They're being

systematically slaughtered. We're getting reports of companies with fifty percent casualties. They can't advance. They can't even dig in."

Another officer, a major from G-3, looked up from his map, his eyes bloodshot.

"Sir, the barrage is... it's perfect. Kesselring has every approach bracketed. We have to pull them back. We have to regroup. We can't take the summit like this. We're sacrificing them for nothing."

Retreat. The word hung in the air, a cold, logical poison.

Hays stared at the map, but he wasn't in this cellar. His mind was a battlefield of ghosts.

He was at Cisterna, seeing the ghost of Will Darby, a gifted soldier broken by bad intel and a single, arrogant mistake.

He was at Cassino, reliving his failure, the grinding, bloody sacrifice of the 34th Division against a mountain that would not yield.

He was at the Ardeatine Caves, seeing the cold, smiling face of Kesselring—the man who saw war not as a duty, but as an administrative act of murder—the master chess player.

This "ring of fire" was Kesselring's signature checkmate move—a perfect, arrogant fortress designed to bleed his enemy's will.

To retreat was to prove Kesselring right. To retreat was to admit that the Germans' cold, murderous arithmetic was superior.

To retreat was to let Kesselring win.

Just then, the *thump-thump-thump* was punctuated by a high-velocity shriek.

It was a specific, tearing whistle, a sound Hays hadn't heard this close since the Marne.

A German 88 shell, searching for the command post's radio antennae, slammed into the farmhouse wall just feet above the cellar.

The room exploded in a shower of stone dust, splintered wood, and dirt.

The lanterns went out, plunging the room into darkness and chaos.

"Medic!" Hampton yelled, his voice choked with dust.

In the pandemonium, as men scrambled for cover, Hays did not move.

He stood, unblinking, in the dark.

He calmly struck a match and re-lit the lantern on the table.

The flare of light illuminated his face, which was now a mask of cold, white dust and pure, terrible resolve.

He looked at his officers. They were waiting for the inevitable order to withdraw.

Hays slowly raised his hand.

The room went dead.

"No," he said. His voice was quiet, low, and dangerous.

Hampton stared at him. "Sir?"

"No," Hays said again, his voice a low rumble, building. "We are not retreating. We will not be broken."

He looked up, his eyes blazing with a cold, terrible fire.

He slammed his fist onto the map table, the sudden crack making the lanterns jump.

"Kesselring thinks he can bleed us. He thinks we'll break. He will not break this Division. Not today. Never! We are not giving him... one... goddamn... inch!"

The voice was a roar that drowned out the guns.

Hays commanded, his voice now the clipped, precise

instrument of a general who had just made his final, terrible choice.

"We are going to break his line, or we are going to die on this mountain. Those are the only two options."

He turned to his Air Officer. "Get the Air Corps on the net. I want 'Rover Joe' on station at first light. I want that little Piper Cub buzzing the ridgeline like a mosquito. The Germans will laugh at a fragile prop plane right up until it directs a P-47 to drop a 500-pound bomb down their throat."

An aide scrambled for the field phone. But before he could lift the receiver, the Division's radio operator ripped off his headphones, his face pale with disbelief.

"General, flash report!" the operator shouted, his voice cracking. "From Belvedere! Sir, I... I've never seen a report like this."

"Report!" Hays roared.

"Sir, the 87th is still pinned. But... a squad. Sir, a part of the line is broken! A lieutenant reports... a sergeant and his squad just ran through the 'ring of fire'!"

Hays stared at the operator. "What?"

"Sir, the report says... 'Subject NCO made a straight run through the barrage with his squad. Didn't even dodge. Just ran through the gauntlet.' The lieutenant says he's on the objective, sir! They are on the objective!"

A terrible, profound silence filled the command post. Hays was about to grab the handset from the stunned operator when the operator shouted, "Sir!"

His voice cracked with disbelief. "It's the 85th! They've taken the summit!"

"Operator, what's the name of that sergeant?"

The operator scanned his notes, his hand shaking.

"A staff sergeant, sir. Name is... Grey. Johnnie Grey."

In that moment, in the middle of his failing battle, a single NCO had just defied the laws of physics to give him the victory.

A fierce, terrible joy seized him. The line was broken.

Hays looked at the map, then at his officers, his granite face cracking into a wolfish grin.

"Goddamn brilliant!" he roared.

He grabbed the handset for the main artillery line, his voice no longer a rumble but the sharp, joyous bark of a hunter.

"All batteries. You have your targets. Fire."

51

ROVER JOE

0655 HOURS, FEBRUARY 22, 1945

Querciola / Mount Belvedere

The sun broke over the Apennines, revealing the cost of the night. The slopes of Mount Belvedere were scarred and blackened, but the 10th Mountain Division was still there.

In the regimental command post, the relief was palpable, but the danger was peaking. Daylight meant the Germans could see them again. It meant the inevitable counterattack.

"General," the radio operator called out, his voice sharp with a new kind of energy. "We have 'Rover Joe' on the net. The Cub plane is overhead."

Hays grabbed the headset. He wasn't listening to a panicked lieutenant on the ground; he was hearing the clipped, calm voice of an aviator in a liaison plane buzzing directly over the German positions. It was the "Rover Joe" system—a tactical innovation that put an air controller in the sky to talk directly to the infantry on the ground.

"Red One, this is Rover," the pilot's voice crackled, tinny

but clear. "I have visual on Jerry mortar pits in the defilade behind Hill 1036. Adjusting fire... now."

For the first time since Cassino, the artillery and air power were not fighting separate wars; they were a single, integrated fist. The controller in the air called down grids with terrifying precision, walking airbursts onto the German gun pits that were trying to fire back.

A Fifth Army observer, a weathered colonel who had watched three previous assaults on this sector fail, lowered his binoculars. He looked at Hays with a mixture of disbelief and respect.

"Three times," the observer murmured. "We tried to crack this sector three times with veteran divisions, with ten times as many men. We failed every time. And these... these kids just walked right over it."

"They didn't just read the doctrine, colonel," Hays said, watching the smoke rise on the horizon. "They rewrote it."

Up on the ridgeline, the victory was not being celebrated with cheers, but with sweat. Staff Sergeant Johnnie Grey didn't wait for orders.

"Dig!" he roared at his squad. "Dig deep and roof it! The counter-barrage is coming!"

They weren't digging standard foxholes; they were carving bunkers with overhead cover, a survival adaptation learned the hard way during the D-Series maneuvers. As they dug, Johnnie saw movement on the trail behind them. It wasn't mules.

A second line of men was trudging up the steep incline, bent double under wooden pack-boards stacked high with ammunition cans. They were the "human mules," a tactical innovation to keep the guns fed where the animals couldn't go. They stepped over the exhausted assault troops, dropping fresh bandoleers and grenades right at the fighting positions.

Johnnie paused to wipe sweat from his eyes and looked across the valley to the right flank. On the neighboring peak of Mount Castello, he saw silhouettes moving against the skyline.

He brought his binoculars up and caught a flash of green and yellow shoulder patches.

"Brazilians," Mineo said, spotting them too. "The BEF. They took Castello."

Johnnie watched the "invisible" allies, the men from the tropics fighting in the snow, securing the 10th's flank. He raised a tired hand in a wave. Across the gap, a Brazilian soldier waved back.

Then, they both picked up their shovels and went back to work.

52

THE PROMISE

MARCH 1945

London, England

The air in the small London flat was quiet, smelling of coal smoke and damp, a world away from the Highland mist. Will Darby stood in the doorway, in his colonel's uniform with full ribbons. He was in London on a "tour" with General Hap Arnold's staff—a respectable, high-profile assignment for an officer "recovering" from the strain of combat.

Annie opened the door, and for a moment, they just stared. The Will she had kissed in Scotland was gone. The haunted ghost from the Pentagon was also gone. This man was someone new: quiet, lean, his eyes holding a calm, focused intensity she had never seen.

"Will," she breathed, her hand on the doorframe. She had been working at the liaison office in London, and the fatigue of the long war was plain on her face. "You're here."

"I'm here," he said. His voice was steady. "The tour starts tomorrow. We're in London for a night."

Annie didn't say a word. She simply reached out, grabbed the lapels of his pressed tunic, and pulled him across the threshold. She kicked the door shut behind him, sealing out the London fog, the war, and the ghosts that had followed them both for so long.

She led him not to a chair, but into the center of the small room, under the warm glow of a single lamp. She reached up, her hands trembling slightly, and touched his face. Her fingers traced the new lines around his eyes, the hardness that had settled in his jaw—the geography of his penance.

"You look tired," she whispered. "Not the exhaustion of a climb. The exhaustion of a long fall."

"I landed," he said softly, covering her hands with his own. His palms were warm, rough, and undeniably real. "You were the net, Annie. You caught me."

She kissed him then—not the playful, testing kiss of Scotland, nor the desperate, comforting kiss of the Pentagon. This was a collision of souls. It was slow, deliberate, and terrifyingly sweet. It tasted of salt tears and the vanilla scent she always wore, a promise of peace and joy.

Will groaned, a low sound of surrender, and swept her up into his arms. He carried her into the small bedroom, where the coal fire had burned down to glowing embers.

He set her down on the bed as if she were made of something far more precious than glass. He undressed her with a reverence that broke her heart, his hands shaking from an overwhelming gratitude. When he shed his uniform, stripping away the silver eagles of his rank and the ribbons of his campaigns, he was just Will.

He came to her in the firelight.

In Scotland, their lovemaking had been a discovery, a

spark in the dark. Here, in London, it was a benediction. It was slow and aching, every touch a silent conversation about what they had lost and what they had found.

He didn't hold her like a conqueror claiming territory. He held her like a drowning man finding the shore. He kissed the hollow of her throat, her shoulder, her mouth, worshipping the life in her.

"Annie," he whispered in the dark, his voice ragged. "You are the only true thing I have found in this whole damn war."

"Then stay," she breathed, arching into him, wrapping her legs around him, pulling him deeper into the sanctuary of the moment. "Stay here until the end."

They moved together in the rhythm of a heartbeat, a desperate, fluid dance to keep the morning at bay. For a few stolen hours, there were no generals, no orders, no broken tablets. There was only the heat of their skin, the sound of their breath, and the fierce, unbreakable tether of a love that had survived the fall.

Later, as the embers faded to gray ash, they lay tangled together under the heavy wool quilt. Will held her close, his hand gently stroking her back in the quiet of the night.

"I have to go back," he whispered into the silence, the words heavy with regret.

"I know," she said, closing her eyes against the tears.

"But this," he said, pressing a kiss to her shoulder. "This is where I live now. No matter where they send me. I live here."

They slept then, a fitful, clinging sleep, holding onto each other as the world turned toward a dawn that would take him away.

~

In the morning, Annie stood by the kettle, her back to him. She was making tea, her movements slow, deliberate. The yellow bow that he loved was in her hair.

"The car is here," Will said softly.

Annie turned. Her big brown eyes were swimming, but she forced a smile. It was the bravest thing he had ever seen.

"So," she said, her voice trembling slightly. "The Observation Tour. Very prestigious. Shaking hands. Inspecting runways."

"Yes," Will said. He walked over to her, taking the kettle from her hand and setting it down. He took her hands in his.

"Annie... look at me."

She looked up, and the facade crumbled. She knew him. She knew the strength of the soldier inside him.

"You're not just going to inspect runways," she whispered. "You're going to the friction. You're going to find the fight."

"I have to," Will admitted, his voice low and intense. "I don't know where the plane lands first. But I know the evil is still there. I can't sit in the VIP stands while the Nazis are still standing."

He pulled her close, wrapping her in his arms. The scent of her overwhelmed him. This was home. This was the peace he had denied himself for so long.

"I love you so much," he whispered into her hair.

"I love you more," she sobbed, clutching him tight.

But as she held him, Annie felt a profound, aching clarity —a realization of the soldier's sacrifice. She had saved him. She had taken the broken pieces of the man and helped him forge them into something stronger. But in doing so, she had made him fit for service again.

She pulled back and looked at him, memorizing every line of his face, the way his blue eyes crinkled, the strength in his jaw. She touched the bow in her hair, a small attempt to be beautiful for him one last time.

"Will," she whispered, her voice fierce through the tears. "Promise me."

"Anything."

"When you get there… stay safe… don't go to the front. Just do the work. And know that I am with you. Every step."

"I know," he said. He kissed her—a desperate pouring out of his soul. It was a kiss of gratitude, of apology, and of undying love.

"Goodbye, Annie."

"Goodbye, my love," she whispered.

She kissed him.

He picked up his bag. When he left in the cold, gray London dawn, he walked with the steady, unburdened steps of a man who was, at long last, at peace. Annie watched from her window, her hand pressed against the cold glass, until he disappeared into the smoke and fog.

53

THE BLACK DAYS

APRIL 14-16, 1945

Castel d'Aiano, Italy

The Spring Offensive did not begin with a sprint; it began with a slaughter.

Before they could chase the Germans across the Po Valley, the 10th Mountain Division had to break out of the mountains one last time. The obstacle was a series of rugged hills around the town of Castel d'Aiano and a bowl-shaped valley known as the Pra del Bianco—the White Meadow.

But two days before the jump-off, a different kind of darkness fell over the assembly area.

The news hit the column like a physical blow, passing from jeep to truck to foxhole in a hushed, incredulous ripple.

Roosevelt is dead.

Johnnie sat in the mud of the staging area, watching the stunned faces of his squad. For most of these boys, FDR was the only President they had ever really known. He was the voice on the radio, the steady hand on the wheel since they were children in the Depression.

"Who's flying the plane now?" Miller whispered, looking at the sky as if expecting it to fall.

"Truman," Mineo said, though the name sounded foreign, unsure on his tongue.

Johnnie looked at the formidable ridgeline of Castel d'Aiano looming above them. The "Father" was gone. The generals were grieving. The world was tilting on its axis right before the final push.

But the Germans on the hill didn't care who the President was.

"It doesn't change the hill, Miller," Johnnie said, standing up and checking his bolt, his voice cutting through the uncertainty. "The President is gone. But we're still here. And we still have a job to do."

By the end of the first day, the snow in the White Meadow was gone, replaced by churned earth and blood.

Staff Sergeant Johnnie Grey lay pressed into the mud of a shell crater, the ground shaking violently beneath him. The air was a solid wall of noise—the *crump-crump-crump* of German mortars walking back and forth over their position.

"Medic! Up left! Medic!"

The scream was barely audible over the barrage. Johnnie looked up, sand grit stinging his eyes.

To his right, a new replacement—a kid named Henderson who had joined them only a week ago—was staring at his legs. Or rather, where his legs used to be. A 'Bouncing Betty' had triggered, springing into the air and detonating at his waist.

"Don't look at it, Henderson!" Johnnie roared, crawling toward him. "Eyes on me!"

Mineo was already there, ripping open a packet of sulfa powder, his hands slick with blood. He worked with a frantic, terrifying efficiency, his face a mask of grim determination.

This wasn't the tactical precision of Riva Ridge. This wasn't the silent, snowy warfare they had mastered. This was a brute-force collision, a grinder of mines and pre-sighted artillery.

For three days—April 14th, 15th, and 16th—the division threw itself against the German defenses. The enemy, realizing this was the final push, fought with the desperation of men who had nowhere left to run.

In seventy-two hours, the 10th Mountain Division suffered nearly 1,300 casualties. Two hundred and eighty-six men were killed. It was a stretch of unrelenting slaughter, a desperate toll demanded by a war that refused to end quietly.

Johnnie watched as a stretcher team sprinted low through the smoke, carrying another poncho-covered form. He didn't ask who it was. He didn't want to know.

He looked at Luby. The squad's joker was huddled against the crater wall, trying to light a cigarette with trembling hands. His face was gray, his eyes hollowed out by three days of constant concussion.

"Remember what the Chaplain said?" Luby rasped, the unlit cigarette dangling from his lip. "About Saint Andrew going into foreign lands? 'Places that didn't speak his tongue'?"

Johnnie nodded, wiping mud from his eyes. "Yeah. I remember."

Luby finally got the match to catch. He took a deep drag, the cherry glowing bright in the gloom.

"I don't think he mentioned the mines, Johnnie. I feel like he left out the part about the lousy mines."

It was a weak joke, but Johnnie forced a smile. It was the only currency they had left.

"They're chewing us up, Johnnie," Mineo yelled, sliding back into the crater, his hands wiped clean on his trousers. "We can't stay here! We're sitting ducks!"

"We're not ducks, we're the squirrels," Johnnie corrected, his voice a low growl. He touched the St. Andrew's cross beneath his tunic. "And we aren't staying."

He looked at the ridgeline ahead. The German guns were dug in deep, hammering the basin. The "Squirrel Run" on Belvedere had been about speed. This was about stubbornness.

"We push!" Johnnie ordered, rising to a crouch. "If we stay in this bowl, we die. We have to break the rim!"

He blew his whistle, the sound thin and sharp.

"Forward! Move! Move!"

They surged up the slope, slipping in the mud, stepping over the bodies of the men who had fallen minutes before. They threw grenades into machine-gun nests, clearing them with a savage, exhausted fury.

They fought past the town of Castel d'Aiano, past the minefields, past the point of exhaustion.

By the evening of April 16th, the firing finally slackened. The German line, hammered by the relentless assault, shattered.

Johnnie sat on a stone wall overlooking the Pra del Bianco. His uniform was torn, his hands shaking from the adrenaline crash.

The valley below was littered with the detritus of the

fight—burning vehicles, discarded packs, and the white markers of the medics.

Mineo sat down beside him, uncorking his canteen. He took a swig and handed it to Johnnie.

"We broke 'em," Mineo rasped. "But Jesus... the cost."

Johnnie took a drink, the water tasting of iodine and metal. He thought of the Chaplain's words again. *The world might never know your name, but heaven already does.*

Looking at the White Meadow, now red with the blood of 286 men, Johnnie figured heaven must be getting crowded.

"Yeah," Johnnie whispered. "We broke 'em."

He looked north, toward the flat, hazy expanse of the Po Valley stretching out before them.

The mountains were finally behind them. The vertical war was over.

But as he looked at the empty spaces in his squad, at the fresh graves being dug in the White Meadow, Johnnie felt no triumph. He felt only a heavy, crushing fatigue.

They had kicked open the door to the valley, but they had paid for the key in blood.

Luby sat down on the other side, staring at his boots.

"Hey, Sarge," Luby said softly. "How do squirrels run in the flatlands?"

Johnnie looked at the vast, open plain of the Po.

"I guess we're about to find out," Johnnie said. "Get some sleep. Tomorrow, we run."

54

THE BLACK MARCH

MID-APRIL, 1945

Northern Germany (Near Dannenberg)

They had been walking for three months.

Jimmy thought of the past year. It had begun in the trap at Cisterna, and it had been a slow, freezing descent into hell.

He remembered the iron cage of the "40 and 8" cattle cars that hauled them north from Rome. He remembered the freezing, rattling darkness as they crossed the Brenner Pass—the great stone throat that had swallowed them whole and deposited them 1,200 miles deep into the heart of the Reich at Stalag II-B.

Now, he was walking out the other side of hell. He had been on the road, under German guard, for three months straight.

They were no longer soldiers; they were skeletons wrapped in rags, shuffling along a dirt road near the Elbe River.

The guards were unraveling. That morning, a reservist

named Han had unslung his rifle and aimed it at a prisoner who had stumbled into the ditch, his finger tightening on the trigger not out of discipline, but out of panicked exhaustion.

Only a shout from an older sergeant had stopped the execution. But Jimmy had seen Han's eyes. They were wide, terrified, and dangerous. The Germans were losing, and they were looking for someone to blame.

Jimmy looked at the sky. It was a brilliant, piercing blue. The kind of spring day that made you believe the nightmare might actually end.

Then came the sound. The low, throat-vibrating growl of engines.

Someone screamed, "IT'S THE ALLIES! IT'S US!"

Jimmy looked up, squinting. He saw the elliptical wings flashing in the sun. Spitfires. The most beautiful things he had ever seen.

He started to wave, his weak arm lifting. "Over here! We're down here!"

The lead plane dipped its wing. It wasn't waving back. It was lining up.

"TAKE COVER!" the sergeant screamed, tackling Jimmy into a shallow, muddy ditch.

The world ripped apart. The road erupted as the machine guns and cannons walked a line of death right through the column. The pilots, moving too fast to see the rags or the starving faces, saw only a gray column of men in German territory.

When the roar faded, the silence was worse. It was filled with the moans of men who had survived Anzio, survived the trap at Cisterna, and survived the winter march, only to be cut down by Allied bullets.

Jimmy lay in the mud, staring at the boot of a man who wasn't moving. Ten more of their men were gone.

He closed his eyes against the blue sky. There was no safety. They were unarmed prisoners, marching in the kill zone.

55

THE WIRE

APRIL 21, 1945

Panaro River, Italy

Private First Class Angelo "Smitty" Renzulli of the 126th Mountain Engineers was lying on his stomach, the cold, rusted steel of the Bomporto bridge pressing into his gut. The world had shrunk to the four square inches of darkness under the I-beam where his hand was working, entirely by feel.

The air smelled of river mud, rust, and the sharp, sudden tang of ozone. A German sniper was playing a tune on the girder just above his head.

Ping... tzzzing!

The sound of the ricochet was a high-velocity whine that made his teeth ache. He didn't flinch. Flinching got you killed. Shaking got you killed.

"You good, Smitty?" a low voice rumbled just behind him.

"Got it, Sarge," Smitty muttered, his arm shoved up to the shoulder into the bridge's guts. His fingers, raw and numb, were brushing the cold, smooth casing of the first Teller mine. He could feel the "spider"—the pressure-plate igniter. And he could feel the wires. Two of them. A "daisy chain." The Germans had wired the whole damn bridge to blow.

"They're gettin' awful curious," Sergeant "Grizz" Miller said. Grizz was lying parallel to him, his body partially shielding Smitty's, calmly firing his MI rifle at the stone farmhouse on the far bank. He was a target, deliberately, to keep them from focusing on the man with the wire cutters.

B-r-r-r-r-i-p-p!

An MG42—"Hitler's Buzzsaw"—opened up. The steel around Smitty didn't just ping anymore; it screamed. Sparks flashed in the gloom under the bridge, illuminating his hands, which were now slick with grease and sweat.

"Just like training, kid," Grizz said, firing again. "Find the primary. Don't you pull, just... snip."

Racing up the muddy embankment fifty yards away, Staff Sergeant Johnnie Grey saw the situation instantly through his binoculars: the sparks flying off the bridge steel, the engineer sergeant using his own body as a shield.

"Everyone drop!" Johnnie roared, throwing himself into the mud. "Mineo, Luby! Light up that farmhouse! Now!"

He glanced back at the idling MIO, its crew watching through the open turret. "Tell that TD to hold its fire! If that three-inch gun opens up, the concussion will set off the daisy-chain and drop the whole bridge before the engineers even get a hand on the wire!"

The engineers were their lifeline. Johnnie and his squad would be damned if they let it break.

Johnnie, Mineo, and Luby opened fire in a coordinated, rolling volley. Their rounds slammed into the farmhouse, chipping stone, shattering the window, and forcing the German gunner to duck.

"Those engineers are the craziest bastards in this whole man's army," Mineo said, chambering another round.

"They're the best," Johnnie corrected, his gaze locked on the bridge. "Just like at Riva Ridge. Without their tramway, we'd have died on that rock."

Under the bridge, shielded by the sudden storm of infantry fire from the bank, Smitty's fingers traced the wire. One was the primary. One was a booby trap. He held his breath. The entire Po Valley, the entire 10th Mountain Division, the whole war, shrank to this. Two wires.

Zzzzzing! A round skipped off the girder and tore a hot line across Smitty's pack, ripping the canvas. He didn't move.

He felt it. The slight, rough patch on the primary. He got his wire cutters into the cramped space. His hand wasn't shaking. He was a professional. He was a 126th Engineer.

He cut the wire.

The *B-r-r-r-r-i-p-p* of the MG42 stopped completely as Luby's BAR chewed up the windowsill.

A profound vacuum of sound fell. Smitty slowly, gently, pulled his arm back. His hand, now that it was over, was cramped so hard he could barely hold the cutters.

"One down, Sarge," he whispered, his voice cracking.

"Good lad," Grizz said, reloading his rifle. "Now, let's go find the next one."

Down on the bridge, the engineer sergeant gave a quick "all-clear" wave. The charges were disarmed. He and his private scrambled back to the bank, and a moment later, the first

M10 tank destroyer rumbled across the bridge, its engine roaring.

Johnnie and his squad rose from the mud, their part in this small, vital battle over. As the engineers passed, Johnnie gave them a sharp, unprompted salute.

Mineo cupped his hands around his mouth and bellowed, "You saved us again, THANK YOU!"

Smitty, exhausted and still shaking, looked up, a stunned, grimy grin splitting his face, and returned the salute. The connection was made.

"Look at 'em," Luby muttered, his usual sarcasm replaced by a quiet awe. "They just... walk out there and get to work. Like they're fixing a tractor back home."

They watched the engineers, already packing their gear to move to the next river, the next booby-trapped bridge.

"Alright, boys," Johnnie said, slinging his rifle. "Let's follow them. They had our backs. It's our turn to have theirs."

Luby's eyes met Johnnie's. "Amen," Luby murmured, and the others echoed him, the word a shared, solemn understanding.

56

THE PARADE

APRIL 23-24, 1945

The Po Valley, Italy

The Gothic Line was a memory of ice and blood. The war was no longer vertical; it was a flat, desperate, high-speed chase.

The 10th Mountain Division, having shattered Kesselring's fortress, was now the spearhead of the entire U.S. Fifth Army, a blue arrow plunging through the mud of the Po Valley, relentlessly hounding the retreating German army.

On April 23, at San Benedetto, the chase collided with the wide, brown expanse of the Po River. But the water didn't stop them. Hays watched as the 126th Engineers launched their flotilla, comprising storm boats, rafts, and DUKWs—amphibious trucks nicknamed "Ducks" that could be used as boats—churning the brown water.

As he watched the chaos, Hays felt a phantom echo of the Marne. In 1918, he'd been a lone rider, fighting to swim parallel to a German rip current that wanted to drag the whole line under. Now the geometry had flipped. He was the rip current.

His command post was the front seat of his jeep, parked at a muddy crossroads, its radio handset perpetually in his fist. Around him, the division had become a ragtag, high-speed caravan.

In the struggle to keep pace with the retreat, his men had commandeered everything with wheels. Hays watched a surreal parade of German trucks, draft horses hitched to farm wagons, stolen Italian Fiats, motorcycles, and even bicycles, all surging north in a cloud of dust.

At a narrow bend, a Sherman tank swerved to miss an elderly farmer frantically dragging a terrified dairy cow into the ditch—a jarring collision of steel armor and livestock that reminded them this battlefield was someone's front yard.

As the column roared through villages, the war briefly transformed into a parade. Crowds stood at every crossroads, cheering wildly. Young women in bright dresses ran alongside the slow-moving trucks, their arms full of spring blooms, pelting the "liberators" with flowers and passing up bottles of wine and loaves of bread.

In the back of a requisitioned truck, Luby suddenly grabbed Mineo's shoulder, shaking him hard.

"Mineo! Look! Three o'clock!" Luby shouted over the roar of the engine, pointing at a dark-haired girl in a yellow dress who was blowing kisses to the convoy.

"There she is! That's her! The girl you've been dreaming about since Camp Hale!"

Mineo scrambled to the side of the truck, a wide grin breaking through the grime on his face. He waved frantically, catching a red poppy she threw toward him.

"I see her! I see her!" Mineo yelled back, laughing. "Tell the driver to stop! Stop the truck!"

But the truck didn't stop. It accelerated, the gears grinding as the convoy surged forward to keep pace with the retreat.

The girl and the village receded into the dust. Mineo slumped back against the sideboards, still clutching the flower, his smile fading into a look of wistful longing.

Johnnie watched as another bouquet hit the side of a tank and fell, instantly crushed into the gray mud by the grinding treads.

It was a chaotic, beautiful, violent parade—flowers and steel churning north in a cloud of dust.

57

THE RETURN

APRIL 25, 1945

South of Verona, Italy

By April 25, the column was skirting the smoking outskirts of Verona. Hays didn't stop to celebrate. He knew the rail links were now severed, another escape artery closed. With the exits to the Reich choking off one by one, the enemy wasn't just retreating—they were trapped, and his division was the wall closing in.

His path was now a rutted, muddy track, and he was driving his men with a merciless, relentless fury.

"Don't let them breathe!" he roared to an officer directing traffic. "Don't let them dig in. Don't let them sleep. Run them to ground!"

The 10th was now the hammer, the Germans were the anvil. And Hays was bringing everything to bear to crush them.

The war had become a race through the most beautiful spring the men had ever seen. They sped down long, straight avenues lined with towering Lombardy poplars, their new leaves shimmering like green coins in the sun.

The air was thick with 'summer snow'—the white cotton fluff drifting from the poplar trees, swirling in the wake of the tanks, catching in their eyelashes and clogging the radiator grilles like warm, sticky confetti.

"Mineo! Mineo!" Luby screeched, mimicking Hogan's high-pitched panic from two years ago. "There's a feather in my throat!"

Mineo laughed, a short, sharp bark of recognition. For a second, they weren't in a stolen truck racing across Italy; they were back in the freezing barracks at Camp Hale, young and immortal.

"At least this time it isn't Hogan's down sleeping bag molting," Mineo shouted back.

As the truck bounced over a rut, Luby started thumping a rhythm on the side of the truck bed. He began to sing, leading the men in the bitter, mocking anthem of the "D-Day Dodgers." Their voices rose in unison over the grind of the gears, throwing the "Italian holiday" accusation back in the brass's face with every sarcastic note about the "sunny" Italian weather and the wine they were supposedly enjoying.

He grinned at Johnnie, gesturing to the dust-choked, war-torn landscape around them. "See? Just a vacation, Sarge. Living the life of Riley while the real soldiers are in France."

"Yeah," Johnnie said, looking at the graves lining the road. "A vacation."

The laughter died down as the truck hit another rut, replaced by the hum of the tires and the drifting white fluff. Luby wiped his face, his smile fading into a thoughtful look.

"I wonder how he is," Luby said quietly. "I hope he's still

one of the lucky ones. Maybe that shattered leg kept him out of this hell for good."

"You think he married her?" Mineo asked, looking at the passing fields.

"That girl he met in Elkins?" "Hogan?" Johnnie grinned. "He probably married her and bought the whole damn bar."

On either side of the road, the unplowed fields were a sea of red poppies, stretching to the haze-blurred horizon. The treads of the Shermans crushed them by the thousands, leaving wide tracks of mashed green and scarlet pulp.

The air was heavy, humid, and smelled overpoweringly of the sweet, honeyed scent of the acacia trees blooming along the canals—a perfume so thick it almost masked the diesel exhaust.

Hays sat with his Assistant Division Commander, Brigadier General Robinson Duff, as the main column of the 86th raced past them toward the front.

As a beat-up old truck passed, its bed crowded with muddy, exhausted infantrymen, General Duff pointed to a staff sergeant, his legs precariously dangling over the gate as it raced by, a map in his lap.

"General, there he is," Duff shouted over the roar of the engines.

Hays, his mind on the next river crossing, looked over, annoyed at the interruption. "There who is?"

"Sergeant Grey—the one from Belvedere. The one who made the straight run."

Hays's gaze locked onto the sergeant. For a fleeting heartbeat, the Italian dust seemed to vanish, replaced by the gray mist of the Marne. Hays felt a sudden, cold jolt in his chest—a flash of recognition that had nothing to do with the present. He saw a set of eyes, weary but defiant, that mirrored a ghost from 1918.

The image shattered as the truck rumbled on, leaving only a haunting sense he couldn't name. Hays gave a single nod of acknowledgment.

Staff Sergeant Grey, seeing the general's jeep, pushed himself up and snapped a crisp salute. Hays returned it, a flicker of respect on his granite face.

The truck rumbled on. "He's the tip of the spear," Hays said, his voice a low rumble. He grabbed the radio handset from his operator.

"Get me Hampton," Hays barked. "86th. Now."

The line crackled. "Hampton, Hays here. That Staff Sergeant Grey in your command. The one from Belvedere. You find him. You promote him. Next time I see that man, he'd better be a Technical Sergeant. He's earned it. That's all."

Hays clicked off the radio and handed it back, his gaze already scanning the road ahead. He turned to General Duff. "That man, general, is the future of this Army. See that he—"

He never finished the sentence.

The world suddenly disintegrated from the ground up. There was no whistle, no warning from the sky—just a deafening, earth-shattering roar from beneath the wheels. The jeep had struck a buried German antitank mine. The blast threw the vehicle sideways, a geyser of black mud and twisted steel exploding over the road.

Hays was already out of the jeep, his .45 in his hand, his face a mask of cold rage. He was untouched.

His ADC, however, was not. Brigadier General Duff was

slumped against the dashboard, his eyes wide with shock, a dark, spreading stain on his tunic.

"Medic!" Hays bellowed, his voice a force of nature. "Get him out of here! Get a litter!"

As the medics lifted the wounded officer, Hays turned to his radio operator, his command now logistically fractured. "Dammit! I'm blind! I need an ADC now. Get me G-1. Tell them I want the best man they've got, and I want him here an hour ago!"

The radio operator's voice crackled back, "Sir, G-1 reports Colonel Will Darby is in-theater. He's on an observation tour with General Arnold's staff, inspecting the captured airfield at Villafranca. That's less than ten miles south of us, sir. He's the highest-ranking, most experienced combat officer available. Should I...?"

Hays froze. Will. He thought of the V-Mail he'd received weeks ago, after his own letter. The raw, honest confession. *'I'm not asking for a command... I'm not asking for anything but a chance to serve, in any capacity. I'm just trying to get back on the right path.'* He was here. He had kept his word. "Get him," Hays barked into the mic. "Get him now."

Forty minutes later, another jeep—caked in fresh mud—skidded to a halt. A lone colonel stepped out, his uniform sharp from the tour, his boots worn from the trail.

He was leaner than Hays remembered. The old spark in his eyes hadn't gone out; it had compressed into something harder. This was the same steel, retempered.

Will came straight to him and snapped a salute, the gesture so perfect it bordered on punishment.

"Colonel William Darby, sir. Reporting for duty."

Hays returned the salute, but slower—his gaze fixed on Will's face.

"I knew you were in-theater," Hays said quietly.

"I volunteered, General." Will's voice was flat; all the old charm burned away. "To this division. I was told to report to you. To replace your ADC."

Hays held him there a beat longer than a salute required. He saw what Cisterna had taken—and what it had left: a man not asking to be forgiven, only to serve.

Hays let his hand come down to rest on Will's shoulder. A weight. A claim. An acceptance.

"Welcome back to the climb... Will." Hays's voice returned. "We'll finish it."

And for the first time, Will's face moved—just a fraction, the smallest release of air, as if he'd been holding it since Cisterna.

"Yes, sir," Will said.

Hays thrust a map into his hands. "You wanted the 10th Mountain? You got it. We're pushing for Lake Garda." He handed the map case to his new ADC.

"I need a Ranger's eyes."

58

THE GATE

NIGHT, APRIL 25, 1945

West of Verona, Italy

The command post was a requisitioned farmhouse kitchen that smelled of stale garlic and the high-octane sweat of a racing army.

General George P. Hays poured two tin cups of "liberated" Chianti. He slid one across the rough-hewn table to his new ADC.

"To the 'D-Day Dodgers,'" Hays toasted, a wry, tired smile crinkling his eyes.

"To the Dodgers," Will Darby replied, clinking the tin. He took a drink. It was rough red wine, but it tasted better than the filtered water of the Pentagon.

Hays leaned back, studying his protégé. The frenetic energy of the chase had paused for a few hours while the fuel trucks caught up.

"We make quite a pair, Will," Hays mused, swirling the wine. "I'm the general who couldn't take a monastery at Cassino because I followed the rules too closely. And you're the colonel who lost a regiment at Cisterna because you didn't follow them at all."

Will let out a short, sharp laugh. "We're a hell of a command team, George. Marshall must be drinking heavily."

"Maybe," Hays chuckled. "Or maybe he figured that between my brakes and your gas pedal, we might actually stay on the road."

The humor faded, leaving a comfortable, heavy silence between them. They were two men defined by their worst days, trying to carve out a better one.

"I read the reports on Cassino," Will said softly. "You didn't fail. You were given a hammer and told to paint a masterpiece. Kesselring built a wall. You did your duty."

"And I read the reports on Cisterna," Hays countered gently. "You didn't fail either, Will. You were given a gap that was actually a mouth. We both walked into traps set by the same man."

Will looked down into his cup. The wine looked like blood in the lantern light.

"That's why I'm terrified, general."

Hays sat up straighter. "Terrified? You?"

"Not of dying," Will said, looking up, his eyes intense. "Of not getting there in time. Every instinct I have screams to drive faster, to kick down the door and grab my men before the clock runs out."

He paused, his hand tightening on the cup.

"But I heard the rumors in London. About Hammelburg. Oflag XIII-B."

Hays nodded grimly. "The end of March. Patton's raid. Task Force Baum."

"It was a disaster," Will whispered. "Everyone said he was

trying to pull out his son-in-law. He sent an armored column fifty miles behind the lines before the German army was truly broken. They reached the camp, but they couldn't fight their way back. The column was cut to pieces."

Will looked at the map on the wall, his voice dropping to a hollow rasp. "Three hundred and fourteen soldiers went on that mission, and only thirty-five came home. The rest were either captured or are just more names for the crosses. And the POWs they were trying to save? Probably caught in the crossfire—killed by the rescue itself."

He looked at Hays, the anguish raw on his face. "What if my officers were there?"

Hays reached across the table and put a hand on Will's forearm. The grip was solid. The Rock.

"We aren't Patton," Hays said firmly. "And this isn't a raid. We aren't going to snatch them. We are going to finish this. We are going to break the German army so completely that they can't march anyone anywhere."

"Methodical," Will said, the word tasting like penance.

"Relentless," Hays corrected. "We don't rush into the trap. We dismantle the trap. We close the Brenner Pass. We cut the fuel. We make Kesselring surrender the keys. That is how we get them home."

Will took a deep breath. The ghost of Hammelburg receded, replaced by the clarity of the mission.

"Relentless," Will agreed, raising his cup. "We close the gate."

"We close the gate," Hays echoed.

They drank, the pact sealed in cheap wine and hard truth.

Outside, the engines of the fuel trucks began to roar. The pause was over.

59

THE FIRE

NIGHT, APRIL 25, 1945

West of Verona, Italy

Johnnie watched as the road to the Alps became a highway of nations.

It wasn't just the 10th Mountain Division anymore. To their right, a dust-caked column of Shermans roared past, the crews shouting in Portuguese. They were the 'Smoking Cobras' of the 1st Brazilian Infantry Division, racing to cut off the German 148th Division.

Behind them, a heavy transport convoy rumbled north, the drivers swapping cigarettes in the clipped accents of the British Eighth Army. And on the eastern horizon, the radio nets were buzzing with reports of the Polish II Corps smashing through Bologna.

Farther down the line, Johnnie spotted the distinctive slouch hats of the New Zealanders and the turbans of the Indian 8th Division moving up the line, while the deep, mechanical roar of South African armored brigades shook the ground to the east.

"Look at them go," Luby said, leaning against a broken stone wall, watching the Brazilians tear north.

"I heard their patch is a smoking snake," Luby continued, "because Hitler said it was more likely for a snake to smoke a pipe than for Brazil to fight in Italy. Now look at 'em. I respect that kind of spite."

Mineo shook his head, watching a jeep filled with Nisei soldiers from the 442nd—the famous "Go for Broke" regiment—weave through the traffic.

"It's a traffic jam," Mineo grumbled. "Every army in Europe is trying to fit on this one road."

"You know," Luby said, watching the endless stream of taillights fade into the dust. "I think the whole world turned out for this dance."

Johnnie nodded. "Yeah. Let's move. Let's join the dance."

Later that night, for the first time since they had entered the Apennines, they built a fire.

They weren't hiding anymore. They were insulated by a river of steel, surrounded by thousands of Allied troops on all sides. The need for the cold, dark discipline of the ridge had finally passed.

Tech Sergeant Johnnie Grey sat with his back against the wheel of their broken-down truck, staring into the flames. The heat on his face felt strange, almost intoxicating, after months of freezing nights. Mineo and Luby huddled close, mesmerized by the dancing light.

A shadow fell across the firelight, blocking the warmth.

"American?" a voice rasped.

Johnnie's hand flashed to his .45, but he stopped.

Standing at the edge of the light was a man who looked more like a scarecrow than a soldier. He wore a ragged wool jacket, a mismatched pair of German boots, and a distinctive red kerchief tied around his neck.

He held a rusty Carcano rifle, but the barrel was pointed at the ground.

"Partisan," the man said, tapping the red scarf. "Garibaldi Brigade."

He didn't ask for food. He reached into his coat and pulled out a crumpled, hand-drawn map. He crouched next to the fire, smelling of woodsmoke and old sweat.

"Avanti," the partisan said, pointing a grimy finger north toward the mountains. "Tunnels. Tedeschi... Germans... they wait. Boom." He made an explosive gesture with his hands.

"We know," Johnnie said, offering the man a cigarette. "We're going to clear them."

The man took the cigarette with a trembling hand. He looked at Johnnie, his dark eyes brimming with a terrifying intensity in the firelight.

"My brother," the man whispered, struggling with the English. "He was in Roma. The Caves. Ardeatine."

Johnnie froze. He had heard the rumors of the massacre —335 civilians executed in the dark.

"Kesselring," the partisan spat the name like a curse. He locked eyes with Johnnie. "You finish him? You finish the... *bastardo*?"

Johnnie looked at the man's shaking hands, at the grief carved into his face. The heavy woodsmoke from their fire drifted over them, and suddenly, the dust of Italy vanished.

Johnnie was a boy again, alone in a snow-covered hollow in the Intervales. He was tending a small, defiant fire against the gnawing chill, clutching his slingshot like a rifle. He remembered the feeling that always haunted him in those woods—the phantom scent of something acrid burning in the clean mountain air.

The ghost of a war he had never seen.

He remembered the boyish promise he had made to the silence of the forest: that he would be strong enough to save the father he barely remembered. He couldn't save him then. But looking at this partisan, he knew he could finish the fight now.

Johnnie lit the man's cigarette with a twig from the fire, his hand steady.

"Yeah," Johnnie promised, his voice low and hard. "We'll finish him."

The partisan nodded once, a sharp, martial jerk of his chin, and vanished back into the shadows as quickly as he had come.

"Jesus," Luby breathed, the sarcasm gone.

"I swear to God," Mineo muttered, poking at the congealed 'meat' in his K-Ration tin. "My mother's dog eats better than this. And it's cold. I thought Italy was supposed to be sunny? All I've seen is mud, mountains, and now this... this..."

Luby, with a mouthful of SPAM and a smile on his face, countered, "Better than Texas, at least we're not getting bit. Remember Camp Swift? The ant swarms? Had to sleep with the legs of my cot sitting in tin cans of water just to get a night's rest."

Johnnie turned back to his rifle, meticulously, almost obsessively, cleaning the bolt. Luby just watched him with a curious look on his face.

"Honest to God, Sarge. I don't get you."

Johnnie didn't look up, his oil rag moving in small, perfect circles on the bolt. "What's to get?"

"Back at Belvedere," Luby said, lowering his voice. "The 'straight run.' I was there. I saw you. We all ran straight, but you ran with your head up at the 'ring of fire' while the rest of us were running in a crouch with our heads down. You got a death wish or something?"

Johnnie stopped cleaning. He was silent for a long moment, staring at the rifle in his lap.

"Just doing the job, and that's the way I run the fastest," he said quietly. "Get it done, get it home."

"Bull," Luby said, not unkindly. "That was more than 'doing the job.' You were trying to win the war all by yourself. What's the hurry?"

Johnnie took a deep breath. "My old man... he was in the last one. The Great War."

Mineo, about to complain again, shut his mouth. This was new.

"He was at the Marne," Johnnie continued, his voice flat, his gaze distant. "Got mustard gassed. He... he came home, but... he never really came home, you know?"

Luby and Mineo just nodded. They knew.

Johnnie looked at his two men, his eyes as hard and clear as the mountain ice they'd left behind.

"My old man never got to finish his fight. He just... faded... died when I was just a boy. I'm finishing mine. I'm not gonna 'never really come home.' I'm gonna win. And go home. The real way."

He clicked the bolt of his M1 back into place, the sound a sharp, final clack in the quiet.

A heavy silence fell over the squad. Luby and Mineo exchanged a look. They finally understood the fire that drove their sergeant. It wasn't ambition. It wasn't glory. It was a ghost.

"Well, hell, Sarge," Mineo said quietly, breaking the tension. He reached out and gripped Johnnie's shoulder, his hand steady for the first time all day. "Pass the oil. If we're gonna finish this thing, we'd better have clean rifles. We got your back."

"Amen to that," Luby added, his usual grin replaced by a look of fierce, quiet loyalty.

Johnnie nodded, a small, tight smile on his face, and passed them the rag. Around them, the fire crackled, its light reflecting off the steel of three rifles being readied for the last battle.

60

THE TUNNELS

APRIL 28–29, 1945

Lake Garda, Italy

The chase had ended at the mouth of the Alps. The 10th Mountain Division, having run the Germans to ground, now faced the vertical walls of Lake Garda.

It was the southern gate to the Alpine Redoubt, and Kesselring's retreat had funneled into a single, lethal choke point. The Germans held the heights, and the only path north was a narrow ribbon of asphalt blasted into the cliff-side—a path that was currently buried under rubble and sighted by artillery.

General Hays stood in the makeshift headquarters—it made him sick to think about what he was about to ask.

"Gentlemen," Hays began, his voice hoarse. "The Germans have blown Tunnel #1 to hell," he said, grimly tapping the map. "And that's just the first obstacle. Ahead of us is nine miles of solid rock. Six tunnels between Malcesine and Torbole. To clear Tunnel #1, I'm considering ordering the 126th Engineers to take on an unimaginably risky operation: bring in heavy equipment to clear that rubble under direct fire from the Monte Brione batteries."

A cold knot tightened in Colonel Will Darby's stomach. It was the feeling from Cisterna all over again—listening to his men being fired on in an open field, without cover, while he stood powerless.

He looked at the engineers, realizing many of them were about to be sacrificed for a similar daring frontal assault.

There was no 'King's Stone' here. There was only the cost.

No more, he thought. *Not again. Not my plan. I cannot let this happen again.*

Will looked at the map, then at the vast, dark expanse of the lake. He thought for a moment, not of roads... but of trails.

Will stepped forward.

"General," Will began, his voice firm, "may I propose a different path? The Germans blew up Tunnel #1 to lock the front door. They expect us to clear the rubble. They want us to send the engineers in so they can tie us up and pick us off one by one. This isn't a road problem," Will said, his voice cutting through the pessimism. "It's a 99th Artillery (Pack) problem. Fort Hoyle, 1940."

The room went silent. They looked at him as if he were mad.

"In the 99th," Will explained, "when the trail died, we didn't sit there and wait for the engineers to rebuild it. We packed around it. We broke the guns down."

He looked at Hays, his expression intensifying.

"But it's also the letter you sent me, general. About the surfman... Coste?"

Hays looked up, surprised by the reference to his past.

"You wrote that Coste died because he fought the ocean's power head-on," Will continued, his voice quiet. "You said the only way to survive a rip current is to swim parallel. To find the angle."

Will pointed to the blue expanse of the lake on the map.

"The blocked tunnel is the rip current, general. We can't fight it head-on. The DUKWs... they're how we swim parallel."

General Hays looked at his aide. A slow, knowing smile touched his lips.

"The mules would approve," he murmured.

"The DUKWs... are our mules," Will said, "We use them to ferry the main force to a point just south of Tunnel #3. We bypass the blocked Tunnel #1 entirely, land behind their demolition, and clear Tunnel #2 then Tunnel #1 from the rear. We don't break down the front door; we come in through the back door."

It was insane. It was brilliant. It was the Ranger way, born on a mule path in Oklahoma.

General Hays looked at his aide. He saw the fire, but this time it was tempered by purpose, not ambition. The glory-seeking officer from Gela and Salerno was gone, replaced by a commander who had seen the cost.

His plan was about saving the 126th Engineers. If more men walked out of this alive because of his plan, that was enough.

"I agree," Hays said. "It's your plan, Colonel Darby. It's risky, but it's worth it to drive these bastards back to hell. Lt. Col. Hampton, assemble your squads. Make it so."

Hays paused over the map. "But I want insurance. While the main force rides the DUKWs past Tunnel #1, I want two companies to go over the top from Tunnel #3—night move —up Monte Baldo. They bypass Tunnels #4 through #6 and come down near the rear of Tunnel #6, south of Torbole. If the Germans have the tunnel mouths blocked, our men will already be inside, opening the back doors for the main body."

The last-ditch gamble codenamed "Task Force Darby" had begun.

∾

1200 Hours, April 28

Johnnie and his squad—Mineo and Luby—found themselves crowded onto one of the DUKWs, the amphibious vehicle groaning as it slid from the shore into the shimmering, sunlit waters of Lake Garda.

Near the water's edge, a gaunt small boy sat on a pile of rubble, clutching the handle of a wooden cart filled with scavenged firewood. He watched the soldiers on the strange, amphibious trucks with wide, unblinking eyes, not moving, not waving—just tracking the soldiers with the grave, heavy stare of a child who has seen too much and eaten too little.

The DUKWs bobbed in water that was a shocking, jewel-tone emerald. The air was surreal, heavy with the perfume of blooming lemon groves—the *limonaie* terraced into the cliffs. For a moment, the sweet scent masked the diesel fumes, smelling more like a wedding than a war.

Then the spell broke. On this bright, unforgiving mirror, there was nowhere to hide. Johnnie gripped the cold steel gunwale as the first high-velocity whistle tore through the perfume.

He felt the concussion through the hull of the DUKW a split second before an airburst snapped above them and a geyser of water erupted fifty yards to port—a tower of spray fifty feet high that misted over them.

German observers on the high ground of Monte Brione had a clear view of them in broad daylight.

"Well, I feel naked," Mineo whispered, clutching his rifle to his chest as if the wood and steel could stop an 88mm shell. He stared at the mountain cliffs that pressed the road tight against the lake. "There's no cover. No trees. It's just... open."

"It's a shooting gallery," Luby muttered, his usual grin gone. He watched the water falling from the geyser. "And we're the plastic ducks."

Another shell screamed past, closer this time, shaking the boat violently. They were a slow-moving target, churning through the emerald water at a painfully sluggish pace.

"Hey, Johnnie," Luby said, his voice tight. "If this tub gets hit... how are we going to swim with 75-pound rucksacks on our backs?"

Johnnie looked at him. They had climbed cliffs in the dark, run through artillery barrages, and cleared minefields. The idea that water might be the thing to take them seemed absurd, yet terrifyingly real.

"You won't have to swim," Johnnie said, his voice calm, trying to anchor them. "Because we aren't getting hit. We're going to land on that beach, and we're going to walk into that tunnel."

"I prefer climbing," Mineo said, squeezing his eyes shut as another shell landed starboard. "I hate the water... come to think of it, I hate tunnels too."

"Hold on to the boat, Mineo," Johnnie commanded. "Just hold on."

They landed safely on a small, secluded beach just south of Tunnel #3, which was empty. The relief of solid ground beneath their boots was palpable.

On Lt. Col. Hampton's signal, they struck.

The assault on Tunnel #2 was a whirlwind of controlled chaos.

Johnnie tossed a grenade, the concussion a deafening, echoing boom that seemed to suck the air from the rock tube. Muzzle flashes from their rifles lit the darkness in strobing, terrifying bursts, illuminating the shocked faces of the German soldiers for a split second before they fell.

The Germans, caught entirely by surprise, were thrown into chaos. They had prepared their positions to repel a direct, frontal assault coming up the road from the south—they had no time to reposition their heavy weapons to face the attack from the north. The tunnel became a tube of deafening noise, the roar of rifles and screams echoing off the rock.

They cleared the second tunnel, then they cleared the first. By 1530 hours, Tunnels #1-3 were secured. They jogged, widely dispersed, zig-zagging up the thin road under the weight of their rucksacks. Next, they attacked and cleared Tunnel #4, where they spent the night.

0600 Hours, April 29

The morning of 29 April, an eerie silence hung in the air as they approached Tunnel #5.

Johnnie felt it first—a wrongness in the air, the smell of

fumes of high explosives mixed with something else, something sweet, iron, and sickening.

Inside, the tunnel was a mangled tomb. It was filled with the twisted remains of dozens of German soldiers, their uniforms still holding fragments of their elite SS Mountain Warfare School insignia. They had been rigging the tunnel with explosive charges to collapse it on the Americans, but the explosives had detonated prematurely, killing them instead.

"Jesus," Luby whispered, covering his nose with a rag. "They did our job for us."

"Let's just get through it," Johnnie said, stepping over the bodies.

They moved quickly through the carnage, eager for the clean air on the other side. As they emerged into the daylight at the northern mouth, Johnnie didn't stop to celebrate. He applied the ingrained lesson: never bunch up at an exit. He signaled his squad to move fast and wide, pushing them fifty feet past the mouth in a dispersed, zig-zag formation along the edge of the cliff road.

Johnnie paused, looking back. He saw the battalion command group ducking into the stone archway, seeking cover.

At that moment, the sky didn't just split; it collapsed.

There was no whistle. Just a sudden, violent overpressure that sucked the air right out of the valley. The 88mm shell slammed into the archway, turning the stone ceiling into a downward-firing shotgun.

The blast wave hit Johnnie like a physical wall, throwing him face-first into the ground. He felt the shock rattle his teeth, a vibration so deep it seemed to crack his bones.

Then came the silence—a high, screaming void in his head.

"We're buried!" a voice screamed, tearing through the ringing in his ears. "Get the medics up here! We are buried!"

Johnnie blinked, trying to focus on the carnage. Through the settling dust, he saw the battalion commander, Major Drake, being dragged back, his face ashen. The blast had decimated their entire command group, seeking cover in the archway. Five American soldiers lay dead, and almost fifty were wounded, their blood bright against the gray dust.

A medic, his face streaked with tears and grime, looked up at Johnnie.

"It's a goddamn tomb," he choked out. "It's a Death Tunnel."

Their radio operator was slumped against the wall, his set smashed. Johnnie looked at the chaos.

His battalion commander was out. The radio was dead. They were deep in enemy territory.

And they were blind.

61

THE SECOND TRAP

0800 HOURS, APRIL 29, 1945

Bletchley Park, England

The war in Italy was a war of maps, and Annie's job was to find the one that was lying. She was back in her true fortress: a cold, damp wooden hut in Buckinghamshire.

Annie was staring at a wall covered in cork and paper. She was hunting Field Marshal Kesselring's mind one last time. She stood before two grids pinned to the damp wood.

The first was the "Known Map." It showed the official G-2 intelligence picture from Allied Force Headquarters in Caserta.

Pinned to the center of the corkboard, dominating the blue arrows of the Allied advance, was a fresh clipping from *The Stars and Stripes*. The headline shouted in bold, celebratory caps:

NAZIS IN ROUT: GERMANS RACE FOR ALPS

It was the story the world wanted to believe—a simple footrace to the finish line. Annie looked at it, her stomach tightening. It wasn't just a headline; it was a blindfold. With a sudden, sharp movement, she ripped the newsprint from the board, the tearing sound cutting through the clatter of the typewriters.

She crumpled the "victory" in her fist and threw it into the wastebasket. It depicted Kesselring's forces in a full, panicked retreat toward the Brenner Pass, the main alpine artery into Austria. The arrows were big and red, sweeping north. It looked like a rout.

The second was the "Intercept Map." It was Annie's private project, a map of whispers built from hundreds of low-level Enigma decrypts—logistics orders, fuel requisitions, and hospital supply requests.

And the two maps told a different story.

"It's wrong," Annie whispered, the cold dread pooling in her stomach.

She traced the line of the 10th Mountain Division's advance. They were pushing hard along Lake Garda, chasing what they thought was a fleeing enemy. They were driving straight for the tunnels.

She picked up a decrypt from that morning. It was a request for 88mm anti-aircraft ammunition—not for the Brenner Pass, but for the northern tip of Lake Garda. She picked up another: a requisition for fuel.

"He's not running," she realized, her hand trembling as she reached for a red pin. "He's *luring*."

Annie's hand measured the scale on the map—between Torbole and the relative safety of Tunnel #6, there was exactly one mile of exposed, cliff-side road.

She looked at the fresh decrypts again—the pre-registered 88s high above the road. Panzer fuel. It was beginning to dawn.

"Jean," Annie whispered, her voice cracking. "How many men in a full mountain battalion?"

"Paper strength? Seven hundred and seventy," Jean replied without looking up.

The number hit Annie like a physical blow—770. At Cisterna—761. The math was a mirror of the massacre she had been forced to watch in silence a year ago.

"It's happening again," she hissed.

She closed her eyes, and for a terrible second, she was back in 1944. She heard the phantom static of the radio, the silence of seven hundred and sixty-one men vanishing into a mouth she had seen opening but had been forbidden to stop.

She glanced at a decrypt she had pinned to the corner of her board—a routine G-1 Morning Report she had intercepted three days ago. It was a single line of administrative text that had stopped her heart:

Reassignment Orders:

COL DARBY, W. ... RELIEVED OF OBSERVER STATUS ... ASSIGNED ASST DIV CMDR, 10TH MTN DIV ... EFFEC-TIVE 25 APRIL

Will was there now. He was with Hays. They were walking into the same buzzsaw.

"Not this time." She ripped the intercept log from the wall. She didn't care about the shift change. She didn't care about the celebration outside. She grabbed her coat and marched out into the rain.

62

THE ECHO

1230 HOURS, APRIL 29, 1945

Near Navene, Italy

A field phone and radio crackled on the crate beside him. "What's the status, Will?" General Hays demanded, his knuckles white on the edge of the map table.

"Static," Darby said, pressing the headset to his ear. "I've got nothing from the 3rd Battalion command. That shell at Tunnel Five didn't just kill men; it killed the net. We're blind."

"They aren't moving," Hays muttered, looking at the map where Company I should be. "Without a link, they're stalled in the dark. If they don't drop on that town soon, the whole timeline collapses."

Then, the static broke. A voice crackled through, thin and desperate.

"Be advised... am approaching the town square... wait..."

It was the commander, climbing down from the Mount Baldo ridge toward the town of Torbole.

"... moving past the boathouse..."

The voice spiked an octave. "CONTACT! Heavy contact! They have a gun in the square!"

Will Darby froze. His blood went cold.

"Say again, I Company," the radio operator shouted.

"It's a 20! They have a 20-millimeter flak gun dug in right by the fountain! It's firing point-blank down the main street! We're about to be cut to pieces!"

The radio erupted in a roar of explosions and static—the terrifying, supersonic crack of a high-velocity anti-aircraft shell being used against infantry.

"We can't move forward!" the commander screamed over the noise. "We have to fall back! We have to retreat to the tunnel! I can't—"

Click.

Silence.

Hays slammed a fist on the jeep. "Dammit! They were waiting for him."

Will just stared at the radio, his face pale. *The square. 20s. We're about to be cut to pieces.*

63

THE MESSAGE

2100 HOURS, APRIL 29, 1945

Bletchley Park, England

"You are asking me to overrule the Theater Commander from a hut in Buckinghamshire," Alistair said, his voice calm, maddeningly reasonable. He tamped his pipe, not looking at the map she had spread over his desk.

"I am asking you to look at the math!" Annie cried, slamming the intercept log down. "The G-2 in Caserta is reading the generals. I am reading the supply trucks. Kesselring isn't retreating to the Brenner Pass. That is a ghost story he is feeding us. He is digging in at Torbole."

She pointed to the timeline. "The 10th Mountain Division is entering those tunnels right now. If they come out the other side thinking the town is clear, they will be annihilated."

Alistair looked at her, his bird-like eyes devoid of sympathy. "Annie, we have been over this. The 'Ultra' source is sacrosanct. We cannot risk exposing that we have broken the

Enigma cipher just to warn a single division about a tactical ambush. We cannot compromise the Allied victory for... for a personal crusade."

He knew. He knew about Will. He knew she wasn't just an analyst right now; she was a woman trying to save a man.

"It is not personal," she lied, her voice shaking. "It's the men of the 10th."

"The file is closed, Annie," Alistair said, turning his back to her to look out the window at the rain. "You were told to stand down at Cisterna, and I am telling you to stand down now. You will not send this cable. You will return to your hut. Is that clear?"

Annie stared at his back. She remembered the 761 Rangers. She remembered the letter Will had written her from the darkness of his own failure.

She realized then that "Protocol" was just a fancy word for letting people die so you didn't have to make a hard choice.

"Perfectly clear, Alistair," she said.

She walked out of his office. She didn't go back to her hut.

She walked through the driving rain, her heels clicking on the pavement, past the guard post, and straight to the main Signals Building.

The room hit her with a wall of heat—the scent of hot Bakelite, copper, and sweat. It was a cacophony of clacking teletypes, the machine-gun fire of information connecting England to the world.

She walked to the dispatch desk. A young corporal looked up, tired and bored.

"I need a FLASH priority signal to Italy," Annie said.

"Allied Force Headquarters, Caserta – for Fifth Army, 10th Mountain Division.

"I can't just send a FLASH straight to a division CP, ma'am," the corporal said. "I need a routing order from London or Caserta."

Annie grabbed a "FLASH" priority form—the red-bordered paper reserved for the highest level of emergency. Her hands were trembling, but her mind was ice cold. She was about to violate the Official Secrets Act. She was about to end her career. She was about to commit treason to save a life.

She wrote the message quickly, her pen tearing the paper.

MAJ. GEN. GEORGE P. HAYS. FWD COMMAND POST. 10TH MTN DIV. ... SUBJECT: KESSELRING KILL BOX. URGENT...

She signed it with the Theater G-2's authorization code —a ciphered callsign she'd memorized from a file she wasn't supposed to see.

Then, at the very bottom of the message text, she typed one final line—a breach of protocol that was a message to one specific man:

SENDER: ANNIE MCKENNA

Somewhere in Italy, she feared Will Darby's hand might be frozen by the weight of the past. So she picked up her pen and carried the burden for both of them.

She handed the form to the Corporal.

He looked at the "FLASH" header. He looked at the unauthorized signature. He looked at her pale, wet face.

"Ma'am, this is... this breaks the chain of command. If I send this..."

"If you don't send it," Annie whispered, leaning in, her brown eyes fierce and terrifying, "men will die in the dark because you were waiting for a stamp. Do you want that on your soul, Corporal? Because I already have enough on mine."

The Corporal hesitated. He looked at the clock. Then, he took the paper.

"Send it," she breathed. "Send it now."

64

PROTOCOL

2120 HOURS, APRIL 29, 1945

Bletchley Park, England

She didn't even make it back to her desk.

Major Sterling, the British Section Chief and Alistair's direct superior, was waiting for her as she walked out of the signals room. His face was a mask of cold, imperious fury.

"Miss McKenna," he said, his voice clipped and precise. "A word. Now."

He didn't wait for a reply. He turned and marched toward a small, private office—a glass-walled box at the end of the corridor that offered silence but no privacy. Annie followed, her heart hammering, but her footsteps steady.

When she entered, she saw he wasn't alone. Alistair, her handler, was standing by the window, his back to her, staring out at the darkened courtyard. This was the end.

"Sit down," Major Sterling said. He remained standing, looming over the desk, the King's uniform imposing in the small space.

"Do you have any idea what you've done?" Sterling began, his voice a low, controlled hiss. "You, a junior liaison officer, have taken unvetted, uncorroborated intelligence, and you have, in direct violation of the Official Secrets Act and the BRUSA Agreement, sent it directly to a front-line divisional commander."

Alistair turned from the window. His face was not angry; it was worse. It was disappointed.

"You've gone rogue, Annie," he said, his voice quiet. "After Cisterna, I expected... discipline. You were told to stand down then, and you have defied a direct order from the Crown now."

"That's not the half of it," Major Sterling cut in, his eyes hard. "You didn't just 'defy' orders. You bypassed the entire chain of command. You have endangered the intelligence-sharing framework with the Americans at a critical juncture of the war."

He leaned in. "If General Hays diverts his main force at Lake Garda based on your hysteria...." Sterling straightened, adjusting his tunic. "The blood of that failure, young lady, will be on your hands. You will not just be dismissed. You will be facing a tribunal. You will be in a cell by morning."

The air in the small office was suffocating. This was it. The end of her life as she knew it.

Annie looked at the major's furious face. She looked at Alistair's cold, resigned eyes. She thought of Will, a ghost in the Pentagon, and now a soldier on the line. She thought of the men who died in the trap she had been forced to watch in 1944.

She would not let it happen again.

"You're wrong," she said, her voice clear and steady in the small room.

Major Sterling stared, stunned by her defiance. "I beg your pardon?"

"I said, you're wrong," Annie repeated. She stood up, her gaze meeting his, level and unafraid. "It's not hysteria. It's the plumbing. And you're all reading it wrong."

She turned to Alistair. Her voice was no longer that of a subordinate. It was the voice of an equal.

"I did what I had to do. I failed to act at Cisterna, and 761 men were killed or captured because we were too polite to interrupt the generals. I will not fail again."

She picked up her cover from the chair, her movement final.

"You're right about one thing, major," she said, her hand on the doorknob. "I did break protocol. But I didn't send that intel on a 'hunch.' I sent it to the only man I knew who might listen."

She opened the door and walked out, leaving the two men in a stunned, furious silence.

She knew she'd painted a target on her back, trading a safe future for this one, thin chance. There were prison cells waiting for troublesome women who broke the Secrets Act.

So be it. If Torbole did not become another Cisterna, she could live with that.

She walked back through the grand hallway, past the maps of the "Known War," her career in ruins, but her conscience, for the first time, perfectly clear.

She had done her part. The rest was up to "The Rock."

"Please, George," she whispered, her voice tight with fear and hope. "Read it right."

65

THE SHADOW

2214 HOURS, APRIL 29, 1945

Torbole, Italy

The daylight assault was a bloody failure. But the 10th did not break.

Under the cover of darkness, Johnnie Grey's exhausted, ragged squad infiltrated the town and took out the men manning the 20 in the square. What followed was a brutal, house-to-house fight. They used grenades to clear enemy nests and BARs to sweep alleys.

By 22:14, they had done it. They fought their way to the town square and linked up with the remnants of L Company.

"We're in," Johnnie radioed back, his voice a raw whisper. "Square is secure. I think... I think we've got it."

He sat on the edge of a dry fountain under the shadow of a pine tree, his rifle across his knees, and for a single, gasping second, he allowed himself to breathe.

In the command post miles away, General Hays tracked the situation. Looking up from the reports, he spotted a 10th

Mountain trooper with a tattered paperback Western tucked into his blouse.

Hays allowed himself a faint, tired smile. Somewhere, Julia would be pleased to know her Zane Grey cowboys had made it all the way to the shores of Lake Garda.

Down in the square, the moon was just past full, casting long, dancing shadows over the villas. Johnnie sat cleaning his rifle when a commotion erupted near the boathouse.

It wasn't enemy fire. It was cheering.

The partisan with the red scarf—the one Johnnie had met on the road to Verona—came sprinting into the piazza, waving a piece of paper like a flag. He was weeping, screaming a phrase over and over.

"Hanno preso il Duce! È morto! È morto!"

Johnnie looked up. "What's he saying?"

"He says they got him," Mineo said, lowering his rifle. "Mussolini. He's dead."

A roar went up from the Italian civilians emerging from their homes. They hugged the Americans, pouring wine into canteen cups. The nightmare of Fascism was physically, undeniably dead.

"It's over," Luby breathed, looking around at the celebrating town.

Johnnie looked at the partisan dancing in the street. He wanted to believe it. He fingered the St. Andrew's cross around his neck. *Il Duce* had fallen. Surely the fighting would stop.

Then Johnnie heard it.

It started as a low, deep vibration through the cobblestones.

The Italians froze.

They knew that sound better than anyone. The cheering

vanished, replaced by a collective gasp of terror. In seconds, the piazza was empty again, the wine spilled on the stones as the civilians scrambled back into their homes, slamming the doors on the false dawn.

Then a rumble from the northern entries. Two massive dark shapes breached the streets leading to the square. To the left, a tank began its grind along the Via Benaco promenade; to the right, a second monster was heading towards the tight carport corridor of the Hotel Geier. The heavy gears locked in place as the turrets began to rotate, hunting for targets in the dark.

"Tanks," Luby yelled. "Blocks away, but they're fighting their way in. We're pinned against the lake."

"Panzers," Mineo hissed, his eyes wide, looking through binoculars. "God, I hate tanks."

Behind them, a wave of German infantry surged toward the square.

There was no way out.

The radio at Hays's CP exploded.

"COUNTERATTACK! Panzers heading towards the square! Two of them, moving into position! We're trapped— repeat: we're trapped! All we've got up here are rifles and grenades! We can't hold!"

Will Darby stood by the radio, his body shaking. It was not a ghost. It was not a memory. It was happening. His men. His plan. He was listening to his own failure, replaying note for agonizing note.

66

THE THIRD PATH

0025 HOURS APRIL 30, 1945

Torbole, Italy

"They're being annihilated," General Hays said, his voice a low, terrible growl. He stared at the map, at the blue icon for the battalion, hopelessly isolated in the streets and houses of Torbole.

This was Cisterna all over again.

Will Darby stood next to him, frozen, his face ashen. He was a spectator to his own nightmare, listening to the same radio calls, the same sounds.

Hays grabbed the radio handset, his voice devoid of all emotion. "This is Hays. I am not sacrificing that battalion. The operation is compromised. Colonel Hampton, order your men to withdraw. Pull them back to Tunnel Six. That is a direct, final order."

The radio crackled with static, then the voice of Colonel Hampton speaking from the forward edge came through, tense but steady. "General, with respect, sir. My men are in and behind the buildings. They have cover. Give us a delay. Give us time. "

Hays thought of the lesson from Cisterna—light infantry cut off, even in the hands of two Ranger battalions, was no match for heavy armor. It would be the end of his men.

"General!" A signals clerk burst in, his face in shock, ignoring all protocol. He held a dispatch. "Sir, FLASH! EYES-ONLY! It's from Bletchley, routed to you personally."

Hays ripped the dispatch from his hand. His eyes scanned the text.

> **SUBJECT: KESSELRING KILL BOX. URGENT. ...HEAVY ARTILLERY BATTERIES 88s ARE REGISTERED AND HIDDEN IN THE MOUNTAINS ON THE SOUTHERN EXITS AND ROADS... ...PANZERS ARE A FLUSHING FORCE... ...INTENT IS TO FORCE WITHDRAWAL FROM TORBOLE SOUTH INTO OPEN KILL ZONES FOR THE 88s ... RETREAT WITH CAUTION.**

The words—*Batteries Registered On Exits*—seemed to jump off the page. Hays looked at the radio, which was still screaming about Panzers.

"Sir," Colonel Johnston said, his hand hovering over the radio. "We have to pull them out. We have to retreat to Tunnel Six before they're overrun. All our heavy weapons are still back on the road, south of the blown tunnels."

Hays stared at the map. The old habits screamed at him to pull back. The book demanded a clean arc of fire and a neat withdrawal line. It demanded he reset the board.

But then his eyes dropped to the bottom of the message. Beneath the cold military syntax, there was a name.

SENDER: ANNIE MCKENNA

Hays froze. He remembered Will's letter from Washington. *An analyst... her name's Annie... she told me the other half of the story.*

Then the tactical memory clicked into place. This was the woman who had predicted Cisterna. Will had written it clearly: *She saw the trap, general. She called it a kill box when we all saw a gap.*

This wasn't a generic report from a faceless G-2 officer. This was Will's Annie. The woman who didn't miss. She had found them.

If she was risking treason to send this, it was real. Annie's words—*Batteries Registered on Exits*—locked him in place.

He looked at the tangled streets of Torbole. It wasn't a grid; it was a maze. Suddenly, the map of Italy blurred, overlaid by the memory of a rain-soaked trench in 1918. He saw the face of his old friend Lieutenant Dubois pointing to a hidden depression in a field of fire.

A trail for a rider who knows when to disappear, the Frenchman had said. *A ghost path.*

Hays realized then that the "ghost path" wasn't always a safer route through the battle. Sometimes, it was the eye of the storm.

Cassino had taught him that doctrine without humanity was slaughter; Cisterna had taught Darby that ambition without caution was suicide.

Lake Garda would demand something else entirely—a third path, the one that lay between.

If they retreated, they walked into Kesselring's maw. To live, his men had to do the one thing the German artillery computers couldn't calculate. They had to hunker down inside the trap, hugging the enemy so tight the big guns couldn't fire.

He decided, finally and absolutely, to trust his men, not the doctrine.

"No," Hays whispered, the realization hitting him with a force.

"That's exactly what Kesselring wants."

He handed the dispatch to Will.

"Look. She says the artillery is aiming at the road in and out. The Panzers aren't there to retake the town. They're there to flush us out. If we retreat we walk right into the barrage she's warning us about."

Will stared at the paper from his beautiful Annie, and for one dizzy second, the burning town map vanished. All he saw was her name on the message. She had risked everything to send this. She was reaching across the continent to stop him from making the same mistake twice.

The chaotic map suddenly resolved into a simple, deadly current. "Coste," Will whispered, the name rising unbidden.

Hays looked at him, a fierce pride burning in his eyes. "Exactly."

"The only safe place..." Will said.

"...is to tread water inside the trap," Hays finished, his voice hardening into absolute certainty.

He closed his eyes and listened... to the still voice within him. When he opened them, he crushed the dispatch and grabbed the handset from his stunned radio operator.

"Done," Hays barked.

"Request approved. Delay the withdrawal. Hold your ground. The exit is the kill zone. You are safest where you are. Hug the enemy. Help is on the way. But if that perimeter breaks..."

"It won't break, sir," Colonel Hampton replied.

"Then give them hell," Hays ordered.

Hays turned to Colonel Johnston, his mind racing two moves ahead. "But we can't tread water forever. If Kesselring has batteries in the mountains targeting the road, we have to go get them."

He pointed to the rock faces looming above the town of Torbole on the map.

"Tell Colonel Hampton. Tell him to send the remnants of Company I—the men who just got pushed back—tell them to scale those cliffs tonight and silence those guns. It's Riva Ridge all over again. We clear the heights, we break the trap."

"Yes, sir," Johnston replied, relaying the order.

Will grabbed his helmet and a rifle. He thought of the vertical rise he had always coveted. He remembered Hays's warning about the fall. Now, he was being offered one last chance. No more lifts. Just the ground beneath his boots, and a walk into the dark to stand and serve with his men.

He finally understood Annie's story. It wasn't a climb to glory; it was a trail toward redemption.

"I'm not staying here," he said, his voice quiet, resolved. "I'm going up there."

Will reached into his map case and pulled out the small, brittle sprig of dried purple heather, the trophy of a kingship he no longer wanted.

He walked to the edge of the square, where a statue in a dry stone fountain stood amidst the rubble. He held his hand over the basin. With a single, deliberate motion, he opened his hand and let it fall. "The King is dead," he whispered to the dust. "Long live the man."

It fluttered down into the dust, the trophy of a reign that

never happened. He didn't need the rock. He was ready to carry the shards. There'd be no headline in this. No Gela, no Salerno—just exhausted men in the dark and the hope that with his help, a few more of them would make it home.

67

THE SERVANT

0040 HOURS, APRIL 30, 1945

Exit of Tunnel #6

The road between the tunnel mouth and the town was a bottleneck of terror.

A supply jeep, its driver panicked by the roar of the Panzers ahead, had tried to turn around on the narrow lakeside track. It was stuck, blocking the only artery to the front. Behind it, a queue of ammo carriers and reinforcements was stalled, creating a chaotic jam.

Men were shouting. Some were throwing down their crates, ready to flee back into the safety of the tunnel.

"Panzer!" a corporal screamed. "Turn it around! Go!"

The lifeline to the men in the square was severed by fear.

Colonel Will Darby stepped out of the darkness.

He didn't run to the front to find glory. He ran to the friction.

He grabbed the bumper of the stalled jeep. He didn't yell at the terrified driver. He looked at the men frozen in the jam —engineers, supply clerks, replacements.

"This jeep moves," Will said, his voice calm, cutting through the panic. "Or the men in town die. Lift."

He didn't order them to lift. He bent his knees, grabbed the steel fender, and heaved.

The sight of a full colonel straining against the weight snapped the men out of it. Three soldiers jumped forward. Together, they physically bounced the heavy vehicle clear of the road.

The artery was open. But the flow had stopped. The men were still running backward, toward safety.

Will saw a crate of bazooka rockets sitting in the mud, abandoned. He knew what was happening up ahead. He knew what a Panzer sounded like when it faced light opposition.

He walked over and picked up the crate. It was heavy, a dead weight of steel and explosives.

"We're taking this to the line," Will said, hoisting it onto his shoulder. He looked at the supply sergeant. "Who's coming with me?"

He started walking toward the sounds of the battle. He didn't look back.

For a moment, no one moved. Then, the sergeant grabbed a crate of rifle ammo. A private grabbed a box of rifle grenades.

Will led them up the road. He stopped at the casualty collection point, just outside the kill zone, where the runners from the line were screaming for ammo.

He dropped the crate at the feet of a runner from Company K.

"Fresh rockets," Will said, wiping sweat from his eyes. "Get them to the Bazooka teams."

"Who... who are you, sir?" the runner gasped, grabbing the rockets.

"Just the delivery service," Will said. "Go."

He watched the runner sprint into the darkness of the town. He heard the *crump* of a grenade, the roar of a BAR.

The old Will Darby would have followed that runner. He would have wanted to pull the trigger.

But the new Will Darby turned around. He went back to the tunnel exit. He grabbed another crate. He organized the flow. He calmed the wounded coming back.

He spent the night in the shadows, doing the heavy lifting, ensuring the men in the square had the tools to win their own victory.

He just wanted to be their foundation, not their spire.

68

THE TANK HUNTERS

0115 HOURS, APRIL 30, 1945

Torbole Town Square

The square was a roaring, flashing hell of tank and machine gun fire. Johnnie Grey and his squad were pinned behind the stone fountain, rifle rounds sparking off the stone while the crack-boom of the Panzers deafened them. Above, the shredded branches of the pine tree showered the men with a rain of needles, providing a thin, dusty screen against the enemy optics.

"We've got nothing!" Luby yelled, firing his BAR at the German infantry. "We're dead!"

"Not yet!" Johnnie roared. "Look! On the water!"

Through the smoke, the rhythmic splash of oars cut through the mechanical roar. A wooden rowboat heavy with men from Company K surged across the gap from the jetty. The men had bypassed the blocked road by water, rowing like madmen while the lake mist shielded them. The boat hit the quay with a jar, and the men tumbled out.

"It's Company K!" Luby screamed.

The lead private from Company K didn't just run; he slid. He hit the cobblestones hard, hooking his leg and sliding into the square like he was stealing second base. He came to a stop in a cloud of dust, directly in the path of the steel monster.

The Panzer was accelerating on the left, driving straight for the fountain—straight for them. The main gun lowered, the black muzzle growing larger by the second. The massive steel prow rose and fell as it hit a heave in the road, tilting the hull back just enough to expose the grease-dark seam at the turret base.

The kid from Company K leveled his weapon right at its face.

FWOOSH.

The rocket streaked across the dark, a razor-thin line of smoke meeting the charging hull. The rocket slammed into the turret base with a flash of white-hot light as the copper jet of the shaped charge sliced through the turret gears.

The Panzer shuddered as if it had hit a brick wall, its tracks locking up and skidding to a halt just yards from the fountain.

A second Panzer was grinding from the right, its machine gun traversing. A squad of German infantry used its bulk for cover, advancing in its wake.

"Bazooka! Up right!" a corporal screamed, but the response was cut short by a jagged burst of machine-gun fire. The loader crumpled, his shoulder a spray of red, as his teammate lunged forward to drag him behind the iron sanctuary of the first tank's carcass. Pinned behind the wreck, they had no angle on the second Panzer.

"Luby! Strip the infantry!" Johnnie ordered. "Stop them!"

Luby shifted his aim, skimming the BAR's fire along the

steel flanks of the Panzer. The heavy *thunk-thunk-thunk* became a metronome of suppression, shredding the air around the soldiers huddled in the tank's wake. The infantry froze and dove for the nearest doorways, leaving the tank isolated and blind.

"Mineo! The flanks!"

Mineo's Garand cracked with surgical rhythm, picking off the exposures—a helmet in a window, a runner trying to cross the street.

The tank, buttoned up and stripped of its eyes, hesitated as it squeezed under the stone archway of the Hotel Geier's carport. Johnnie looked at the raw wound on the second floor, then the central support pillar, which was shivering and cracked from the previous shelling.

"Mineo! Get down, now!" Johnnie yelled as he ripped a rifle grenade from his belt and aimed.

He didn't need to destroy it. He only needed to finish it. He sighted the stressed support pillar and squeezed the trigger.

THUMP-CRACK.

The explosion was a sharp, focused hammer-blow that snapped the weakened stone. With a slow, grinding groan of ancient mortar, the entire front face of the Hotel Geier's three-story carport buckled. Tons of limestone and timber cascaded down, burying the Panzer's engine deck and slamming onto the turret. The engine let out a strangled wheeze as the air intakes choked with debris.

"Finish it!" Johnnie roared, flagging the bazooka team out from the carcass of the first tank.

A private stepped out into the open and slid a white phosphorus rocket into the tube.

WHOOSH.

The 'Willy Pete' blossomed into a spray of chemical fire that poured into the tank's damaged ventilation. Inside the 25-ton Panzer, the darkness was suddenly replaced by a blinding, unquenchable light.

By 0200, the elite German paratroopers had retreated.

A profound, eerie stillness descended on the square—a vacuum of silence shattered only by the cries of the wounded.

Johnnie Grey slumped against the fountain, his hands shaking so hard he could barely reload his rifle. He looked up at the ruins of the Hotel Geier.

In a jagged hole on the third floor, a shadow moved.

Johnnie's instinct snapped. He jerked his rifle up, his finger tightening on the trigger, hunting for the shape of a German helmet.

He froze. It wasn't a soldier.

A small, pale face peered out from the masonry. It was a boy, no older than ten, his eyes wide in the gloom. The child hesitated, then raised a trembling hand and waved.

Johnnie let out a breath that felt like it had been trapped in his chest for hours. He slowly lowered the barrel of the M1. He didn't smile—he didn't have the energy—but he touched two fingers to his helmet brim in a short, weary salute.

It was the same soft, knowing salute Mr. Sandford had given him every morning at the bus stop—a silent language of survival shared by his father's generation, now passed to a child who had lived through his own storm.

The boy waved back, his voice drifting down, small and clear in the sudden quiet.

"*Grazie!*"

Johnnie nodded and whispered "*Prego,*" letting his head fall back against the cold stone of the fountain.

The Germans were gone.

The 10th had won.

69

THE LAST SHOT

0700 HOURS, APRIL 30, 1945

Torbole, Italy

At 0700 hours, victory was a ragged, gasping breath in the new morning light. The town square of Torbole was a wreck. The buildings were missing jagged chunks of masonry, and the streets were choked with debris.

Tech Sergeant Johnnie Grey sat with his back against the fountain, his rifle across his knees. He was caked in filth from the tunnels, his ears still ringing, his body one solid, screaming ache.

A jeep, its engine grinding, rumbled into the square and skidded to a halt. Major General Hays got out. He was followed by his ADC, Colonel Will Darby.

Hays, his exhaustion palpable, walked into the center of the town. His eyes scanned the destruction. He saw Grey, recognizing the NCO who had led the "straight run" on Belvedere.

"Tech Sergeant Grey, well done," Hays said, his voice a low rumble.

Grey pushed himself to his feet, snapping a weary but correct salute. "General."

"This is my ADC, Colonel Darby," Hays said, gesturing to the man beside him.

Johnnie's head snapped toward the colonel, his eyes narrowing. The name felt like a fresh wound.

Will, seeing the younger soldier's grief-stricken reaction, lost his command stiffness. "Sergeant?" Will asked, his voice quiet.

"Sorry, sir," Johnnie said, his voice thick. "It's just... my best friend. From home. Lake Placid. His name was Edgar Darby. A West Point man, too."

Johnnie swallowed, the loss of his friend hitting him again. "We... we lost him at the Bulge, sir."

A profound, shared understanding passed between the two men. Will looked at Hays, then back at Johnnie—a soldier who had lost his best friend, just as Will had lost his Rangers.

"There were a lot of good men lost at the Bulge, sergeant," Will said, his voice raw. "I'm sorry for your friend."

Johnnie nodded, seeing not a colonel, but the eyes of a man who profoundly understood. "Thank you, Sir. He... he always said he'd 'see me at the top.'"

Will's eyes held his. "Looks like you made it, sergeant."

Will leaned back against the grille of the jeep, the adrenaline fading, replaced by a heavy, pleasant fatigue. He looked around the ruined square, at the dust motes dancing in the shafts of morning light cutting through the smoke.

"You ever taste anything this good, sergeant?" Will asked, wiping a smudge of grit from his lip.

Johnnie looked at him, confused, tasting only limestone and cordite. "The dust, sir?"

"The quiet," Will said, closing his eyes for a second, tilting his face toward the sun warming the cobblestones.

He opened his eyes and looked past the smoking rubble. The late afternoon sun hit the wisteria vines draped over the ruined wall of the Hotel Geier, illuminating the purple clusters that hung like grapes, miraculously untouched by the shrapnel.

Beyond them, the lake was a deep, bruised indigo. The beauty of it was like a fresh breath; the air smelled not of war, but of the wisteria and the lake water—a scent of peace that felt like a violation amidst the ruins.

"It tastes like... Sunday morning. No maps. No radio static. Just... morning."

His eyes were a brilliant, startling blue against the grime of his face. He smiled—not a conqueror's grin, but a boy's smile, light and unburdened.

"It's a beautiful day to be alive, Johnnie."

Hays nodded, letting the two soldiers have their moment, before turning his attention back to his aide.

A second jeep rumbled into the square. "General Hays! Colonel Darby!" A brigadier general got out, followed by a tough-looking sergeant major. "That's General Ruffner, Div Artillery," Hays said. "And Sergeant Major Evans of the 86th. They're here to coordinate the final push into the Town of Riva."

Evans stepped forward, a wide grin of respect on his tough face, and clapped Darby on the shoulder. "Colonel Darby, that was one hell of a plan with those DUKWs, sir."

Will offered a tired, grateful smile. "You fought all the

way from Belvedere, sergeant major. I just got to stand on your shoulders—the shoulders of giants."

The four men—Hays, Darby, Ruffner, and Evans—huddled over a map on the hood of the jeep. Johnnie Grey watched from the fountain.

Colonel Darby stood in the center of the chaos, his face streaked with sweat, but his eyes... his eyes were clear. The haunted, hollow look from the Pentagon was gone. His DUKW plan had worked. It had shattered the German line. It had saved the engineers from a suicide mission.

Hays walked over to him and put a heavy hand on Will's shoulder. "Nicely done, Will," Hays said, his voice rough with pride and exhaustion. "You saw the path forward."

Will looked at his mentor, his general. He didn't smile. He just nodded, a single, sharp motion of profound, unburdened relief. He had become the man Annie had challenged him to be.

"We—" Will started to say.

He never finished the word. The square had been quiet for hours, the battle seemingly over. It was a silence that invited safety. From across the lake, from the shadows of Riva del Garda, a distant, hidden 88 fired. The last shot—a ghost of the Gothic Line—soared across the water.

There was no scream. There was no tearing whistle. The shell was supersonic, outracing its own noise. It arrived just as the climbers on Riva Ridge had arrived: in total, absolute silence.

"INCOMING!" Hays, the "Rock of the Marne," bellowed from pure, thirty-year-old instinct as he saw the muzzle flash on the distant shore.

The death was already there before the air could warn them. The final CRACK of the explosion arrived at the same instant. The world dissolved into white light, unbearable sound, and the percussive, suffocating blast of stone and smoke.

An eerie stillness fell.

Johnnie Grey pushed himself up, his ears bleeding, his vision swimming. He looked across the square. General Hays was on his knees, stunned, covered in dust, but alive.

Hays looked at the men who had been standing next to him. Sergeant Major Evans lay on his back, still. He was gone, killed instantly.

But Colonel Darby was moving. He was on his feet, swaying, a hand pressed to his chest. His face was drained of all color, a mask of shock, but he was standing.

"I'm... I'm all right, general," Will gasped, though his voice was thin, wet. He took a step toward the command post, a commandeered hotel lobby just off the square. "Just... need to sit down."

Hays scrambled to him, wrapping an arm around his waist. He felt the hot, slick wetness on Will's tunic. It wasn't just a scratch.

"Medic!" Hays roared. "Get him inside! Now!"

They got him into the lobby, away from the dust and the noise. They laid him on a table. A medic was there instantly, cutting away the tunic.

It was a single piece of shrapnel. A small, dark hole. But the damage was done.

Will survived for five minutes.

He did not spend them screaming. He spent them looking at his general, his friend. The pain was there, etching lines into his face, but his eyes were clear. The "King" was gone. For the man who remained, the world was falling away, leaving only the essentials.

As the medic tried frantically to save him, Will reached out. His hand, cold and trembling, found Hays's.

"General..." Will whispered, his breath coming in shallow, ragged hitches. "The Pass... did we... close the gate?"

Hays leaned in close, his voice thick with tears. "We closed it, Will. The line is cut. They're trapped."

A look of profound, settling peace washed over Will's face. The tension he had carried since Cisterna finally left his body.

"The clock stops...," Will breathed, a faint smile touching his lips. "The boys in camps... we bought them time..."

He struggled for air, his chest rising with a terrible, rattling effort. He squeezed Hays's hand one last time.

"Tell Annie... I kept... not crown... I went... for them..."

He paused, gathering the last of his strength, his mind drifting back to a rainy morning in London.

"...Tell her... I love her *more*."

"I'll tell her, Will," Hays promised, gripping him tight. "I'll tell her."

"Home," Will sighed.

The breath left him in a long, final release. The chest did not rise again.

The medic checked for a pulse, waited a long moment, then looked up, his eyes sad. "He's gone, Sir."

Hays reached out and gently closed Will's eyes.

He stood there for a long time, his hand resting on the shoulder of the bravest man he had ever known. Hays straightened, wiping the dust and tears from his face. He turned to leave the lobby.

Standing in the doorway, covered in the filth of the tunnels, was Tech Sergeant Johnnie Grey. He had witnessed it all.

Hays stopped. The memory of the "ghost" he had seen on the road to the Po Valley returned, colliding with the comment Johnnie had made earlier in the square about Lake Placid.

He had to know.

"Sergeant," Hays said, his voice rasping with grief.

"Sir?"

"You mentioned Lake Placid earlier," Hays said, searching the younger man's face. "Your father... did he serve? In the Great War?"

Johnnie straightened, surprised by the question. "Yes, Sir. He was at the Marne."

Hays felt a chill that had nothing to do with the mountain air. "Do you know his unit, son?"

"The 28th, sir," Johnnie replied quietly. "He was a replacement, the Keystone Division. But... he didn't talk about it much. The gas got him. He died when I was a boy."

The air in the Italian square suddenly vanished. The smell of wisteria and lake water was replaced by the stinging, garlic-rot stench of mustard gas.

Hays wasn't looking at a sergeant in 1945. He was looking into the eyes of a Private in 1918—eyes that were terrified, burning, and yet utterly selfless as he handed over the reins of a Morgan horse.

Take him, sir. You have to hold the line.

The ghost wasn't haunting him anymore. The ghost had sent his son to finish the job.

Hays closed his eyes for a brief second. The 28th. The Adirondacks. The gas.

It was him. The debt had not been forgotten; it had just been waiting for this moment.

The general looked at the sergeant. He saw the father

who had given him a horse to save the line, and the son who had broken through on Belvedere to save the division.

"He would be so proud of you, sergeant," Hays whispered, his voice thick with emotion. "I know I am."

Hays stood tall, pulled his shoulders back, and raised his hand in a slow, deliberate salute.

It was not a salute to a subordinate. It was a salute to a savior.

Johnnie Grey, his eyes shining, returned it.

Hays nodded once, then walked out into the light of the square.

Later that night, the command post had been moved to a villa overlooking the lake. The sounds of battle had faded, replaced by the rhythmic lap of water against the stone quay. Hays sat alone at a desk, a single lamp illuminating the map of Northern Italy.

The war was ending. He could feel it in the stillness. But the silence in the room felt heavy, a physical weight pressing against his chest.

A knock at the door broke his reverie.

"Enter," Hays said, his voice a low rasp.

A lieutenant stepped in, his face pale in the lamplight. He held a clipboard.

"Sir, a report on the crossing to Riva Del Garda—one of the DUKW's went down... it was the storm, sir. It whipped up out of nowhere. We saw a flash of lightning illuminate the boat... it was heavily loaded with men and artillery. It was listing, taking on water over the gunwales. When the next flash came, the boat was gone. Twenty-four men, sir. Swallowed by the lake. The other boats made it. The Germans in Riva Del Garda have fled or surrendered."

Hays closed his eyes for a long moment. Twenty-four more of his men. Twenty-four more families broken on the very last day.

"Get me a list of the men, Lieutenant," Hays said softly, the grief a fresh, heavy stone in his chest.

With the Brenner Pass secured, the last major supply artery for the German war machine in Italy—including its critical fuel pipeline—was severed. All remaining Axis formations south of the Alps were now trapped.

With no fuel, no supplies, and no routes left for retreat, the estimated one million Axis soldiers and personnel in Italy had two choices: ditch their weapons and surrender in place, or be annihilated in pockets. They chose the former, and Italy's war ended on 2 May.

After 114 days of continuous battle, the fight was over. The 'Rock' had held, the 'Ranger' had found his peace, and for the mountain soldiers who survived them both, Italy was finally free.

70

THE EMISSARY

MAY 2, 1945

Caserta, Italy

Major General George P. Hays stood in a grand, vaulted hall in the Royal Palace at Caserta, the Allied Force Headquarters. The air was cool and still, smelling of polished antique wood and old tapestries, a world away from the cordite and filth of the front.

It was Hays's greatest victory. The culmination of his long, lonely climb.

But the victory was sour. His mind was not in this grand hall, accepting the congratulations of staff officers. His mind was in the shattered, smoking piazza in Torbole, kneeling in the dust, his hand over the small, dark hole in Will Darby's chest.

His war was won. His man, and so many of his men, were lost.

An aide, his uniform impossibly clean, approached, his

footsteps echoing on the marble. "General Hays, sir. They are ready for you. General Von Senger is waiting."

"Thank you, Captain," Hays said, his voice a low, empty rumble.

It was his final duty. As the commanding general of the division that had broken the line, he had been given the formal, symbolic task of delivering the German emissary to the signing table.

He thought of Will. A man who had so desperately tried to be a king, who chased the glory all the way to his ruin at Cisterna. And yet, in the end, he had returned. He had chosen the other path. He had died as a servant, saving his men. That, Hays thought, was the only true kingship.

He walked alone down a long, echoing corridor.

At the far end, two American MPs stood guard outside a set of tall, ornate doors. Standing between them was Lieutenant General Fridolin Von Senger und Etterlin and his staff.

Hays slowed his pace, his eyes narrowing as he took in the enemy. He had expected field grey, the high collars, the iron crosses—the armor of the Wehrmacht.

Instead, the German officers were in civilian clothes, their uniforms removed by the victors. In the ill-fitting suits and shirts, they looked smaller, almost impotent—a look that belied the carnage they had inflicted, the utter havoc they had initiated against the world.

If they were monsters, they had left their claws in the uniform. Here, standing in the light of day, they looked unremarkable—middle-aged, pale, anxious—like bureaucrats caught in the wrong government line. It was a terrifying banality—evil stripped of its rank, revealing only diminished, defeated men standing in a hallway.

As Hays approached, the MPs came to attention. Von Senger looked up. Despite the civilian attire, his posture was rigid, his face pale but pressed and severe. He was defeated, but he was not broken. He was a professional, clinging to the last shreds of his dignity.

Hays looked at him and thought of Will Darby lying in the dust of Torbole. Will had died in a dirty uniform, but he had looked like a giant. This man stood here in a clean starched suit, alive and arrogant, and yet he looked hollow.

Hays knew the man's G-2 dossier. Fridolin Von Senger und Etterlin. A Rhodes Scholar. A lay Benedictine monk who reportedly despised Hitler and the Nazis.

And yet, here he was.

He wasn't a fanatic; he was something perhaps worse. He was a man who knew better, a man of faith and culture who had nonetheless used his brilliance to hold the Cassino line and prolong a genocidal war for two bloody years. He was the ultimate proof that "duty" without morality was just a fancy word for complicity.

Hays gave a single, curt nod. "General."

Von Senger met his gaze, offering a nod of his own. "General."

The MPs opened the doors. The two men, victor and vanquished, began the long, silent walk through the antechamber toward the surrender hall.

Von Senger, his voice quiet, spoke not as a prisoner, but as a colleague. "I must congratulate you, general," he said, his German-accented English precise. "You have a very fine division."

Hays kept his eyes forward, his face a mask of stone. He said nothing.

"I have commanded troops on all fronts," Von Senger continued, as if discussing a map. "Russia, France... and here. Yours was the best division I have ever encountered. You completely destroyed five of my divisions. Five. They were no longer effective combat units."

The words landed. This was the validation. The proof. They'll call them what they like, Hays thought. D-Day Dodgers.

We know what they did here.

He inclined his head in the barest of nods.

"My men did their duty," he said. "That's all."

It was the respect his men had earned, the prize at the end of the climb. It should have felt like triumph. It felt like nothing.

He wondered what Julia would make of a German general praising his division. She'd probably just tell him the staircase had led exactly where it was meant to: to the boys who needed him most.

"Your division broke completely through two of my Panzer Corps," Von Senger said, permitting himself a small, bitter smile. "You forced me personally and my staff to jump from our tanks and swim the Po River."

He paused, then added, "Field Marshal Kesselring has already sent his assessment to Berlin. He characterized your division as 'highly efficient.' It is a German understatement, general. By seizing the peaks, you pierced the defensive structure between the Panaro and Reno Valleys. You forced us to commit the 29th Panzer Grenadier Division—our last strategic reserve—into a fight we could not win."

Hays stopped, his feet echoing in the great hall, one yard from the final door.

He turned and looked at the man. He saw the truth of it in his enemy's face.

He realized then the true scale of what his men had achieved in the dark on Riva Ridge and Belvedere. They hadn't just taken a cliff or a mountain range; they had cracked the hinge of the entire Gothic Line. They had opened the gate to the Alps.

They had won, absolutely.

But the victory offered no comfort. It didn't change the image of Will in the dust. It didn't silence the ringing in his ears. It was just... a fact.

"Thank you, general," Hays said. His voice was flat, hollow.

He turned and, with the MP, escorted the German emissary into the hall to sign the unconditional surrender. It was 1840 hours. He stood alone afterward, watching the German delegation being led away. The Allies had won.

He thought of the risks—the night climbs, the unloaded rifles, the open boats on the lake. "We always fought with an exposed flank, sometimes three," he whispered to the empty hall.

"The good Lord had guided us by His hand."

Later that night, Hays walked alone to the grand window of the palace, looking north toward the mountains. The sun was setting on the first day of the new world. Somewhere, the Army's printing presses were already humming, churning out a special edition of *The Stars and Stripes*.

He pictured his valiant men—thousands of them scattered across the valleys and ridges—waking up to the first morning where the only thing falling from the sky would be the truth.

His second Great War was over.

71

THE LAKE

MAY 3, 1945

Lake Garda, Italy

The way the mountains ran down to the shore reminded Johnnie of his home in Lake Placid. He sat for a long time, his gaze fixed on the shimmering expanse. The breeze moved through the grass. He clasped the cross Ellie had given him, its chain still resting against his throat, letting it swing gently between his fingers. He let himself hear her laughter again and felt the ghost-warmth of her embrace.

In the silence of the morning, looking across the water, he finally understood what had carried him. The cross at his throat. Ellie's love. The faith she'd pressed into his hands as surely as the metal itself. Not charms. Not luck. Trail marks —the only signs he could follow through Belvedere's fire and the tunnels' dark, when every map he knew went blank.

He thought of his father. He didn't have many memories of the man—just the faint recollection of a voice teaching him to sand a piece of ash wood. Most of the rest had come from Mr. Sandford on the porch: how his father had given up his horse—his only ticket out of the mustard gas—to an officer so the line could hold.

His father had come home, but the war had followed him in his lungs, stealing his breath and his voice until there was nothing left. He had sacrificed his future so others could have one.

Johnnie made a promise then, watching the ripples fade. He would not let that sacrifice be the end of the story.

The easy way was to let the grief hollow him out, to let the war finish what it started with his father. The hard way was to take this life he had been given—this second chance his father never got—and live it fully.

He would go home alive. He would go home with stories. The war would not be a ghost that haunted his house; it would be the ground he stood on to build something new. He would live the long, full life the gas had stolen from his father.

A low, heavy drone vibrated through the soles of his boots. Johnnie looked up, shielding his eyes against the glare. High above the lake, a lone B-17 Flying Fortress banked lazily over the Alps. Its bomb bay doors yawned open. Johnnie flinched, instinctively grabbing for his rifle, but no iron bombs fell.

Instead, a shimmering white cloud was released into the slipstream, fluttering down like a winter snowstorm. It was paper. Thousands of leaflets drifted onto the lakeshore, spiraling in the updrafts to coat the water and the grass. One landed next to his hand. Johnnie picked it up.

It wasn't a warning; it was a newspaper, a special air-drop edition of *The Stars and Stripes*. The ink was still dark and fresh. He read the banner headline, his breath catching in his throat:

NAZI ARMIES IN ITALY SURRENDER

His eyes welled up with joy. It was over.

He pushed himself up, his legs holding. He slung his rifle.

His fingers found the familiar, smooth sphere in his pocket, wrapped in its tattered cloth. He unwrapped his "silver bullet"—the polished steel bearing from his slingshot—from its pouch.

It had served its purpose. It had kept him and his family alive. He thanked his dad for having the foresight to help him build the slingshot—a small tool that had carried them through the leanest years of the Depression.

He thought about his childhood friend Edgar Darby. He thought about how much they all had lost. He weighed the cold sphere in his hand—a symbol of a life that felt a million miles away.

"See you up top," he whispered, the words ragged, torn from his throat.

He skipped the silver sphere like a stone into the lake, retiring it, thanking it for helping him put food on the table. He would never use it to kill again. He watched the ripples spread outward, disturbing the perfect reflection of the mountains.

The fighting here was done. He didn't know yet how long the Army would keep him, or what oceans he might still have to cross. But he knew one thing for certain.

He had survived the fire. He would go home to survive the peace.

72

THE LIBERATION

APRIL 28, 1945

Westertimke, Germany

The guards were gone. They had vanished in the night like smoke, leaving the gates of the camp wide open.

But the men didn't run. They couldn't. They huddled in the barracks, listening to the ground shake. It wasn't the sharp crack of artillery this time. It was a heavy, mechanical grinding. Steel on pavement.

Jimmy Tolliver dragged himself to the window. He was too weak to stand, so he pulled himself up by the sill. He ran a hand over his jaw. It was smooth. Even in the freezing barns, even when they had no bread, the sergeant had made them shave with cold water and sharpened steel. We are Rangers, he had said.

We are still Rangers.

A tank rounded the corner of the wire. It wasn't a Panzer. It was square, ugly, and green.

A British Comet.

The hatch popped open. A man in a black beret poked his head out, looking at the scarecrows crowding the doorways. He saw men in rags, but he saw men who were standing, men who had shaved that morning despite the hell they were in.

The tanker didn't raise a weapon. He reached into his tunic and tossed a handful of chocolate bars onto the ground.

"Alright, mates?" the Brit shouted, his voice casual, as if he were asking about the weather. "War's over for you lot. Who's hungry?"

Jimmy slid down the wall until he hit the floor.

He put his head in his hands. He tried to say "thank you," he tried to cheer, but nothing came out.

He just sat there on the rough floorboards, amidst the lice and the filth, and wept.

They had made it.

73

THE LETTERS

MAY 3, 1945

Caserta, Italy

He sat at a broad oak desk, the grand, silent room at Caserta a stark contrast to the shattered piazza in Torbole. To his left lay a copy of *The Stars and Stripes*, just delivered by courier.

The headline screamed in massive, bold type:

NAZI ARMIES IN ITALY SURRENDER

He looked at the date on the newspaper: May 2, 1945.

He closed his eyes, picturing the lakeshore he had left behind. He imagined the papers tumbling out of the sky against the cliffs, the boys of the 10th finally holding the proof in their hands.

The victory was total.

It lay inches away from the casualty report he had just filled out for Colonel William Darby.

The peace had arrived exactly forty-eight hours too late.

An aide knocked softly on the heavy oak door.

"General? A communique from SHAEF. Just came over the wire."

Hays took the slip of paper. It was short.

Adolf Hitler. Suicide. Berlin Bunker. April 30.

Hays stared at the date. April 30.

The same day Will had stood in the sun at Torbole.

Hays looked at the two reports side-by-side. The Architect of the war had died hiding in a hole, putting a pistol in his mouth to escape the consequences of his ambition. He had died a coward, pulling the world down on top of his head.

And at the exact same hour, Will Darby—a man who had conquered his own ambition—had died standing in the open, after organizing a supply line, and helping to save his men.

The world would remember the date for the monster who died in the dark. Hays would remember it for the man who died in the light.

He crumpled the Hitler communique and dropped it into the wastebasket. It didn't belong on the same desk as Will.

He had two letters to write. One was an agonizing duty. The other, a debt to the past. He picked up his pen and began the first, his heart aching.

My dearest Annie,

It is with the heaviest heart I must inform you...

He wrote of Will's end, of his last words. He wrote of the man who had returned to the front, of the brilliant

DUKW plan that had saved his engineers from a suicide mission, and of the calm courage he had found in the tunnel.

He paused, looking at the ink glistening on the page. He thought of the defeated German general he had just seen—a man of brilliance who had served a monster for the sake of prestige.

And he thought of Will, who had nearly been consumed by a hunger for a crown, but who had broken free.

He dipped his pen again, the realization crystallizing in his mind.

I have been thinking about the nature of this war, Annie. There are those who get more than they give. And then there are men like Will, who gave more than they got—tenfold.

I know he carried a heavy weight these last months. But he did not let it crush him. He found the strength to stand back up because he wasn't just fighting the enemy; he was fighting to save the living.

You gave him the hope that his Rangers were alive, Annie. You told him they were in the camps. That is part of the reason why he came back to us—to fight his way to them. But in these final months, as dark rumors of POW marches and starving columns drifted out of Germany, Will was terrified that he had run out of time.

He feared they were walking through the snow without food. He died fearing that the long winter of captivity would finish what the ditch at Cisterna started.

But there is one thing Will did not know, and I pray you find comfort in it. Intelligence reports are only now reaching us from the Allied lines in Germany. We have learned that of the 450 men captured at Cisterna, over 400 are still alive—the survivors of Stalag II-B were liberated by the British on April 28th, just two days before Will fell.

But Annie, you must understand—"liberation" was only the last page of a long ordeal. In January, driven by panic as the Russian lines broke in the East, the Germans drove them out at gunpoint. They endured what amounted to a "Black March," a long, deliberate act of desperate cruelty.

For three months, they were driven on foot—day after day, often twenty kilometers or more, six days a week. They slept in open fields and unheated barns while the cold fell far below freezing.

We now see that the enemy had no intention of freeing them; they were determined to keep them under guard. Many of our intelligence officers believe they were being held as hostages— human bargaining chips the Reich hoped to trade for its own survival.

Hays paused, his pen hovering over the inkwell. He looked to the corner of his desk, where *The Stars and Stripes* lay open.

It wasn't the victory headline that caught his eye now. It was the photograph below the fold.

It was a grainy, horrifying image from a place called Dachau, liberated just days ago by the 45th and 42nd Divisions. It showed a railcar filled not with soldiers, but with skeletons—the bodies of Jews and political prisoners stacked like cordwood, starved and discarded.

Hays felt a chill that had nothing to do with the drafty palace. He looked at the report on the Rangers—men who had been marched for three months on starvation rations.

He knew the moral abyss between them was vast: the victims in the railcar were innocents systematically targeted for erasure; the Rangers were soldiers held as pawns.

He thought of Kesselring and the prisoners killed in the caves at Ardeatine.

The enemy they had been fighting wasn't just holding ground; they were operating a machine of torture and annihilation. If the war had lasted another week, if the Axis had been allowed to retreat to the Alps and consolidate, the "expendable" mouths of the POWs—already nearly starved —might well have been the next lives that machine consumed.

Will hadn't just interrupted a retreat. He had helped to stop the machine.

Hays returned to the letter, writing with renewed conviction.

In the weeks before they were found, the men were skeletons, starving and exposed on the roads. The German guards had grown frightened and unpredictable; rumors ran through the columns that they would simply shoot the prisoners rather than let them be recovered if the war dragged on.

For three months, they had been in the kill zone. What kept them alive in the end was not mercy; it was the sudden collapse of the German command.

Will helped stop the heartbeat of the enemy. By breaking the line here, by cutting the Brenner Pass and stopping the retreat to the Alps, he denied the Germans the long war they wanted. He forced the surrender that stayed the executioners' hands.

If Will had been cautious—if he had taken even three more days to clear Lake Garda—I am convinced the war would have ground on, and that those whispered threats of execution might well have become reality.

I cannot prove it, but I know it in my bones. He didn't just buy them time, Annie. He bought them their lives—and he never knew it.

The problem is, it is not arithmetic—it is war—and there is no way to balance the equation, even for a single life lost. That is the burden we soldiers carry until the day we die.

Will carried it better than any man I ever knew, and in the end, he laid it down with honor. He died carrying a second tablet up the mountain. He died serving the men. And that is how I will remember him.

Hays paused again. He thought of his own darkness from the Marne, and the book of hours Julia had pressed into his hand—a map that had guided him when the world went black. He realized then that Will hadn't found his way back alone. He had been guided.

He dipped the pen again.

I know he found that path because of you, Annie. Every soldier needs a map when the fighting stops, and the silence begins. My wife, Julia, gave me mine a lifetime ago. I believe you gave Will his. You didn't just love him; you anchored him. You saved the man, so the man could save the soldiers.

He sealed the envelope, his grief for the man he considered a son a heavy, cold weight in his chest.

His mind then turned back to the square. To the other man who had been there. Technical Sergeant Johnnie Grey.

Hays's mind snagged on two words. *Lake Placid.* He looked at Grey, truly seeing him. Grey. From the Adirondacks.

The memory hit him with the force of a shell. July 1918.

The Marne. He was in the mud, the air tasting of fear and wet horse. He remembered the feel of his first mount, Traveler—his great heart hammering against his legs—running with a desperate, terrified courage he was demanding to the last beat.

Then, the acrid smell of mustard gas. Then, when he lost his mount, the face of a brave young private—Grey—from the Adirondacks, pressing the reins of a horse into his hand.

Take him, sir. You have to hold the line.

The ghost wasn't haunting him anymore. The ghost had sent his son to finish the job.

Hays, the "Rock of the Marne," looked at his hands.

He had held the line in one war because a father named Grey had given him a horse. He had broken the line in this war because a son named Grey had shown him the way.

It was a mark left in the mud of France, followed twenty-seven years later in the snow of Italy.

He took a fresh sheet of paper. This was not a letter of condolence, but a letter of commendation, to be entered into the Technical Sergeant's permanent file.

He wrote of the "unconventional courage" and "brilliant tactical leadership" displayed at Belvedere.

He signed it, *George P. Hays, Major General.*

Then, he picked up his pen again and added a handwritten postscript at the bottom.

P.S. Technical Sergeant Grey, when this war ends, I would very much like to tell you your father's full story. Your father was the valiant Private Grey who gave me his horse—his only way out of the gas—so that I could ride for the guns. Because of your father, I made it to the guns. The line held. He saved my life,

Johnnie. And he saved thousands of others. I believe I owe your family a debt I can never repay.

Hays put down the pen.

For the first time in twenty-seven years, Hays's debt to Johnnie Grey's father felt, if not balanced, at least a little closer to level.

He sealed the second envelope. The past was not dead. It wasn't even past.

It would be a debt, finally honored.

74

THE BELLS

MAY 8, 1945

Charleston, South Carolina

On May 8th, the bells began to ring in Charleston. V-E Day. The war in Europe was over.

People poured from shops and homes, their faces a mixture of disbelief and dawning, explosive joy.

The Charleston Library Society was closed for the celebration. The main reading room was empty, the only sound the muffled, joyous roar from the street outside.

Julia Hays stood in the center of the room, surrounded by the quiet, orderly stacks. She felt a profound, bone-deep relief. The slaughter, the casualty lists... it was over.

But she felt no joy.

Her "war" wasn't finished. Her husband was still a world away. She had not had a letter from him since the final offensive had begun. The bells celebrated a victory, but her personal war was still being fought in the terrible, agonizing silence.

She walked to the window and watched the celebration

in the street, a witness, not a participant. Her victory was not here, in the ringing of bells. It was in the quiet, desperate hope that the man she loved would one day walk back through that library door.

She was still at her post, her face calm, waiting.

75

ANNIE

MAY 15, 1945

Spean Bridge, Scotland

In a small, stone cottage in the Scottish Highlands, Annie received the letter.

She was no longer 'Liaison Officer McKenna.' She was just Annie again.

The dismissal from the service had been quiet, cold, and absolute. There had been no court-martial—the intelligence service preferred silence to scandal. Instead, she had been stripped of her clearance, erased from the rolls of Bletchley Park, and sent home with a permanent mark on her file: *Insubordinate.*

It was the price of the 'FLASH' cable. She had traded her career to break the trap at Lake Garda. She had sacrificed her ascent to ensure the men on the ground didn't pay the ultimate price.

She had no regrets.

The letter bore an American general's return address.

She knew, the moment she felt the weight of the envelope, that Will was not coming back.

She walked to the small, silvered mirror hanging near the hearth. She looked at her reflection—the shadow of the girl who had assessed a Major in a pub three years ago.

With steady hands, she reached for the drawer and pulled out the yellow bow and carefully pinned it into her hair. She primped the edges, a small, defiant ritual for a man who wasn't there to see it. It was her way of lighting a lamp for him.

She didn't read it in the cottage. She couldn't let that news live within those walls. Instead, she took it, unopened, and stepped out into the Highland morning to begin the seven-mile trek toward Achnacarry.

She walked with a steady, unhurried pace, her boots on the same road that had once echoed with the rhythmic boots of the 1st Ranger Battalion. By the time she reached the entrance to the Mile Dorcha, her legs ached, but her mind was clear.

She stepped under the heavy canopy of ancient beeches and pines where the sunlight was instantly swallowed by the thickness of the moss and the arching branches.

When the dense woods gave way to the remote vista of Loch Arkaig, the light was almost blinding. The water was a dark, mirror-still expanse, reflecting the mountains. The air was cool and clean, carrying the scent of pine.

She sat on the large, flat rock and broke the seal. It was not a form letter from the War Department. It was a personal, handwritten note from Major General George P. Hays.

~

He wrote of the end—not the grand strategy, but the quiet truth of Will's final days.

He described the brilliant plan with the DUKWs, the way Will had saved the engineers from a suicide mission, and the calm courage he had shown in the tunnel.

And then, she read the words that stopped her breath.

"Will died hoping he had bought them time," Hays wrote. *"And he was right. Intelligence reports confirm that over 400 of the men captured at Cisterna are alive. They survived the camps. They are coming home."*

Annie lowered the letter, a sob catching in her throat.

He had done it. The information she had given him—the terrifying truth about the boxcars—hadn't crushed him. It had driven him. He had stopped the clock.

She forced herself to read on.

"He asked me to tell you that he kept the pact," the letter continued. *"He said: 'No headlines. I didn't go for the crown. I went for them.'"*

Then, at the bottom of the page, Hays delivered the final promise he had made in the dust of Torbole.

"And his very last words, Annie, were for you. He asked me to tell you: 'I love you more.'"

The tears came then, hot and fast, blurring the view of the Highlands.

The wind sighed through the oaks, a sound like a held breath finally released.

She thought of the two stories she'd given him—one about a ladder to the stars, a crown the world could see; the other about climbing back up the mountain and a second chance. Will had chosen the second. It cost him everything —but it saved his men.

She reached down and picked up a small sprig of purple heather—the "trophy" of glory.

She looked at it for a long moment. The King was dead, but the man—the man she loved—had found his way home. And because of him, hundreds of others would find their way home, too.

She opened her hand and let it fall.

It was caught by the wind and carried out over the loch, a small, purple ripple that was, finally, at peace.

It didn't matter that her name would never appear in a history book. It was enough that it had appeared at the bottom of one cable—and that the men had lived.

76

HOME
AUTUMN 1945

Charleston, South Carolina

General George P. Hays, his uniform sharp, his duty finally laid down, walked down the familiar, sun-dappled street in Charleston.

The air was thick with the sweet, heavy scent of jasmine and the salt of the harbor. He walked with the slight limp he'd carried since the Marne, a "Rock" now weathered by two World Wars.

He walked past the Hibernian Hall. He noted its proud, white columns, the site of so many cotillions, a symbol of a life and a social "staircase" he had once been expected to climb.

He did not stop. He did not pause. He kept walking.

His path did not end there.

He turned the corner and walked two blocks to the Charleston Library Society. He stood before its quiet, unassuming stone facade. This was the place.

This was the staircase he had been climbing his whole life.

He walked up the worn, stone steps, his hand on the wrought-iron rail. He opened the heavy oak doors.

The familiar, hallowed silence wrapped around him. The air smelled of old paper, leather, and lemon oil.

He walked past the stacks, past the "Books for Soldiers" posters, now faded and yellowed. He walked to the main reading room.

She was there.

Julia Hays sat at a long, oak table, her back to him, a book of medieval maps open before her, her mind a world away.

He stood, his heart hammering against his ribs. He was the soldier, the boy, the man who had run into the surf, the general who had come home.

He said one word, his voice rough. "Julia."

She froze. The book of maps was forgotten. She turned, her hand flying to her mouth. She saw him, not the general, but her Price Hays, his face older, his eyes weary, but home.

Her eyes, the ones that had guided him across an ocean of blood and fire, met his.

A slow, radiant, tear-filled smile spread across her face.

The general, his long, lonely climb finally at its end, had come home.

Weeks later, he sat with her in their library, helping Julia sort through the last of the book donations.

He had started this life on a horse running coordinates through France in the Great War, judging range by the height of a hedgerow. He had helped turn loose the greatest artillery barrage over Omaha Beach on D-Day, then stepped into its bloody wake on D+1. But in the Italian mountains, with a few dozen batteries and a climbing division, it felt almost human again.

He had his file open on the table, a small stack of papers from his command. "I came across this," he said quietly, pulling a carbon copy of a letter from the file. "I wrote it to a man in Chicago. A Mr. Douglas. To... well, to make sure the records were straight."

Julia took the thin paper. She began to read, her eyes widening as she scanned the lines.

"George," she breathed, looking up at him. "This... this praise. From General Von Senger himself? "'The best division I have ever encountered'?"

She read on, her voice filled with awe. "And this British officer? Lieutenant Colonel Freeth? He says he supported seventeen different British and American divisions during the war, but he wants to wear your patch. He's asking permission to identify his regiment with the 10th Mountain Division forever."

She looked up, her eyes shining. "And this... the DUKW operation in broad daylight at Lake Garda. Will's plan. You wrote it was 'one of the most daring operations I have ever witnessed.'"

She placed the letter on the table, her heart full. "My goodness. They... they must be the most celebrated division."

Hays was silent for a moment. He looked away from her, out the library window at the quiet street, his face hardening just slightly.

"They weren't," he said, his voice flat. "For all of that, the division was never awarded a citation." He remembered Will's fierce vow: *I'm not here for the headline.*

He gently took the letter from her, the official record of his men's valor, and placed it back in his file with a quiet finality. His boys had helped give the world a victory no one could ignore. He had fought for their recognition, and still, it had fallen short. He turned back to the box of books.

"The world might not know," he said. "But heaven already does."

AUTHOR'S NOTE

This novel is my humble tribute to the soldiers of the 10th Mountain Division and the U.S. Army Rangers. It is a story about the burden of command, the price of glory, and the courage it takes to find a new path when the old one has failed.

Above all, it is about the calculus of sacrifice: the willingness to trade one's own life to buy time for another.

It is a work of historical fiction, inspired by the parallel lives and converging destinies of two authentic American heroes: Major General George P. Hays and Colonel William O. Darby. While the personal conversations, private letters, and the thematic thread of the "Broken Tablet" have been imagined, the historical framework—and the astonishing bravery of the soldiers they led—is very real.

The story of General Hays is rooted in his Medal of Honor actions as a young lieutenant at the Second Battle of the Marne in 1918 and his later brilliance as a commander of artillery in Normandy and Italy.

The story of Colonel Darby is based on his legendary

founding of the 1st Ranger Battalion and his hard, costly campaigns in North Africa, Sicily, and Italy.

Their paths show two very different arcs of leadership. Hays, born in 1892, climbed the long, steady staircase of the professional soldier, receiving his first star as a brigadier general at forty-nine and going on to serve as the High Commissioner for Germany and Commander of U.S. Forces in Austria, eventually retiring as a three-star lieutenant general.

Darby, born in 1911, was a meteor. He was thirty-four when he was killed in action—the same age at which he was posthumously promoted to brigadier general.

It has been the deepest honor of my life to tell the stories of these most courageous men and women. I must admit that I felt guided by them throughout, because although they may be gone, they will forever be close to my heart.

The story isn't over. Turn the page to learn the true story behind the legends—and to meet the soldier who inspired these stories.

THE LETTER

Shortly after the campaign in Italy concluded, Major General George P. Hays wrote the following letter. It stands as a contemporary testament to the events depicted in this novel and to the extraordinary nature of the 10th Mountain Division's achievements.

HEADQUARTERS
10TH MOUNTAIN DIVISION
APO 345 U.S. ARMY
Italy, 14 May 1945

DEAR MR. DOUGLAS:

Now that I have a few minutes to spare during the whirlwind life we have all been leading since our jump of a month ago, I want to write you more fully of the operations of this Division to date. Have just re-read my short note to you of May twelfth which, on second reading, seems to be curt and ungracious which I assure you was unintentional. I thought you might like me to summarize what I consider to be the highlights of the operations of the Division, as follows:

I personally participated in the Battle of the Marne and the Meuse Argonne offensive in the last war; in the Battle for Cassino with the 34th Infantry Division–landing on Normandy on D plus 1 with the 2nd Infantry Division, the subsequent break through in Normandy, the attack of the fortress of Brest. Also witnessed part of the fight in the Anzio beachhead. As I have told my men, the battles of the 10th Mountain were as strongly contested and as bitter, and in many instances more intense than any I had experienced hitherto.

During our operations we were invariably opposed by the major elements of two or more German first rate divisions. We completely destroyed the five divisions, marked by an asterisk, as effective combat units. The German divisions which opposed us in various phases of our operations were, *232 Infantry Division, *114 Jaeger Division, *2nd Panzer Grenadier Division, *334 Infantry Division, *90 Panzer Division, *94 Infantry Division, 8th Mountain Division, 65th Infantry Division, and 305th Infantry Division. With their supporting troops my one division has been opposed at some time throughout the entire operations by approximately 100,000 German troops.

Lieutenant General Von Senger who commanded the 14th Panzer Corps (emissary whom I delivered to Fifth Army Headquarters in regard to the surrender), congratulated me on having a very fine division, the best he had encountered on all fronts (Russia, France, and Italy). He stated that my division broke completely through two German Panzer Corps and forced himself personally and his staff and many of his troops to swim the Po River on the same day that we crossed in assault boats.

The Commanding General of the 90th Panzer Division, on a statement to his troops, said that in their surrender they had the consolation of surrendering to a very worthy opponent, the 10th Mountain Division.

The Division has encountered and overcome every type of natural obstacle as follows: innumerable rugged mountains of the Apennines and Alps, Po and Adige Rivers, canal region of Po Valley and Lake Garda, also every type of artificial obstacle, to include the old walled city of Verona and pre-war frontier defenses of the Italian-Austrian border along Lake Garda; and one of the toughest positions I oversaw taken was four mutually supporting tunnels with precipitous mountain cliffs on the right and Lake Garda on the left. We took these tunnels by an amphibious movement of a company, in slow moving DUKWs, which captured them from the rear in one of the most daring operations I have ever witnessed.

During our entire operations our Division always had one flank exposed and during the last operation of April fourteenth on had both flanks and frequently our rear exposed. The Chief of Staff, of our IV Corps, stated to me that our crossing of the Po River was one for the record. I was attacking on my right and left flanks, defending my rear and crossing the Po River simultaneously.

As I told my troops, in a recent talk I gave them when the Germans surrendered, no one except those in the Division will ever believe them when they get back home and discuss the operations we have been through. We had a British Lieutenant Colonel Freeth commanding the 178th Lowland Artillery Medium attached to us. He told me that he had supported seventeen British and U.S. Divisions during the war; and that the 10th Mountain was outstanding in its aggressiveness and boldness in taking objectives. He is trying to get permission to identify his regimental insignia with the 10th Mountain Division so as to have lasting recognition for his support of our operations.

As you see from the above, I am very proud of the magnificent work of my gallant soldiers, and am happy that there are people like yourself interested in seeing that they get the recognition due them.

With best wishes,

(Signed) GEORGE P. HAYS
Major General, U.S. Army

THE FORGOTTEN FRONT

By 1945, as the crushing vise closed on Berlin from the east
and west, a brutal and decisive war continued to rage in Italy.
Here, the German Army under Field Marshal Albert Kesselring built some of the most formidable defensive lines in
military history.

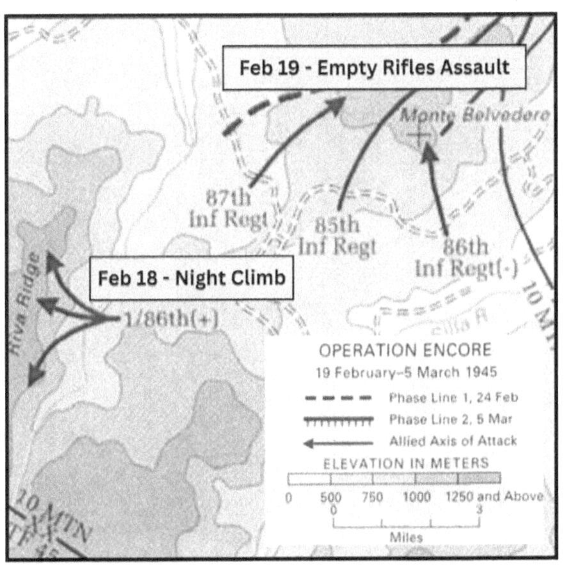

Map: Operation Encore. This map illustrates the 10th Mountain Division's assault on Riva Ridge and Mount Belvedere.

The Gothic Line, Kesselring's masterpiece, was a fortress of rock and concrete thrown across the Northern Apennines. In the central sector, key positions like Riva Ridge and Mount Belvedere commanded the high ground over the roads leading toward the Brenner Pass—the all-weather life-line from Italy into the Reich. To seize that pass and trap Army Group C, the Allies had to break this last mountain barrier.

In this vital sector, that task fell to the men of the 10th Mountain Division. In a relentless 114-day push, they did what conventional tactics had not: they cracked the Gothic Line and drove the Fifth Army's momentum into the Po Valley—a relentless push that helped cut the northern escape routes. For the first time in the Italian campaign, the dynamic finally reversed.

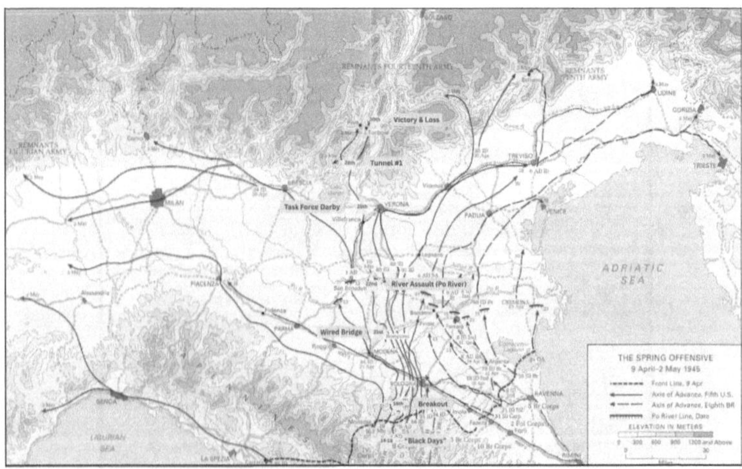

Map: The Spring Offensive. This map depicts the final Allied thrust into northern Italy between 9 April and 2 May 1945.

The Race to the Alps

While the 10th Mountain Division cracked the Gothic Line in its sector, the final race to the Austrian border was a massive, coordinated effort. By late April, the Allied advance had formed a steel trident designed not just to chase an army, but to slam the door on its escape.

On the left, the 1st Armored Division swept wide toward Lake Como to seal the Swiss border. On the right, the 85th Infantry Division drove past Verona to block the eastern exits.

But the 10th Mountain Division drove the center. General Hays's men became the spearhead that pointed the way to final victory: the roads leading toward Bolzano and the Brenner.

To seal the Brenner Pass, the Allies didn't have to march all the way to Austria; they had to shut the gate at the bottom.

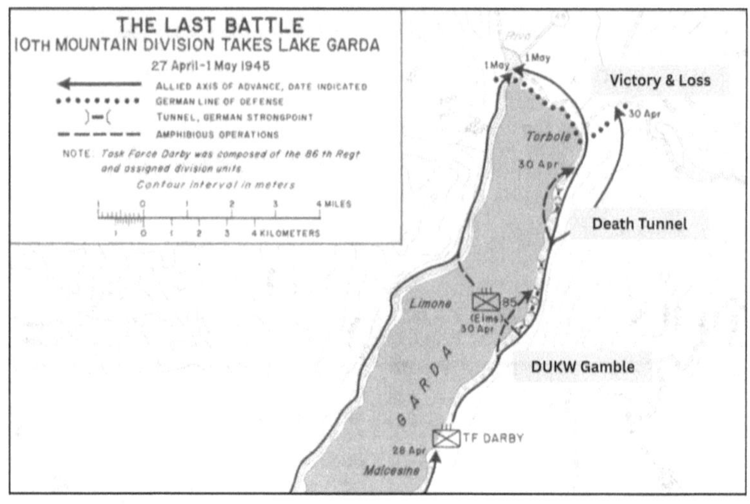

Map: The Last Battle. This map details the final obstacle
of the Italian Campaign at the northern tip of Lake Garda.

It was here, along the precipitous cliffs of Lake Garda,
that Task Force Darby surged north to cut the final artery.
While units like the 88th Infantry Division would eventually
pivot east and physically reach the frontier days later, it was
the 10th's relentless pressure in the center that helped finish
the race north. By the end of April, the escape route was cut.
The climbers had sealed the pass.

And, as the map of the Spring Offensive shows, this last
drive into northern Italy was not a solitary climb, but a
symphony of nations fighting together against a common
darkness.

From west to east, this line was held by a brotherhood of
the willing. It was a coalition of the U.S. Fifth Army and
British Eighth Army; the brave men of Poland, New Zealand,
and India; the armored brigades of South Africa; the

Brazilian Expeditionary Force on the western flank, whose victory at Collecchio–Fornovo forced the surrender of the German 148th Infantry Division and attached units; and the Italian Liberation Corps fighting to redeem their soil. Together, this diverse legion did what had once been called impossible: they broke through.

Born from the "impossible courage" of the climbers on the Apennines, that effort gathered momentum like a snowball rolling down a mountainside, becoming an avalanche that helped trigger the collapse of Germany's southern front.

The massive surrender in Italy was not an end in itself, but the beginning of the end. It was the first torrent released from the dam, unleashing a cascade of capitulations across Europe:

- **2 May 1945 (Caserta):** Nearly one million Axis troops surrendered in Italy. Field Marshal Harold Alexander, the British commander of Allied forces in Italy, later argued that this unconditional surrender shortened the war in Europe by six to eight weeks and saved tens of thousands of lives.
- **4 May 1945 (Lüneburg Heath):** Roughly one million German soldiers surrendered to the British in Holland, Denmark, and northwest Germany.
- **7–8 May 1945 (Reims & Berlin):** Germany signed the final, unconditional act of military surrender.

History rightly honors the heroes of Normandy who stormed Fortress Europe from the west. This story also honors the men who, at the very same time, were shattering the southern gate.

As *The Stars and Stripes* declared on May 2:

"In the theater where the western Allies made their first breach in Adolph Hitler's Fortress Europe, the fighting has ended with the surrender of an entire front." The article went on to note that the victory saved Allied forces from the "heart-breaking task of conquering the mountains" leading into Austria.

Far from being a sideshow, the Italian campaign became a catalyst. By breaking the Gothic Line and racing through the Po Valley toward the Alps, Allied forces didn't just win a local battle; they helped force the unconditional surrender of German Army Group C, hundreds of thousands of enemy troops who might otherwise have been thrown against the Americans and British advancing from France.

The term "D-Day Dodgers" was a bitter, ironic joke among the troops in Italy—men who were dying in the ice and the mud while much of the world watched France. But the record offers vindication: the "Dodgers" fought one of the war's hardest fronts, and the surrender in Italy on May 2, 1945, was the first of the final great theater-wide capitulations. The chain of surrenders that followed at Reims and Berlin began with them.

And the men of the 10th didn't just hold the line; they crossed it first.

General Hays, "the Rock," survived to witness the final peace in May 1945. Colonel Darby, "the Ranger," tragically did not; he fell at the very moment of triumph, after volunteering to rejoin frontline action in Italy.

Their fictional counterparts in the narrative, soldiers like "Johnnie Grey" and intelligence officers like "Annie McKenna," symbolize the countless real men and women whose courage and sacrifice in those final months will never be fully recorded in history books.

It took all of their efforts to write the concluding pages of World War II in Italy. Their intersecting paths, and their sacrifices, were the threads of the last, brutal chapter that helped bring about the collapse of the Axis in Italy and, ultimately, the total defeat of Nazi Germany.

For them, and for the world, this wasn't only a matter of capturing ground; it was also a fight to uphold basic principles of human dignity and decency. By forcing a million-man Axis army in Italy to surrender and sealing the passes through the Alps, the Allies blunted Germany's last hope of holding the southern front and prevented countless further deaths.

Their race to the frontier struck a final blow against a regime that, in its last weeks, was still starving and murdering people in its camps.

Their story deserves to be remembered in full and in proportion to the price they paid.

THE COST

To understand the true magnitude of the sacrifice, one must look at the brutal mathematics of the 10th Mountain Division's brief, violent 114 days of combat in Italy.

The Division

While the division maintained an authorized "paper strength" of about 14,000 men, the sheer intensity of the campaign required about 20,000 men to serve under its banner to maintain that combat effectiveness.

- Total Battle Casualties: 5,212—roughly one out of every four men who wore the 10th Mountain Tab.
- Killed in Action (KIA): 992.
- Wounded in Action (WIA): 4,154.
- Missing in Action (MIA): 38.
- Prisoners of War (POW): Despite the chaotic, vertical terrain, only 28 men were ever taken prisoner.

The 85th Mountain Infantry: A Calculus of Attrition

The cost was heaviest within the individual infantry regiments that spearheaded the assaults on the Gothic Line. The 85th Mountain Infantry serves as a harrowing example of the price paid by the regiment that climbed Belvedere with unloaded rifles in the dark:

- Total Personnel Served: 3,563 men.
- Total Casualties: 1,528.
- The Attrition Rate: A staggering 42.8% of the regiment became casualties.
- The Replacement Toll: To remain in the fight, the 85th required 1,713 replacements in less than four months. This means the original combat force was essentially destroyed and rebuilt while the mountains were still being won.

THE FATE OF THE RANGERS

In the novel, Colonel Darby is haunted by the silence of the men lost at Cisterna. To the Allied command in 1944, that silence signaled a catastrophic defeat—the tragic result of light infantry being encircled by heavy armor.

Of the 767 Rangers from the 1st and 3rd Battalions who infiltrated the German lines at Cisterna on January 30, 1944, only six ultimately made it back to Allied lines. After a desperate defense that claimed hundreds of lives, the survivors were taken prisoner.

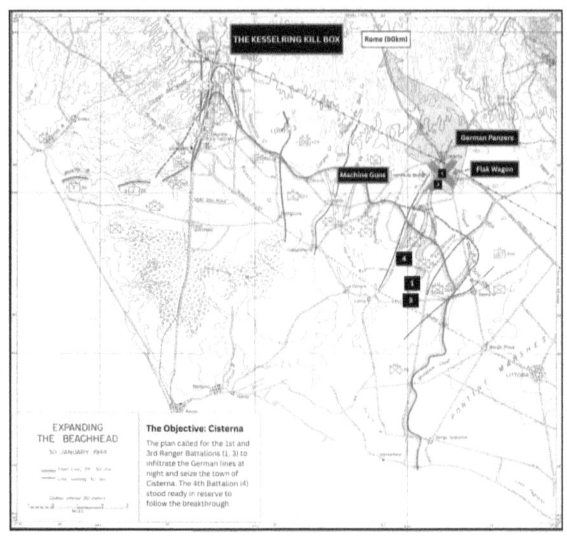

Map: The Trap at Cisterna. The 1st and 3rd Ranger Battalions (1, 3) infiltrated toward the town, only to be cut off and surrounded by German tanks and mobile flak guns. The 4th Battalion (4) attempted to break through to rescue them but was repelled.

But for the men who vanished, the silence hid a remarkable story of endurance.

Eventually, the prisoners were transported to the German POW camp Stalag II-B at Hammerstein in Pomerania—today Czarne, Poland.

For roughly a year, they endured the harsh conditions of the camp.

But their greatest trial began on January 29, 1945—almost exactly coinciding with the arrival of the 10th Mountain Division in Italy. As the Soviet Red Army broke through the Eastern Front, German authorities ordered Stalag II-B evacuated.

What followed was a three-month odyssey known to

history as "The March"—one of the infamous POW death marches of that winter, often remembered by survivors as a kind of "black march" for its brutality.

Under the guard of increasingly desperate German soldiers, the American POWs were forced to march west across northern Germany in one of the coldest winters of the war. They covered an average of 22 kilometers (13.5 miles) a day, six days a week, often sleeping in open fields or unheated barns in temperatures falling as low as −25°C (−13 °F).

As depicted in General Hays's letter, these men were treated as pawns in the collapsing Reich's strategy. Yet, despite starvation, frostbite, and the constant threat of violence and death, the bond forged during their Ranger training held.

On April 28, 1945—just two days before Colonel Darby was killed in action in Torbole—the surviving column of former Stalag II-B prisoners, including many of the Cisterna Rangers, was liberated by the British Army near Westertimke, Germany.

Postwar records indicate that the great majority of the men captured at Cisterna—very likely more than 400 of the roughly 450 Rangers taken prisoner—survived captivity and returned home. Their survival remains one of the great, under-told stories of resilience in World War II.

But it rests forever on the shoulders of roughly 311 Rangers who did not return.

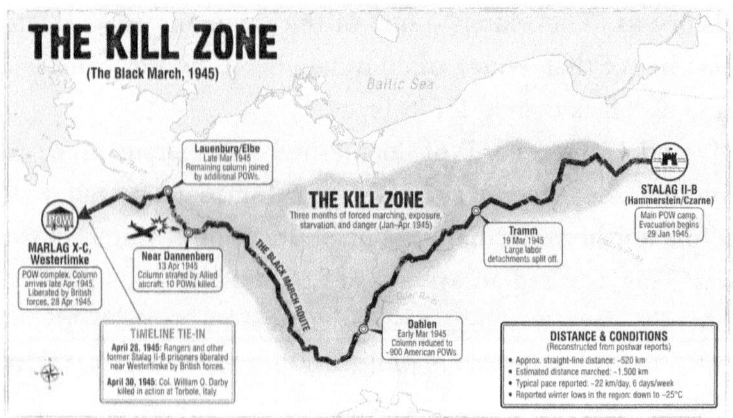

Map: The Black March. This map illustrates the precarious final journey of the Ranger POWs. Many survived because the war ended when it did.

Though British troops unlocked the gates, events seven hundred miles away helped keep men alive inside them by undermining Hitler's hopes of an Alpine Redoubt. By severing the Brenner corridor, Darby and the 10th Mountain Division helped strip the German High Command of its last leverage—the threat of a prolonged holdout in the Alps. This strategic defeat helped accelerate the surrender, staying the executioner's hand long enough for liberation to arrive.

Photo: Rangers from the 1st and 3rd Battalions are marched past the Victor Emmanuel II Monument in Rome by their German captors in February 1944. This propaganda parade, which also took them past the Colosseum, marked the beginning of a brutal fifteen-month captivity.

History honors the Allied forces who unlocked the gates. This story also remembers the men who fought to buy them the time to arrive.

JUDGMENT DAY

Field Marshal Albert Kesselring, the "Smiling Albert" whose defensive genius bled the Allies from Cassino to the Alps, did not escape the consequences of his command. In 1947, he was tried not at Nuremberg, but by a British Military Court in Venice for war crimes committed during the Italian campaign.

Central to the prosecution was the atrocity depicted in this novel: the reprisal execution of 335 Italian civilians at the Ardeatine Caves—a ruthless arithmetic of ten lives demanded for every one German lost.

Kesselring was found guilty and sentenced to death by firing squad, a sentence later commuted to life imprisonment. While he was released in 1952 due to ill health, his conviction stood as a final legal affirmation of the truth General Hays realizes in the story: that military action, divorced from morality, is not soldiering—it is crime.

A NOTE ON REMEMBRANCE

Today, the story of the 10th Mountain Division's sacrifice is not forgotten. It is honored—perhaps most poignantly—by the very people they helped liberate. Each year, on the anniversary of those final days, the Italian people organize the "Col. Darby 40-Miler" Ranger Challenge.

Hundreds of active-duty personnel, veterans, and civilians gather to trace the 10th's path. The forty-mile route begins at the southern end of Lake Garda and follows the eastern shore, ending at the monument to Colonel Darby in Torbole, the town for which he gave his life.

It is a living testament, a difficult and beautiful act of remembrance, ensuring that the final, redemptive chapter of Colonel Darby's story—and the story of the men of the 10th—continues to be written.

ACKNOWLEDGMENTS

This journey, spanning three novels and two world wars, has been a climb I could never have made alone. It has been shaped by the "trail marks" left by those who came before me—mentors, family, and the soldiers whose stories I have tried to tell.

I extend my deepest gratitude to all the individuals and organizations I thanked in *The Tenth Trail Mark* and *The Tenth Station*. Your support laid the foundation for this series, and while I will not repeat every name here, please know that my appreciation for your guidance remains boundless.

Foremost, I offer my deepest love and gratitude to my mother, Nancy Looby. She preserved the physical history of my father's service when the world had moved on. I will always cherish the image of her climbing flights of stairs to our attic at the age of 91 to retrieve not just his personal files, but a trove of countless, perhaps forgotten, 10th Mountain Division records and histories.

Just as he had once climbed into the dark to secure the high ground, she made her own ascent to ensure that his path—and the paths of his brothers—would never be lost. Her act of love placed the seed of this story in my hands, and her unwavering inspiration and radiant light have guided me through every chapter of my life.

This series exists because of the legacy of my father, Jim Looby, and his brothers in the 10th Mountain Division. He left us far too soon at sixty-four, remembered simply as the sweetest man—a gentle father who carried the war quietly within him.

Like so many who came home, he bore physical wounds and unseen burdens that lingered long after the peace was signed. Yet, he never spoke of the specific terrors of the line; he carried that weight in silence so we wouldn't have to.

It is only now, through the clarity of the archives, that I understand the true nature of his path. My father served in Company I of the 85th Regiment (I-85th). While historical narratives often become blurred by time or drama, I wish to set the record straight:

> Unlike the story, it was in fact the ~190 valiant men of Company I (85th Regiment) who spearheaded the climb into the dark at Mount Belvedere.
>
> On the night of February 19, 1945, they were the first wave, designated to take the summit with unloaded weapons. There was no unit in front of them when they crossed the Line of Departure at 2300 hours. Under the strictest discipline, they began an arduous climb of nearly 4,000 feet, ordered not to fire a single shot until first light.
>
> When the assault momentarily stalled on the forward slopes following the death of Company Commander Captain Walter Luther, the men of Company I did not wait for a reserve unit to pass through them. Instead, the "drive through" came from within.
>
> They rallied, regenerated their own momentum, and used grenades and bayonets to breach the German line. They took the Mount Belvedere summit and held it

through one of the fiercest nights of battle in history, securing the objective by dawn despite heavy counterattacks and concentrated artillery fire.

In crafting this narrative, I chose to consolidate the multi-mountain struggle in the Gothic Line sector into a singular, defining climax on the summit of Mount Belvedere. In reality, that assault was only the opening blow in a grueling six-day symphony of courage that echoed across a formidable complex: Riva Ridge and the interlocking peaks of Belvedere, Gorgolesco, and della Torraccia.

While the 85th Regiment led the central charge through the "ring of fire," equal credit belongs to the valiant men of the 87th, who fought up the western approach to seize the Valpiana Ridge.

And while the 86th's night climb up Riva Ridge—backed by the 126th Engineers' lifeline—opened the assault, their 3rd Battalion later moved forward through a second "ring of fire" to reinforce the 85th—cracking the last key position at Mount della Torraccia on February 24, 1945.

To my father, and the valiant men of the 10th Mountain Division who climbed into the dark so that we could stand in the light, we owe a debt that can never be fully repaid.

To the veterans of the 10th who gathered at reunions in Vail, Cranmore, and beyond—thank you for the stories you *did* tell. You shared the humor and the unbreakable bond of brotherhood, while quietly shielding us from the harder truths of the mountain.

To my wife, Connie, my "Trail Mark," my "True Cross," and my constant source of profound love—thank you for your patience, your insight, and for walking this long trail beside me. To our children, Kate, Jack, and CJ, you are the future for which these men fought; thank you for your joy and strength.

This narrative stands on the shoulders of the dedicated historians and archivists at the Denver Public Library's 10th Mountain Division Resource Center, the U.S. Army Center of Military History, and the National Archives. Your tireless work ensures that the voices of the "forgotten front" will never truly be lost.

Special thanks to my sister, Sarah, and my brother, James, for always walking ahead to light the path. To my dear friends, especially "the 914's" and the old "Montclair gang"—your friendship has been a steady anchor.

With enduring gratitude for every step shared on this trail.

See you at the top.

ABOUT THE AUTHOR

Joe Looby, author of *The Tenth Series* (*The Tenth Station*, *The Tenth Trail Mark*, and *The Tenth Command*), draws on a lifetime of outdoor adventures and a legacy of military service to craft compelling historical narratives.

An avid outdoorsman, U.S. Navy veteran, and Eagle Scout, Joe's work is profoundly inspired by his late father, Jim Looby, a 10th Mountain Division World War II veteran and recipient of the Bronze Star and Purple Heart.

If this story mattered to you, sharing your thoughts helps light the path for the next reader.

Review on Amazon

amazon.com/dp/B0FXXR4MVW

goodreads.com/joe_looby

THE PROMISE KEPT

Photo: Jim (I/85th) and Nancy Looby. We stand in the light because you were willing to climb through the dark.

See you up top.

To view historic maps, witness the terrain they conquered, and meet the men of the 10th, visit:

TheTenthSeries.com

IN MEMORIAM

To the Men of the 10th To the soldiers of the 10th Mountain Division—the 85th, 86th, and 87th Mountain Infantry, and the 126th Engineers—who faced the "unclimbable" fortress of the Northern Apennines.

To the 992 men who were killed in action during those 114 days of combat:

From the frozen cliffs of Riva Ridge to the "Black Days" of Castel d'Aiano, and across the deadly waters of Lake Garda, you followed the hardest order of all: *Always Forward.*

You broke the Gothic Line so that others could cross the valley. We stand in the light because you were willing to climb through the dark.

Sempre Avanti.

To the Rangers To the men of the 1st, 3rd, and 4th Ranger Battalions who fell at Gela, Salerno, Anzio, and in the fields of Cisterna:

You laid down your lives in the mud of the "forgotten front"—a hard truth recognized by *TIME* Magazine in 1944

—for Italy's freedom. You were the tip of the spear in a war that often looked away from your sacrifice.

But as the corporal wrote in the letter that guides this story: "The crosses here in Italy stand just as straight as the ones in Normandy."

You are the cost of the climb. You are not forgotten.

To the Wounded And to the thousands who came home bearing the marks of the journey.

To the more than 4,000 soldiers of the 10th Mountain Division—and to their Ranger comrades—who were wounded in action: in the aid stations of Cassino, the snows of Belvedere, and the field hospitals of the Po Valley:

You carried the weight of the war in your bodies and your memories long after the guns fell silent. For you, the climb did not end on V-E Day; it continued in the long recovery back home.

You are the living witnesses of the price of peace. We honor your sacrifice, your resilience, and your enduring strength.

GLOSSARY

Code Names & Intelligence

Enigma — The German cipher machine used to encrypt military communications. Breaking these "Enigma ciphers" was a central task of analysts at Bletchley Park.

FLASH — A priority designation for military cables, reserved for the highest level of emergency. Annie uses a FLASH header to send her unauthorized warning to General Hays.

Operation Encore — The Allied offensive assigned to the 10th Mountain Division to seize Riva Ridge and the Monte Belvedere–Monte della Torraccia complex.

Rover Joe — A tactical system using an air controller in a small liaison plane (like a Piper Cub) to talk directly to infantry and guide bomber strikes onto targets.

Shark Key — Allied codename for the naval Enigma cipher/key used by German U-boat "wolfpacks" in the Atlantic Ocean to coordinate attacks on Allied shipping.

Ultra — The top-secret classification for intelligence

obtained from breaking high-level German encrypted communications. These sources were considered "sacrosanct" and were only used for tactical warnings when their use could be plausibly disguised.

General Terms & Slang

40 and 8 — French railroad boxcars from WWI designed to hold "40 men or 8 horses."

Buttoned Up — A condition where a tank crew closes all hatches and vision ports for protection against small-arms fire or grenades. This significantly limits the crew's visibility, making them "blind" without supporting infantry to act as their "eyes."

Cassandra — A reference to the figure in Greek mythology who was given the gift of prophecy but the curse of never being believed. Annie feels like a Cassandra when her warning about a trap is rejected.

D-Day Dodgers — A bitter, ironic nickname for Allied soldiers fighting in Italy, referencing the misconception that they were avoiding the "real" war in France.

Kesselring Kill Box — In the novel, a name for the kind of trap Kesselring's forces set: leaving a gap in the line to lure Allied units into a zone already plotted for concentrated artillery fire.

No Angle — A tactical disadvantage where physical obstacles or positioning prevent a direct line of sight or a viable line of fire on a target. In the battle for Torbole, the bazooka team is pinned behind a tank carcass, leaving them with "no angle" on the second Panzer.

Paper War — In the novel, a name used by intelligence analysts to describe their war of decryption, reporting, and logistics tracking—fought with pencils and paper rather than bullets.

Partisan — A member of an armed group formed to fight secretly against an occupying force. In the novel, Italian partisans from the Garibaldi Brigade assist Johnnie Grey's squad by providing intelligence on German tunnel defenses.

Red Army — The common name for the military forces of the Soviet Union (USSR). In the novel, the approach of the Red Army from the east triggers the forced evacuation of POW camps like Stalag II-B, leading to the brutal "Black March" across Germany.

Reverse Slope — The back side of a hill, ridge, or mountain, facing away from the enemy. Defenders position themselves on the reverse slope to stay hidden from observation and reduce the effectiveness of long-range fire. In the novel, German troops often used reverse slopes as cover—an advantage that was partly eroded once VT-fuzed airbursts began exploding above their positions.

Smiling Albert — The Allied nickname for German Field Marshal Albert Kesselring, referring to his reputation for maintaining a smiling demeanor that masked a ruthless tactical mind.

Strip the Infantry — A tactical maneuver to isolate an armored vehicle from its accompanying foot soldiers. By using high-volume suppressing fire (such as from a BAR), the infantry is forced to seek cover and halt its advance, depriving the tank of its primary sources of situational awareness and protection against close-range anti-tank weapons.

The Flanks (Order to Mineo) — A directive to provide precision cover fire on the peripheral areas of a combat zone. While other squad members focus on primary targets such as tanks, the soldier assigned to the flanks engages specific targets of opportunity—such as snipers in windows or runners—to prevent the enemy from repositioning or encircling the squad.

The Rock of the Marne — The nickname of the U.S. Army's 38th Infantry Regiment of the 3rd Division, earned for its stubborn defense during the Second Battle of the Marne in July 1918. George P. Hays, then a young artillery officer supporting the division, received the Medal of Honor for his actions in the same battle (the central event of *The Tenth Station*). In this novel, some officers refer to George P. Hays as "the Rock of the Marne," echoing the proud nickname of his old regiment and division.

Vichy French — The government of France from July 1940 to August 1944 that collaborated with the Nazi regime following the German occupation of northern France. In the novel, Will Darby and the 1st Ranger Battalion are tasked with seizing Vichy French coastal batteries at the port of Arzew, Algeria, during Operation Torch. Although these forces flew the French tricolor, they served Axis interests, making them active combatants against the Allied invasion of North Africa.

V-Mail (Victory Mail) — A system used to reduce the bulk of military mail by photographing letters onto microfilm and printing them back onto paper at the destination.

Wehrmacht — The unified armed forces of Nazi Germany from 1935 to 1945, consisting of the *Heer* (Army), the *Kriegsmarine* (Navy), and the *Luftwaffe* (Air Force).

Willy Pete (White Phosphorus) — Slang for an incendiary shell or rocket that produces a brilliant flash and intense chemical fire upon detonation. While often used for marking targets or creating smoke, it is used here as a finishing weapon by drawing unquenchable fire into a tank's damaged ventilation or air intakes, rendering the interior uninhabitable.

Weapons, Vehicles & Equipment

75mm Pack Howitzer (M1/M1A1) — A light, versatile artillery piece designed to be broken down into six mule loads on its standard pack carriage, so it could be led into terrain impassable to vehicles. It was the principal weapon of the 99th Field Artillery Battalion (Pack) at Fort Hoyle, Maryland, where Will Darby first worked with pack howitzers and saw the value of animal transport. The same gun later equipped the 10th Mountain Division's artillery in Italy, allowing them to haul 75s onto steep Apennine positions—and even onto Riva Ridge after its capture—bringing heavy fire support to ground that trucks could not reach. Firing a 14–15-pound high-explosive shell to about 8.8 km (roughly 5½ miles), the pack 75 threw fragments that could inflict lethal wounds within several meters and cause serious casualties out to around 15 meters against troops caught in the open.

88mm (or "88") — A German high-velocity anti-aircraft and anti-tank artillery gun. While distant shells produced a "tearing whistle," the weapon was most feared for its supersonic speed; for targets in direct range, the shell often arrived and detonated before the sound of its approach could be heard.

B-17 Flying Fortress — A massive American heavy bomber with four engines. In the final days of the war, a lone B-17 is used not for bombing, but to drop thousands of leaflets announcing the German surrender over Lake Garda.

BAR (Browning Automatic Rifle) — A shoulder-fired automatic rifle used by infantry squads to provide suppressing fire. Soldiers like Luby use it to sweep alleys and suppress enemy infantry.

Bazooka — A portable, shoulder-fired rocket launcher used by American infantry to destroy tanks.

Counter-Battery Fire — A specialized tactical maneuver focused on the detection and destruction of enemy artillery positions to protect advancing friendly forces.

- **The Science:** It involves using complex trigonometry and coordinates to pinpoint the exact location of hidden enemy guns.
- **The Objective:** Unlike standard suppression, the goal is to "kill" the enemy batteries entirely, silencing the storm of shells to give the infantry a chance to live.
- **In the novel:** General Hays teaches his men this "brutal, forgotten math" to break the bloody stalemate at Monte Cassino, transitioning from a random "carpet of shells" to a surgical, methodical erasure of German gun pits.

Drop Five Zero, Fire for Effect — A tactical artillery command sequence used by a forward observer to adjust range and initiate a full-scale barrage.

- **Drop Five Zero:** A range correction indicating that the previous rounds landed too far past the target; "dropping" adjusts the aim to bring the next rounds 50 units (meters or yards) closer to the observer's position.

- **Fire for Effect:** The transition from the "adjustment" phase to the "destruction" phase of an artillery mission. Once the observer has confirmed the coordinates are accurate, this command orders all assigned guns to fire their full volume of ammunition simultaneously to saturate and destroy the target.
- **In the novel:** During the defense of Chiunzi Pass, Will Darby steps onto exposed rock to act as his own forward observer, using these commands to "walk" twenty-five-pound shells up and down the German line to break their assault.

DUKW ("Duck") — A six-wheeled amphibious truck used by the U.S. military to transport troops, supplies, even an entire Jeep over both water and land.

Flak Wagon — A mobile anti-aircraft platform, often mounting quad 20mm guns. These were sometimes lowered to waist height to be used devastatingly against ground infantry.

Indirect Fire — The practice of firing at a target that is not visible to the gun crew from their position. This requires a forward observer to identify the target and provide coordinates back to the battery. In the novel, Captain Hays teaches the "correct application of indirect fire solutions" during his time as an ROTC instructor at Cornell.

K-Ration — A daily combat food ration for American soldiers, often containing "congealed meat" in a tin.

M1 Garand — The standard-issue American semi-automatic service rifle, fed by eight-round en-bloc clips and famous for the distinctive "ping" as the empty clip was ejected.

M10 Tank Destroyer — A lightly armored American tracked vehicle armed with a heavy gun, designed to hunt enemy tanks. An M10 is the first vehicle to cross the Bomporto bridge after the engineers clear the charges.

MG42 ("Hitler's Buzzsaw") — A German machine gun notorious for its terrifyingly high rate of fire. It produced a distinctive "high-velocity rip" sound (described as *B-r-r-r-r-i-p-p*) that could cut men in half and pin down entire squads.

Panzer — The German word for "tank." The Panzer IV was the most numerous German tank of the Second World War and the only one to remain in continuous production throughout the conflict. By the late-war period, such as the 1944–1945 Italian campaign, the vehicle weighed approximately 25 tons. While originally designed for infantry support, it became the mainstay of German armored divisions and a formidable opponent for light infantry. These vehicles appear during the battles at Cisterna and Torbole.

Pre-Registered Fire — Artillery fire directed at specific terrain features—such as crossroads, ditches, or mountain saddles—where coordinates have been calculated and tested in advance. This allows defenders to call down instant, accurate fire the moment an enemy appears. The German defenders on Mount Belvedere used pre-registered mortar zones to trap the 85th Regiment.

Rifle Grenade — An explosive projectile launched from a standard service rifle using a specialized attachment and a blank cartridge. In the novel, Johnnie uses a fragmentation rifle grenade to exploit structural damage in the Hotel Geier, collapsing the building's carport onto an enemy tank.

Rolling Barrage — A tactical maneuver where artillery fire continuously moves forward in timed increments, creating a "curtain" of steel that advances just yards ahead of the friendly infantry. In the "Hell of the Hedgerows" in Normandy, General Hays uses rolling barrages to erase ancient earthen walls and clear a path for his troops.

Self-Propelled Gun (SPG): Primarily designed for mobile fire support or ambush. They typically lack a rotating turret, meaning the entire vehicle must turn to aim the gun. In the novel, they are used at Cisterna in a "Kesselring's Kill Box" as hidden, static anchors that emerge from barns to provide overwhelming firepower from a fixed position.

S-mine (Bouncing Betty) — A German anti-personnel mine that jumps waist-high into the air before detonating, filling the area with "jagged steel."

Time-on-Target (TOT) — A highly complex technique where multiple artillery batteries, located at different distances from a target, coordinate their firing schedules so that every shell arrives at the objective at the exact same second. Hays describes this as a "symphony of destruction" during the push at Monte Cassino.

VT Fuze (POZIT) – Short for "Variable Time," this was a revolutionary artillery fuze that packed a miniature radar set into the nose of the shell. Guarded almost as closely as the atom bomb, VT/POZIT fuzes were initially reserved for anti-aircraft and naval guns because there was little risk a dud would survive and fall into enemy hands where it could be reverse engineered. VT Fuzes were only released for ground combat late in 1944, beginning with the Battle of the Bulge. Instead of detonating on impact like a standard point-detonating fuze, the VT fuze used radio reflections from the ground to sense its approach and burst the shell roughly 30–50 feet above the surface. These airbursts rained fragments down into foxholes, open trenches, and reverse-slope positions, greatly reducing the protection that uneven terrain usually gave to men on the ground.

Weasel (M29) — A low-slung, tracked vehicle originally designed for snow and rough terrain, later used effectively to haul men and supplies through the mud and broken ground of the Italian front.

Military Ranks

Field Marshal — The highest regular rank in the German Army, equivalent to a five-star general. Albert Kesselring holds this rank.

General (Four-Star) — The highest regular active rank in the U.S. Army during most of the war (e.g., General George S. Patton).

Lieutenant General (Three-Star) — A corps or army commander. Lucian Truscott serves as a Lieutenant General commanding the Fifth Army.

Major General (Two-Star) — Typically the commander of a division. George P. Hays holds this rank as commander of the 10th Mountain Division.

Brigadier General (One-Star) — The lowest ranking general officer. Hays held this rank earlier in the war, before taking command of the 10th Mountain Division.

Colonel (Full Bird) — Insignia is a silver eagle. Will Darby is a Colonel during his service in Italy.

Lieutenant Colonel — Insignia is a silver oak leaf. Typically commands a battalion.

Major — Insignia is a gold oak leaf. Serves as a primary staff officer.

Captain — Insignia is two silver bars. Commander of a company. Will Darby is a Captain when he first meets Hays.

Lieutenant (First/Second) — Insignia is a gold bar (2nd Lt) or silver bar (1st Lt). A platoon leader.

Technical Sergeant — A senior non-commissioned officer rank in the WWII U.S. Army, just below First Sergeant and Master Sergeant. Staff Sergeant Johnnie Grey is promoted to Technical Sergeant after the assault on Belvedere.

Military Acronyms & Organizations

ADC (Assistant Division Commander) — The second-in-command of a division, typically a Brigadier General. Colonel Darby is assigned as General Hays's ADC in the final days of the war to replace Brigadier General Duff after he is wounded.

AFHQ (Allied Force Headquarters) — The command center for Allied forces in the Mediterranean theater, stationed at the Royal Palace in Caserta, Italy.

APO (Army Post Office) — The military mail system used to send letters and packages to troops overseas. Julia Hays manages "APO shipping" boxes for her book campaign.

BSC (British Security Coordination) — A covert intelligence organization established in New York City in 1940 to represent British intelligence (MI6/SIS) interests in the United States. It served as a vital link for intelligence sharing and psychological operations before the U.S. formally entered the war.

BRUSA Agreement — The 1943 Britain–USA agreement that formalized the sharing of signals intelligence (SIGINT) between the two nations. It allowed analysts like Annie to work with American data, though breaching its protocols was a serious offense.

CP (Command Post) — The field headquarters for a unit, where commanders manage the battle. In the text, these range from farmhouse cellars to jeeps.

G-1 (Personnel) — The staff section responsible for personnel management. General Hays contacts G-1 to find a replacement aide after his jeep strikes a mine.

G-2 (Intelligence) — The staff section responsible for analyzing information about the enemy. The plot frequently contrasts the "official G-2 reports" with raw intercepts.

G-3 (Operations) — The staff section responsible for planning and coordinating tactical operations.

GI — Originally an equipment stamp meaning "G.I." (*galvanized iron*), the term was soon reinterpreted by soldiers as "Government Issue" and used for any Army-issued gear. By WWII, it had become an everyday name for American soldiers themselves.

MI6 (Military Intelligence, Section 6) — The British intelligence agency responsible for foreign intelligence. Annie's handler, Alistair, is an officer seconded from MI6.

MP (Military Police) — Soldiers responsible for law enforcement and security. They guard the Pentagon and the surrender ceremony at Caserta.

NCO (Non-Commissioned Officer) — An enlisted leader—such as a corporal or sergeant—who commands soldiers at the squad and platoon level.

PAO (Public Affairs / Public Relations Office) — The office responsible for media relations and official communications. In the novel, they manage Colonel Darby's war bond tour and speeches.

POW (Prisoner of War) — A captured soldier held by the enemy.

ROTC (Reserve Officers' Training Corps) — A college-based officer training program in the United States. Between the wars, George P. Hays served as an instructor at Cornell University's ROTC detachment, teaching future officers the lessons of the Marne.

SHAEF (Supreme Headquarters Allied Expeditionary Force) — The command center in London planning the invasion of Normandy.

SIS (Secret Intelligence Service) — The formal name for the British intelligence agency often known as MI6. Alistair serves as an SIS liaison.

XO (Executive Officer) — The second-in-command of a unit (such as a company or battalion), responsible for day-to-day administration and for taking over if the commander becomes a casualty.

Y Service — The British signals intelligence collection network responsible for the interception of enemy radio transmissions. These raw, encrypted messages were funneled to Bletchley Park to be decrypted by analysts in locations like Hut 6. In the novel, Alistair is on a call with the Y Service when Annie interrupts him to deliver her warning about the "Kesselring Kill Box" at Cisterna.